GO ASK THE RIVER

BY EVELYN EATON

NOVELS
The Encircling Mist (1925)
Desire: Spanish Version (1932)
Summer Dust (1936)
Pray to the Earth (1938)
Quietly My Captain Waits (1940)
Restless Are the Sails (1941)
The Sea Is So Wide (1943)
In What Torn Ship (1944)
Give Me Your Golden Hand (1951)
Flight (1954)
I Saw My Mortal Sight (1959)
The King Is a Witch (1965)
Go Ask the River (1969)

SHORT STORIES
Every Month Was May (1947)
The North Star Is Nearer (1949)

POETRY
The Interpreter (1923)
Stolen Hours (1923)
Birds before Dawn (1943)
The Small Hour (1955)
Love Is Recognition (1971)

NON-FICTION
Heart in Pilgrimage (1948)
The Trees and Fields Went the Other Way (1974)
Snowy Earth Comes Gliding (1974)
I Send a Voice (1978)
The Shaman and the Medicine Wheel (1982)

CHILDREN'S BOOKS
John: Film Star (1937)
Canadian Circus (1939)

EVELYN EATON

GO
ASK
THE
RIVER

CELESTIAL ARTS
Berkeley, California

CELESTIAL ARTS
P.O. Box 7327
Berkeley, California 94707

Cover design by Nancy Austin

Library of Congress Cataloging-in-Publication Data
    Eaton, Evelyn Sybil Mary, 1902–1983.
        Go ask the river / Evelyn Eaton.
            p.   cm.
        ISBN 0-89087-611-8
        1. Hsueh, T'ao, 768–831, —in fiction, drama, poetry,
    etc.
        2. China—History—T'ang dynasty, 618–907—Fiction
    I. Title.
        PS3509.A84G6   1990
        813'.52—dc20   90-37754

First Celestial Arts Paperback Edition, 1990

5   4   3   2   1
94 93 92 91 90

Manufactured in the United States of America

I WOULD LIKE TO THANK Mary Kennedy for allowing me to use her version of Hung Tu's works, copyright to which she retains. My apologies must go to Chinese scholars everywhere, for whom this image of their country in the ninth century may be an obvious never-never land. Yet Donn Byrne wrote his Marco Polo in pure Irish brogue, and if Marianne Moore's imaginary garden has a real toad in it, so this imaginary China has a real poet in it. If *Go Ask the River* helps to bring her work to a wider public, I hope both she and the scholars will forgive me for my errors and blunders. I do not remember the ninth century as well as I once thought I did, when I was in Cheng-tu.

—EVELYN EATON
March 1968

THE PUBLISHER gratefully acknowledges Mr. Chungliang Al Huang, for bringing this important work to our attention for reprint and Terry Eaton for her invaluable assistance in bringing this novel to life once again.

INTRODUCTION

AT ONCE BOTH charming and haunting, *Go Ask the River* is a tale not only of historical China but of the human struggle to discover, as Joseph Campbell put it, "an experience of being alive so that our life experiences on the purely physical plane will have resonances within our own innermost being."

This tale of the female Chinese poet Hung Tu is one such story, rendered here in the seamless prose of one of the twentieth century's most remarkable authors, Evelyn Eaton. Here Evelyn Eaton re-creates China from 760 to 824 A.D. to tell the story of a beautiful woman poet whose adventurous life is the basis for this novel of a majestic and shimmering world of the past.

Evelyn Eaton authored some thirteen novels, five volumes of poetry, two short story collections, works of nonfiction and works for children. She was a regular contributor of short fiction to *The New Yorker*—twenty-five of her short stories appeared in that venerable magazine between 1949 and 1960, making Evelyn Eaton one of the leading writers of the mid-twentieth century.

Perhaps best known for her non-fiction *I Send a Voice*, Evelyn Eaton was a writer of rare skill, with a prose style so effortless that the reader is hardly aware of the authorial presence. In *Go Ask the River*, page after page melt away as the story virtually tells itself—a quality of style that lends the book its curiously haunting mood.

The life of Evelyn Eaton was one of unusual vigor and uniqueness. Born in Switzerland in 1902 to ardently Anglophile Canadian parents, she was educated in England and France, not becoming an American citizen until the age of forty-two. It is this European background that informs her work in a way rarely seen in American literature. The European literary temperament is much less tense than the American, with its rigid concern with moralism and progress, and this unjudging presence is felt in most of Eaton's writing —a willingness to go beyond the surface, to touch, with a gracious subtlety, the essence of an event or experience. Hovering round the edges of Hung Tu's story in *Go Ask the River* is this element of gracious investigation, this quiet examination of the influences that inform cultural life and that make human life interesting.

Her adult life was varied and rich: a war correspondent in China, Burma, and India in 1945; a lecturer at Columbia University from 1949 to 1951; a lecturer at Sweet Briar College from 1951 to 1960; a fellow of the MacDowell Colony ten different years.

As her literary reputation grew, other creative writing posts took her to Mary Washington University in Virginia, The University of Ohio, Pershing College, and Deep Springs College in Nevada.

The jacket copy to her 1974 autobiography, *The Trees and Fields Went the Other Way*, summarizes her life in a fascinating way:

> Her Edwardian upbringing was proper enough on the surface, yet somewhat bizarre. Her career as a poet and novelist began with the publication of a collection of poems when she was twenty-one. What she calls the vital years, from 1919 to 1936, she spent mostly in France, where her daughter was born ... Other adventures range from her reluctant presentation at court in 1923 to a flight over the Hump.

Partly Indian by descent (related to the Algonquin Indians of Nova Scotia through her soldier father), her later life became increasingly focused on Native American culture, but surely this later manifestation of interest in Indian ceremony and mysticism can be traced throughout her life's work. In *Go Ask the River*, a sense of mystery and myth abounds.

This heritage was greatly explored when, in 1960, Eaton moved to the Owens Valley of California. There she forged strong ties with the Paiute and Arapaho peoples, and it was from these experiences that perhaps her most famous work, *I Send a Voice*, was distilled.

Evelyn Eaton spent her final years in the small community of Independence, California, a time that is recalled in her daughter Terry Eaton's memoirs *Joy into Night*. Evelyn Eaton died in 1983. Her papers and manuscripts are permanently housed in the Mugar Memorial Library at Boston University.

—PAUL REED
August 1990,
San Francisco

To Wang Sun

Go ask the river
which are longer,
its eastward-flowing waters
or the thoughts that fill us
at this parting hour.

—Li T'ai Po
(T'ang Dynasty)
TRANSLATED BY HENRY H. HART

PART ONE
Prologue
Circa 1100 A.D.

I

In the Hung Wu Period of the reign of the Ming Dynasty, about the year eleven hundred, a young scholar named T'ien Chu was traveling on foot from Canton toward the city of Cheng-tu, to assume the post of tutor to the Governor's household.

It was twilight when he reached the outskirts of the city and passed within its walls. He was tired and dusty, hungry and thirsty too. He thought it might be wisdom to spend the night at an inn, and present himself in the morning, clean and refreshed, to his employer.

He saw lights on the right side of the road, coming from what seemed to be a teahouse. The gates were open and there were more lights shining on a pathway to the door. He turned in gratefully and was welcomed by a servant, who took the pack from his back and led him to a room where everything was prepared for the comfort of travelers, even to a clean silk robe laid out for his use. After he had bathed and changed, a second servant appeared and showed him to an inner court, where she seated him before a lacquered table, more elegant than any in his father's house. The bowls were of finest jade and the chopsticks of hammered silver.

Wine was brought at once, and before he could express a preference, delicious food, steaming with spicy fragrance. It was obvious that he had come to a superior inn. He seemed to be the only guest, and he was troubled that the reckoning might be beyond his means. He tried to hint to the servant in charge that he was a modest man, a poor scholar, who did not expect to be treated like a rich prince, but his words had no effect. More succulent dishes arrived, with more pretty girls to serve them, more wine was poured, and presently musicians entered with their instruments and arranged themselves at the far end of the court.

When the music began he was astonished at its quality. Canton had excellent musicians, but these were better than any he had heard there. Cheng-tu was a small provincial city, but if this was the standard of food and entertainment at an inn, even the best inn, what must it be like in the great rich houses? And he was going to be living in the greatest and richest, the Governor's Palace!

He listened with added pleasure to the performers. Three of them brushed the strings, one of them played the flute. They had a distinctive style, a pure sort of silken playing, suited to the ancient classics, which these pieces were. He did not recognize all of them and called out after a while,

"What was the name of the song that you just finished?"

The flute player answered, " 'Green Water.' "

"And the one before that?"

" 'The Queen of Shu.' "

"I have never heard them."

She smiled politely. She was young, and if not exactly pretty, very graceful and elegantly dressed. They were all graceful and elegant and skillful, but he was beginning to see them and everything about him through a growing haze.

The smooth rich wine was strong, and he was drinking it by the flagon.

"Play 'The Day of No Fire,' " he said.

They shook their heads. They looked puzzled.

"Never mind," he said thickly, while the room turned about him. "Play anything you like."

The heart-shaking music went on. He shut his eyes and leaned his head down, resting it on his arms, on the edge of the table. Someone brought him a cushion, and hot wet towels for his neck. After a while, he did not know how long, he began to feel better. The room stopped turning about him. He was able to sit up. He glanced shamefaced about him. Now his servant brought him strong tea and poured it for him, with little encouraging noises to put him at his ease.

Suddenly there was a stir in the far end of the room. Coming toward him, with quiet authority, in a flurry of attentive maids, must be the Innkeeper, the Lady of the House, magnificent in green and gold, from the high comb in her hair to the jade shoes on her feet, glimmering as she moved and her jewels caught the light.

When she drew near enough for him to see her face clearly, he was pleasantly surprised. From the stately way she walked and the deference paid to her, he expected her to be old. This was a young woman, very beautiful.

"I am sorry I was not here to pour the first wine." Her voice was as lovely as her face. "I hope you were well entertained?"

"Like the King of Yueh, when he had conquered Wu."

She smiled.

"The King of Yueh got very drunk," he said, "and so did I."

"The King of Yueh said, if I remember well, 'Fill my glass and let it glow in amber.' "

"The King of Yueh had a stronger head than mine."

"I do not think so. Probably you were tired, or the first wine was to blame. This wine will not hurt you." She beckoned. The servants hurried forward with new flagons, bowls of fruit, cakes and sweetmeats, baskets of dates and nuts. He began to worry again, not only about getting drunk, but about the reckoning. He cleared his throat and was searching for the right words to explain the slimness of his purse, when she puzzled him by saying:

"The Governor is unable to greet you tonight. He charged me with his regrets and with the honor of offering you his hospitality."

"The Governor?" he repeated stupidly. "How did he know I would come here?"

"Is he not expecting you?"

"Well, yes, at his Palace," he muttered. "But still, I don't understand. . . ."

Now she looked perplexed, and he thought, "I am not the guest she expected," and then, "Most men I suppose would seize the opportunity. . . ." He said hurriedly:

"I am delighted. It is only that . . . let me explain . . . my name is T'ien Chu. . . ."

"T'ien Chu," she repeated. "It is a well-shaped name, but is it any reason why you cannot drink the Governor's wine?"

She was laughing at him.

"You don't understand," he plowed on. "I am a poor scholar, a tutor for the Governor's sons."

She rebuked him.

"Scholars, rich or poor, and they are seldom rich, T'ien Chu, are particularly welcome, and educators honored here. The Governor's Ya Men will be diminished that T'ien Chu rejects his hospitality, at the hands of this poor shadow, for such a reason."

"No, no," he said hastily. "I do not reject it . . . for any reason. . . . I just wanted you to know who I was, in case you expected another. . . . As you see, I am drinking the wine." He lifted his bowl. "To the Governor's fragrant shadow."

She did not reveal her name, and he did not feel that he should press for it, curious though he was. She was beginning to attract him strongly, with her lilting voice, her painted, heart-shaped face, the charm of her gestures . . . all the subtle enchantment emanating from her.

He tried to remind himself that she must be a trained and skillful performer in the seductive arts, to be the Governor's official Hostess in this inn, where apparently he paid the reckoning for any man who came. No doubt she was the Governor's favorite Flower-in-the-mist, and nothing she did could be sincere. But he did not believe this in his heart, and with every word she said, and everything they shared, every glance, every smile, every sipping of the wine together, in the smooth, swift passing of time suspended between them, on this strange and fortunate night, he was drawn more deeply toward her.

Presently she took up her guitar and began to sing, small haunting songs, in the style he was beginning to think of as the music of Cheng-tu.

The four musicians, shadowy in the background, accompanied her softly in a tune he recognized, a very ancient love song, half rueful, half humorous:

"I will knock down the Yellow Crane House for you, with a hammer. You may upset the Parrot Island too for my sake."

The second was unfamiliar:

6

"The Mountains of Tsang-wu may crumble, the River Hsiang go dry, our tears on the bamboo leaves will not fade forever."

The third he knew well, it always moved him, and he caught in his breath to hear it now:

"Go ask the river which are longer, its eastward-flowing waters or the thoughts that fill us. . . ."

The thoughts that fill us. His must be evident to her.

"T'ien Chu," she said, "shall we sing together some song that you know?"

"I have no voice," he muttered.

She put down the guitar.

"Then shall we harmonize a poem together, composing alternate lines?"

"Willingly."

She clapped her hands. A servant came out of the shadows with brushes and a sheaf of large fine sheets of paper. He took up a sheet to look at the design of pine and plum blossom woven through it.

"How beautiful the texture is," he said, fingering it. "I have never seen a paper as smooth and strong as this. It invites the brush."

She smiled. "Do you like fine paper, T'ien Chu?"

"Yes. Because I am a poet." He shrugged.

"I will give you some. It is made here at our Hundred Flowers Pool. The water at this bend of the Silk River has a special quality. Each of these sheets has been separately dipped into the stream."

"It is beautiful," he repeated.

He was thinking, "If I compose the first line I will introduce the theme of love and the passing of time and then I can sing to her of the new turmoil in my heart. But if she begins . . ."

She smiled as though she caught his thought.

"You first, T'ien Chu."

"Very well."

He wrote down the title:

" 'Harmonizing a poem with the Chance Met Lady.' "

He thought for a long moment.

"Loveliness and compassion cannot be grasped."

He brushed the column down strongly, with bold, thick strokes. Then he pushed the paper toward her. She leaned over his shoulder to brush in the next line:

"The turning year shakes the earth, petals drift . . ." Her script was like her music, complex, detailed, ordered, each glyph complete, a miniature picture, perfect in itself, even without the poem's meaning. No slovenly short cuts or concessions. Few scholars wrote like this today. He wondered how she had acquired the patience and the skill. She was a challenging poet. She had taken the general statement in his line and made it concrete with "shakes the earth" and "petals." Petals blown on the wind, petals from the flowering trees. He would make it harder for her than this. He would put those fallen petals in a specific place and bring her in obliquely. . . .

"flinging a crimson pathway for satin-slippered feet." What would she do with that?

"or cover the ground like frost."

Oh, clever, to bring in the frost, to make loveliness of death, and turn his lament for the fallen into a triumph of escape! But this was leading them a little off the track. He returned to the passing of time, and the need to seize upon love. . . .

"All that is exquisite and frail is evanescent . . ."

She hesitated. Then:

"perfume dispelled, cannot be recalled.
No ghosts of these torn buds will haunt us."

Those were strange lines . . . something poignant, unexpected there. . . . Chance Met . . . Chance Met . . . he leaned toward her urgently.

"There is a lifetime to make up between us," he said. "All the long, lonely hours of this person's life . . ."

"But not in one short evening, T'ien Chu. Now that you have come here, you will come again."

This must mean that she liked him, that he was not just the guest of an evening, imposed on her by the Governor.

"I will come here many times," he said exultantly.

8

"And harmonize poems with me. That will be a pleasure, T'ien Chu. It is too long a time since I composed a new poem."

"Two or three days?" he teased her. "A moon at least, I suppose?"

"Centuries. Let us continue. The lines we have brushed are good. It is your turn to stir up the petals."

"They shimmer in sun. They wilt under rain."

"They fall into the upraised cup of the poet."

"There they go, into my cup, and I am drunk again, but not with wine. I am drunk with joy of you. . . ."

"Into the poet's enameled cup falls the rarest flower of all."

"As a dream melts away, they mingle with the yellow catkin of the willow."

"Versatile petals. They go everywhere, on every wind. Shall we bring them to rest?"

"Not yet, T'ien Chu."

"Very well. *Hold them against loneliness."*

"Let them stay where they have fallen"

"on the steps, on the path into the garden."

"This color is balm for one abandoned"

"who wakes in night and walks in the rustling leaves."

Long lonely night.

The short shared night wore on as they scribbled furiously together, in a fusion of mind and spirit that obliterated everything for him, even the passing of the hours. It was near dawn when the sleeping mat was finally spread and he stumbled into her arms.

II

HE WOKE TO PAIN AND NOISE. Someone was kicking him, someone was shouting. He was lying, naked, on a pile of heaped-up leaves. He sat up groggily. Two angry men stood over him . . . soldiers. . . .

"Wha . . . wha . . . where?"

They struck him. They yanked him to his feet. They were rough-looking brutes with mean faces. One of them, the older, had a scar across his lips that puckered them into a sneer.

"If those are yours, get into them," this Scarface said, tossing him a bundle scooped up from the ground.

They were his clothes. He groped to put them on, shaking with shock, with fear.

"I don't understand. . . . I don't understand. . . ."

He saw his pack a few feet away, hanging from a bush, and stumbled toward it. It was still fastened. He loosened the straps and looked in. His purse was there. He had not been robbed. But something terrible had happened. . . .

"How did I get here?"

Scarface clouted him savagely across the mouth.

"Quiet, Scum!"

The other man laughed. "How did I get here?" he said mincingly. Then they both guffawed.

They took his arms and began to hustle him forward, through a crowd of curious, watching people who made no effort to help him. They halted for a moment, stared, and went hurrying about their business, while new ones came and stared.

He tried to appeal to the nearest. "Wait . . . wait . . . these soldiers are making a terrible mistake . . . help me . . . help me. . . ."

"Come on!" Scarface struck him again.

He staggered a few feet farther, then he stopped and tried to wrench himself free. "Take me to the Inn . . . they know me there . . . they'll tell you. . . ."

"Shut your lying mouth," Scarface said, hitting him once for every word. "Save your strength to move your feet."

"Shall we slice him up a bit? Let's take off his ears."

Someone in the watching crowd laughed. They were dragging him between them now like a sack of stones.

"You'd better stop," he shouted. "I tell you it's a mistake. The Governor will punish you for this. He's expecting me."

"You're an envoy from the Emperor, I suppose?"

"Can't you see, he's the Emperor himself."

"I'm in the Governor's service."

"Ho! It so happens we're in the Governor's service and we never saw you before."

"I've just come from Canton. I'm the tutor for his sons."

They slackened their hold for a moment while they considered this. He looked at them hopefully, but they rejected it.

"A fine tutor you'd make, sleeping off your wine, stark naked in a public place! Are you going to step along, or shall we finish what the wine began?"

"If we have to carry you," the other man said, "we'd as soon tote you dead."

He gave up struggling then and walked beside them, dazed, trying to remember what had happened, what he could have done to be dumped out naked on a pile of leaves . . . who put him there?

The last thing he remembered was rising with his Chance Met Lady from writing the last poem together, following her to a pavilion where the sleeping mat was spread, taking off his robe and sinking down upon her, then her arms around him, then . . . hot shame flooded him, he must have fallen into a drunken sleep, a stupor, on her very breast.

Was that it? Had he insulted her, and was she so disgusted with him that she had her servants throw out the drunken boor?

"No more funny stories?"

"Left his tongue somewhere. At that inn he's raving about."

They guffawed again, winked, made signs to the passing crowd, but they stopped hitting him and twisting his arms.

"Where are you taking me?"

"To the jail."

He knew what that meant. Months, a year perhaps, and meanwhile nobody would know where he had gone or be able to find him. He would rot. . . .

"Take me to the Governor first. . . ."

"Still harping on the Governor."

He looked at their stupid, cruel faces. "Listen," he said, "if you'll take me to a magistrate or any city official, I'll pay you well."

"Ho! In gold, I suppose."

"Yes, in gold. One piece each."

"And what would scum like you be doing with gold pieces?"

"Stolen, perhaps?"

"Well, let's see them anyway."

He undid his pack and handed them his purse. There was some silver in it besides the two gold pieces. They took it all, dividing it between them.

"Hey, what else is in that pack?" Scarface snatched it and started rummaging. T'ien Chu's few belongings fell out, slippers, pen case, clothes, a scroll. . . .

"Give me that!" He struggled with Scarface, who held him off and shook him, while the other undid the ribbon and unrolled the scroll.

"What is it? What's on it?"

"Just some writing."

They looked at each other uneasily, then at T'ien Chu, and the pen case in the mud. They released him. They handed him back the scroll. He stood holding it for a moment uncertainly, then he put it into the pack and began to stuff the other things around it, while they watched.

"Maybe he is some sort of scholar," the younger one said. "That was columns of learned sort of writing."

"What about it?"

"Nothing, only maybe we could take him to some official, if that's what he wants. . . ."

"What's the odds where we take him? He'll get to jail in the end. Scum like him . . ."

"Yes, but after all . . ."

"After all, what?"

"Well, he paid."

"Ho! So why not jail, jail for the plucked crow?"

"There's nothing more in it for us that way. There might be something to pick up from some official for bringing him in . . . it looks well too . . . and if they don't want him then we can take him to the jail. . . ."

"What makes you so fond of officials?"

They took him to Magistrate Wu-tsung, and after an interval of waiting the complaint against him was recorded, the soldiers' statements sworn to, and T'ien Chu had his first chance to defend himself.

He plunged into the story urgently, reliving it as he told it. How he entered the city by the East Gate, and saw an inn on the right side of the road, and then . . . It was the barest outline, with much glossed over or left out, but it was the truth, and as he told it he was seized with anguish, desire, despair. . . . He went stammering on and Magistrate Wu-tsung listened without interrupting him.

It was hard to tell from his expression what he was thinking. He seemed to be a grave man, of the age of T'ien Chu's father, and he looked as though he found it natural to be severe. But still he listened. And when T'ien Chu ground to an end with: "So you see, Sir, I did not go to sleep where I was found. I did not intend any scandal or disturbance. I don't know what happened. It's a mystery. I need your help, Sir, to discover the truth. If you will come with me to the Inn, or send some servant you trust . . ." Magistrate Wu-tsung did not immediately answer. He leaned back and closed his eyes. When he opened them, after a moment of unbearable suspense for T'ien Chu, he did not look at him directly. He looked around the room.

"Let us proceed in an orderly fashion," he said thoughtfully, beckoning to his clerk. "You will go to the Governor and inquire with my heartfelt compliments whether a tutor for his princely sons is expected from Canton, and if the answer is yes, what the name of such a tutor should be."

"You may depart," he added to the soldiers, staring uneasily. "You have done your duty. The delinquent will remain in my custody until we have finished with his case."

They bowed and hurried away, glad to escape before the answer came and while they still had the gold.

He smiled at T'ien Chu, gray-faced and exhausted on his bench.

"While we wait for the Governor's word," he told him kindly, "we will share tea and rice. You must be hungry, after such a day and such a night as you describe . . . whether or not they occurred."

III

THE SUN WAS STILL FAR FROM SETTING when the Governor's answer came, confirming the expected arrival of a tutor named T'ien Chu, requesting further details of the young man's present situation in the house of his old and honored friend, and asking, mildly, but with legitimate curiosity, when the teaching of his sons would begin.

T'ien Chu begged Magistrate Wu-tsung to proceed with the investigation which should clear him of the charges against him and set him free to take up his duties as the Governor desired. He pleaded that they might set out for the Inn at once. Everything, he insisted, would be explained to everyone's satisfaction, as soon as they could get there and question the Lady of the House. Then, he was certain, it would be clearly shown that he was the innocent victim of some strange but natural circumstance.

He was not at all certain of this, or of anything, except that he could not endure to sit for another moment, politely answering questions about his home, his education, and, to prove his scholarship, discuss pedantic niceties of the more obscure classics with this tedious old man. He was trying to conceal the anxiety racking him, his desperate need to see the Chance Met Lady, to ask forgiveness, to set things straight, above all to find out what the catastrophe was. Wild thoughts went chasing through his head. He even imagined the sudden return of the Governor himself to the sleeping pavilion, but if that were so, he would hardly have sent a mild message of inquiry and endorsement to Magistrate Wu-tsung about the young man caught in his Flower's bed . . . unless the Flower's servants had managed to dump the young man out in time. . . .

It might be that, but he did not believe it. There had been no hesitation in her manner, no suggested need for concealment. She moved proudly free. But he must find out.

He hoped that the old man's eyes were not too shrewd, that he saw in his restless prisoner only a young man eager to assume new office, not this burned-up fool of a poet, hopelessly in love.

They set off at last, the magistrate in his litter, drawn by two white oxen, with T'ien Chu walking beside it and an escort of armed servants clearing the way before them, toward the East Gate.

Long before they came within sight of the distant city walls, T'ien Chu was scanning the left-hand side of the road for the first sight of the Inn.

He did not find it as soon as he expected. He was still searching when suddenly they reached the gate itself. He looked up, startled.

"Was the Inn outside the gate?" Magistrate Wu-tsung asked.

"No, no. It was well inside, a li or half a li at least."

"You have missed it. Turn back. Search again."

They returned from the gate toward the city and were almost at the magistrate's house before T'ien Chu would admit that he was lost.

"I must have come through another gate."

"There is none, unless you cross the city to the West Gate. But you came from the east and you did not cross the city?"

"No, not last night. Not until this morning, with the soldiers, as far as your house . . . but then . . . but then it must be there! Let us go back. . . ."

"Very well."

The Inn was not to be found. When they reached the East Gate for the third time, Magistrate Wu-tsung said:

"T'ien Chu, there is one thing you should know. There has never been an inn or a teahouse in the city of Cheng-tu near either of the gates."

"But I tell you . . ."

"It is because you told me, insistently, that such an inn existed, that I came with you to find it. Where is it?"

"I don't know."

"Was it perhaps a private villa?"

16

"I don't know. Perhaps. It isn't here."

"You were drunk. Did you dream or invent the story?"

"I was drunk on the wine I drank there. I had no other wine. I did not invent the story. I did not dream."

"Would you recognize the place where you were found?"

"I don't know. Perhaps."

"Is it over there?" He pointed to a gateway marked by a small stone arch. "Is it this place?" He climbed out of his litter and took T'ien Chu by the arm. "Come here. There is something I want you to see. Read the inscription over the gate."

"P'i-pa Gateway, to the Villa Pi-chi-Fang." He turned inquiringly toward Wu-tsung. Then he saw something else and cried out in surprise: "Look, look, there she is! It is her perfect likeness!" He was staring at a dark stone tablet let into the wall, with the deeply incised figure of a woman holding a sheaf of paper.

"Read the inscription," the older man said, a little grimly.

" 'Hung Tu, the laureate of Shu, who went down to the Terrace of Night at the age of seventy-two, in the T'ao Period of the reign of Wen Tsung, of the Tang Dynasty' . . . Tang Dynasty . . . but that's . . ."

"Four hundred years ago. Go on, finish the inscription."

" 'Offering her famous Hsueh T'ao Poem Pages to the centuries . . .' Those are the very sheets of the scroll, the pine and plum-blossom paper . . . this must be the ancestress of the Chance Met Lady."

"Hung Tu had no descendants, T'ien Chu."

"Then . . . then . . . but the likeness . . ."

"This is the site of the Villa Pi-chi-Fang, built for her by the Silk River, where she poured wine for her friends and harmonized poems. Where she also entertained many guests for the Governors of Shu. It was here that she invented and manufactured paper known by her family name, Hsueh T'ao. And . . . here is her handwriting, on this bronze plaque, T'ien Chu."

T'ien Chu leaned forward to peer at the columns of bold script. Then he fumbled in his sleeve and brought out the scroll. His fingers shook as he unrolled it and held it beside the plaque. He began to compare the writing. Suddenly he sighed deeply, the world turned about him, he fell to the ground.

They carried him home in the litter, his head in the magistrate's lap, the scroll in his hand, rising, falling to the turning of the wheels behind the white oxen.

That night when the moon was high and he was somewhat recovered, lying on a mat in the magistrate's room, watching Wu-tsung's face as he examined the scroll, T'ien Chu said, "One thing troubles me. . . ."

"One? You are fortunate."

"Hung Tu was old when she died. That inscription said seventy-two. The Chance Met Lady is young . . . young. . . ."

"So was Hung Tu's likeness on the plaque. You recognized her at once."

"But . . ."

"Is it not probable, T'ien Chu, that fragrant ghosts beckoned back choose what age they will assume when they pour wine for new friends?"

"But . . ."

"T'ien Chu, do not persist. Remember the saying 'if you see an uncanny thing and do not regard it as such, its uncanniness will disappear.' You are fortunate. Not only did the great Shu laureate come back to harmonize a poem with you, but she left you a scroll to prove it, a literary masterpiece, which will make you rich and famous."

"I will never sell it."

"No, I imagine not." Magistrate Wu-tsung sighed. "Still you have it there, in her handwriting and yours. Men will believe what they are forced to concede."

"Sir," T'ien Chu said, "you have been very patient with the ravings of this stupid person from the beginning."

"I said you were fortunate. You came before the one official who might hear you sympathetically. I too . . . in my day . . . when I was young . . . harmonized a poem with the Chance Met Lady. But my verses were bad. We destroyed the scroll."

After a long pause T'ien Chu said reflectively, "One thing . . ."

18

"Another?"

"I remember that she said she would give me some of the paper when I came back. And she said again, or she agreed when I said it, I don't remember exactly . . ."

"So soon?"

"I was very drunk," he said defensively. "But I think she said that I would come back and harmonize more poems. . . . Did she . . . ?"

"Yes, she also said that to me. I think of it sometimes. And so will you, T'ien Chu."

PART TWO
Circa 760–780 A.D.

IV

BEYOND THE WALL turbulence went rushing by like the River Min, but this was a river of feet, surging into the city. Sometimes the sound was cut by sudden stridencies, laughter, shouted words, street vendors' cries. Mostly it flowed on, a water noise, not friendly like the fishponds in the court, dangerous, deep water.

Behind the wall the safe world was laid out, orderly, with paths to the pavilions, flower beds, and shrubs. Life moved through the garden. Birds flashed by. People came and went, her mother and the other women, aunts and maids; children ran and quarreled, her brothers, who would never play with her; sometimes a man in stiff silk robes rustled gorgeously, her father, to whom they all behaved as stiffly as the robes, as though they were afraid.

She was not afraid. She had a secret strength. When they were alone she could make her father smile. She could even make him laugh and call her teasing names. In front of the others he ignored her. She was a misfortune, inexplicably, for no one would explain it to her, born to be a girl.

But still she was the small daughter of the House of Hsueh, and she was not afraid, of her father, of the world over the wall, of anything. Her official name was Hsueh T'ao, but they called her mostly by her small name, Hung Tu, and she was seven years old, born, the women said, a long way from this garden.

She remembered, or from hearing the women she coaxed tell of it, thought she remembered, snatches of that journey from far-off Chang-an, taken when she was two. There, in the farthest east of the Empire she was born, in the great Capital, Red Phoenix City, glory of the Tang, where the Emperor reigned with all his court . . . "friend and protector of your father."

"Why then did we leave?"

"I've told you."

"Tell me again."

It was a story that could always make her "be good and go to sleep," "be good and eat your rice," "be good and stop your pestering, play quietly."

There was a rebellion. Rebels came and sacked the Imperial City.

"I've told you what sacked means."

The songs the women sang to her, the tales they told, were full of heroic deeds by the Emperor's warriors against Barbarians in the North. There was always war and trouble from the North, but this time it was in the East, in the Capital itself, and it was not Barbarians, it was the Emperor's own army that rose up against him and sacked and looted the city and sacked and looted the Palace. It was mutineers.

"What is mu . . ."

"Hush, Pestilence, and let me do my work."

The Hsuehs fled. So did the Emperor and his court, but the important thing was that the Hsuehs fled, and the most important thing of all was that they carried her with them.

Over hills, on horseback, by palanquin. . . .

"What's pala . . ."

"Never you mind."

By boat, and across scorched plains on foot, through passes where the narrow road clung to the precipice, up cliffs so high you couldn't see the sky, on roads of ladders, and bridges hooked together in the air. . . .

"The yellow crane could not fly over these mountaintops, and the monkeys wail, unable to leap over these gorges; alas how precipitous, alas how high! The road to Shu is more difficult to climb than the steep blue heavens," her father quoted. "That was written for us by the poet Li Po."

"I know," Elder Brother said smugly. "My brother and I are studying the works of my father's friend Li Po."

Hung Tu might have added that she was studying them too,

but at ten she had learned to be silent. There was a value in silence. The privilege of studying the classics with her brothers was a most unusual indulgence. She was nervous that it might be taken from her.

The first time that she marched into the Pavilion of Calm Studies with her brush and scroll and sat down expectantly, her brothers, especially Elder Brother, protested hotly. She was a girl. She had no business there. Honorable Tutor must turn her out at once. But Honorable Tutor was amused, or else he had an inkling of what her father would say.

"Let the small dragon stay," her father said. "She will tire of it soon enough."

When she proved him wrong, he shrugged, as her brothers had to learn to shrug, and she was allowed to practice script and master characters according to p'ai-lü, so long as she kept quiet, in the background where she belonged, and so long as she was properly admiring of her brothers' brushwork and did not put forward her own.

When the day came to advance to a study of the even and uneven tones of the five-character lines of the classics, there was another protest and a much stronger one. This time Elder Brother had a sharper weapon against her. This time she had made a great mistake. She had shown her first completed poem to Honorable Tutor, and he had read it aloud, pointing out the beauty of the brushwork and the sound composition of the form. It was called "Now Alighted."

> *Now alighted on the shadowy pool*
> *two birds float together on the green water.*
> *They rest as one, they move as one,*
> *they cannot be parted,*
> *whose hearts and minds and bodies*
> *know only each other,*
> *who have never had a dissenting thought.*
> *Even the leaves and the rushes*
> *cling together, bending above them.*
> *Happy birds! Happy birds!*

Elder Brother was beside himself. "It is indelicate," he said. "Why should she write of love? How should she know of love? I am contracted in marriage, and I . . . and I . . ."

Hung Tu smiled up at him. "You have been trying to write a poem of love now for a week. You are angry because my brushwork is commended. Shall I lend you my poem, Elder Brother, to send to your betrothed?"

At that he snatched the scroll from the tutor and ran to his father, and Hung Tu trembled, knowing she had gone too far.

When she was sent for, she arrived with downcast eyes and hands in her long sleeves and stood demurely before her father, while Elder Brother sputtered and scolded at his side, and—she could tell this from his feet, tapping beneath the robe—bored him with this vehemence.

Nevertheless, "Eighteen gifted daughters do not equal one lame son," he told her sternly. "A due respect for your brothers is more pleasing than good brushwork." He gave her back the scroll.

To his sons he said, "Teach the parrot to talk, some will do it well. Teach the girl to write, some will do it well. What then? What is changed? It is still a bird, it is still a girl." He shrugged.

To Honorable Tutor he said, "Correct me if I quote the Master with inaccuracy. Did he not once say: 'Women are indeed human beings, but they are of a lower state than men. They can never attain to full equality with men. The aim of feminine education therefore is perfect submission, not the cultivation and development of the mind.'" After a pause he added, "It has never been proved that women have a mind . . . nor disproved." Then to his sons, "Let the small dragon live. It has no wings. What if it try to sing? It is not heard."

He dismissed them. Elder Brother bowed and left the pavilion. Second Brother lingered sulkily.

"My father, when the time comes for me to part the curtains, do not choose for me a wife who can read."

"It shall be remembered. Yet, my second son, a well-informed mind to share the pillow can be a source of strength and of comfort to a man."

There was an awkward silence while they all remembered that his own wives could not read.

And to Hung Tu, waiting in the doorway for her betters to depart, he said unexpectedly, "Give me the scroll."

Later she discovered from some gossip of the maids he had shown it to his friends, boasting of his daughter's talent, and they had drunk toasts to her.

She was at the well when she heard it, with her mother's pitcher to be filled. It was early in the morning, when the latest news went round, while the creaking buckets were hauled up on their ropes and the jostling servants waited, laughing together, relaxed and fresh for the day, the lord and the ladies of the house still safe in bed.

Sometimes they forgot that she was there and she heard things not intended for her, but this they wanted her to hear; they were pleased and proud of this small triumph, reflecting credit on the House of Hsueh.

She managed to smile demurely and to look on the ground as she should, and to make little gestures of polite deprecation to show how well she was trained, but her heart was thumping wildly and she needed all her strength to hold the pitcher steady and to watch it being filled and then to carry it away on her shoulder as though this water for the Second Lady was all she was thinking of, instead of her father's approval of her poem and the knowledge flooding her that she was a great poet, the greatest poet in the Empire probably.

V

HUNG TU'S MOTHER was the Second Lady of the House of Hsueh. She had come from a great merchant's house in Chang-an, where she was only a concubine, as the First Lady often pointed out. Worse, she bore her husband nothing but a slave, a girl. His *sons* were First Lady's.

These unkind public reflections wounded Hung Tu deeply, more than they seemed to hurt her mother, who sat serenely through them, gently acquiescing in anything that Elder Sister chose to say.

When, as a child, Hung Tu was stung to bursts of weeping, disgracing them both, Second Lady would take her quietly away to their own pavilion. She never scolded. She never encouraged rebellion or admitted that Elder Sister was unkind. But once, when Hung Tu in a passion of helpless fury shouted, "I hate her! I hate her!" Second Lady said, "Then do as I do, never give her the satisfaction of your tears."

After that Hung Tu grew more cunning and more observant. One thing she observed, and saw others observing while they pretended to be blind. This was that her father's sleeping mat was spread more often in Second Lady's pavilion than in Elder Sister's. Second Lady was gentle, she was pretty, her mind upon the pillow must have been satisfactory, a source of strength and comfort to her husband, although she had never learned script. When Hsueh Yun emerged from Second Lady's door he was always smiling and content. People could ask him favors then, or tell him disquieting news. When his mat was spread in Elder Sister's pavilion it was better to efface oneself that day, at least until the noon.

These reflections helped Hung Tu to endure the nagging of Elder Sister, the indifference of her brothers, and the rudeness of them all to her mother. Second Lady lived in as much seclusion as

Elder Sister would permit, and in this way the daily life went on, with undercurrents of victory this side or that, beneath a surface of decorum.

Second Lady's small name was Harmonizing Reed. It suited her essence. She could play several instruments—the harp, the lute, the guitar. Her voice was like silver raindrops. She had a prodigious memory for hundreds of songs. Long before Honorable Tutor introduced Hung Tu to the classics, she already knew the words of many by heart, from her mother's songs. This was an advantage her brothers did not have, and one reason why she outstripped them at their lessons. As long as she could remember, Second Lady sang her to sleep with a different song each night. Sometimes her father came to listen. Then Second Lady played and sang for him alone, and Hung Tu was quite forgotten.

This was the union between them, the single mind, the undivided part, the heart the leaves attested of her poem. To their harmonious union she owed her existence and the indulgence with which she was treated in the House of Hsueh although she was a girl.

When she discussed this puzzling question, the misfortune of being born a girl, a disgrace to Hsueh Yun and Second Lady, and what she had done to be so evil, Second Lady paid serious attention, as though the words in her mouth were important. This was soothing to Hung Tu, wilting over what her brothers often said.

"If they were not so unkind, I would like being a girl."

Second Lady smiled at her.

"It is wisdom to enjoy being oneself. When your brothers speak against you rudely, bend as the bamboo does to the breeze. It is but air in their mouths. How can it hurt you?"

"But they say it and say it all the time!"

"A true thing, daughter, need only be uttered once, sometimes not at all, to be evident and acceptable. A doubtful thing is repeated many times, loudly, with anger and with argument. This does not make it true or acceptable."

"But Elder Sister . . ."

"Elder Sister speaks for our good, and sometimes from unhappiness. Remember that."

"If Elder Sister is unhappy, she deserves to be. She makes everyone unhappy, even my father."

"Elder Sister is First Lady of the House of Hsueh," Second Lady said quickly. "We will speak of her with proper respect."

"Well, but I would rather give my husband joy than two dull sons."

"The breath of your mouth is evil," Second Lady said severely, but her own mouth trembled, hiding a quick smile. She changed the subject from Elder Sister to Hung Tu's difficulties as a girl.

"There are precepts to be observed," she said. "A woman must do what she does better than a man would do it, and be sure that it goes unnoticed, to be acceptable to men. It is therefore wise to restrict one's occupations to those a man does not generally desire to do."

"But I want to be a poet," Hung Tu said sullenly. "And when I brush good words I am in disgrace."

"Not because you brush good words. You could brush good words all day and nobody would mind. It is because you jostle your brothers' elbows. You claim attention for your words, while some of the greatest poets let theirs go unclaimed."

Hung Tu pondered this.

"It is never wise to insist on praise from unwilling lips. You would do better to praise your brothers' words and offer to copy them. You might set them to music and sing them to your father, or to all of us, in the garden."

"I had rather sing my own words."

"You may do that too, when they are good enough, and when you have worked harder at your instrument. When I was your age I could play the p'i-pa as well as I do now, and I had already sung before the Emperor."

It was rare that Second Lady mentioned her childhood, and when she did it usually put an end to the conversation. Hung Tu bowed and went about her duties, but she thought about these things and grew more confident.

VI

Hsueh Yun was sometimes depressed that the head of the House of Hsueh was now a minor official in a provincial city far from former greatness and from the Emperor's mind. The mood fell upon him most heavily when envoys arrived from the Court with news of the great world and the happenings about the Golden Throne, gossip of this man's rise or that old friend's disgrace.

Then he would wonder uneasily about his own position. Should he have returned to the Capital when he heard that the revolution was crushed and the Emperor and his court were once more at Chang-an, in the Imperial Palace? But that was a long year after the flight and he had found his position in Cheng-tu. There would be the terrible road to retrace and at the end of the desperate journey no assurance that he would get his old appointment back, or any appointment. There were new faces now about the Emperor, and he would favor those who had stayed with him and fought with him, moving from camp to camp, while Hsueh Yun had struck out on his own.

So he had stayed in Cheng-tu when he reached it, for good or for ill, and was now in a post too small, he hoped, for envy to set the great wheel turning which might crush him from Chang-an. He was still in the Emperor's service, still a government official. His salary was paid from the Imperial Treasury, though not directly to him. It was included in the Governor's monies, who took the customary offering from it, then it went to the minister in charge of his department and then to his immediate superior. After all of them deducted what was proper, he was left with a scarcity of coin, which he in turn made up by extorting gifts and offerings from his subordinates and demanding bribes and payments from anyone else he could.

It was a living, and when travelers arrived from other parts of the land reporting trouble, raids and counterraids, famine and devastation, he was content with his decision. Shu, when once a man could reach it, seemed an oasis of prosperity and peace.

It was an agricultural district, a wide and fertile plain, sheltered by surrounding mountains, watered by a network of ingenious canals devised by an earlier ruler from the meeting of three other rivers with the turbulent River Min. The earth was rich and lavish. Flowers, cultivated with excessive labor in the Emperor's gardens in Chang-an, here were growing wild: hibiscus in so many varieties that some of them were still unnamed, the yulan, the mountain tea flower, the rose, the lilac, the aster, the apricot, the peach, and now in courts and gardens, the tree peony, lately introduced from India.

Cultivated crops grew even more lavishly, and if there were no unnatural floods or droughts or locusts to contend with, Shu would continue to be what the poets called it, a paradise, far from the rest of the starving, struggling world. It was far, and it was hard to reach, almost impossible by the eastern road and nearly as cut off from the north and south. But too many refugees were reaching it, desperate and dangerous men, with nothing to lose but the remnant of their broken lives. Too many were crawling these days into Shu. It was beginning to be a disquieting thing.

They were arriving from all quarters, farmers and peasants driven off their lands, soldiers defeated in battle. So far the Province could absorb them, those who were able-bodied and willing to work in the fields. The rest starved or went back where they came from or—how would one know? The world was always full of beggars, the sick, the unfortunate. It was Hsueh Yun's responsibility to settle the suitable where there was need of them.

So far he had managed to keep them out of the city itself, herded into camps at the other end of the valley. Those who were needed for work inside the gates had special passes, good for the day. At nightfall they must leave. This meant a stream of early morning and late evening traffic to be regulated and supervised, but it also kept Cheng-tu free of disruptive elements.

The City of Silk, Shu's capital, was a walled enclosure of enough great houses and enough established families to make the nucleus of a good society, a replica in miniature of the glittering life in Chang-an, around the Imperial Court. There was wealth here, as there, but the difference was that here a man of reason with only moderate means could mingle with the best, and, if he lived in one of the less fashionable quarters of the city, maintain a good-sized household, safe and fine about him . . . if he kept his post. That was the crux of it, the great anxiety . . . if he lost his post, well, from that no man could recover. That was ruin. Unless he had lands and wealth independent from his office. And what man had those? Not Hsueh Yun.

All this was going through his mind one day as he sat alone in his pavilion. He had come from a meeting with the Governor and some officials from Chang-an. One of these officials he had known in the days when they were studying for their first examination. Now that one was riding high and likely to ride higher. Something that he said made Hsueh Yun uneasy. Was it prudent to neglect his old ties completely, to let himself be entirely forgotten at the Court? On the other hand, would it be prudent to recall himself to attention? So long as his salary continued to arrive with the rest of the Governor's money, should he not let well enough alone?

Perhaps he might rouse himself to send an occasional poem to the Emperor. In the past his poems were well received. He must be careful not to sound too eager to leave or to stay in Shu. A lament of his uselessness to the Throne and a delicate reproach that his political talents were being overlooked might sound the right note. He could determine later whether he would send it.

He went to his tablets and took up his brush.

In my garden the Wu t'ung tree is tall,

That was a good first line, a mighty oak, yes, that described him well. . . .

roots in the earth, head in the sky.

Too lofty, too remote to prop up the Emperor's falling house? Nothing explicit, nothing too overt or wounding, yet the inference was there.

O, for the eyes of an Emperor
to see the phoenix!

Now how to go on to suggest that the tree might better serve the throne, without being uprooted from the court where it was? He did not want to be transferred, only approved and promoted.

Something about its gifts being wasted, on the ants and bees, that was safe, or perhaps its sure support only the ravens know.

That might do. It said nothing much and yet it suggested troubled loyalty, anxious to be doing more for the Golden Throne. Hmm hmm hmm . . . its gifts are wasted . . . he took the brush more firmly toward the inkstone and was about to dip it in when a small commotion beside him swept it from his hand, and two columns of wet lines scrawled themselves beside his own:

> *In my garden the Wu t'ung tree is tall,*
> *birds from the south, birds from the north*
> *are nesting there.*
> *At every passing wind the branches tremble.*

Hung Tu was crouched beside him, leaning over his elbow. She had just completed his quatrain, taking it in a direction he had never meant it to go, and which he could certainly not use for his promotion.

Birds from every quarter? New ideas from wherever they might come? This was a dangerous, revolutionary thought. And whatever winds passed, with the breath of freedom, of unconventional forces sweeping across the narrow decorums of the day?

What bold, preposterous sentiment! How it lifted the whole poem into a proud challenge, instead of the mild resigned reproach he had planned it to contain. How disquieting that a daughter of his house should think in this free way and be able to express it so well!

"The breath of your mouth is evil," he said sternly, looking at

34

the sleek dark head pressed against his shoulder. She did not answer, but when she lifted her face to look at him there was no fear in her eyes; in his, a mixture of pride and consternation. He was afraid for her and of what the future would bring to a girl with such ideas.

They sat together in silence, in front of the completed scroll. Then he said:

"Well, I see that when the time comes to order the Red Candles and the Flowery Chair, we must look for a very brave husband."

He laughed, but he was half in earnest. It was going to be difficult to find a husband for his daughter, not only because she had a free spirit—that might be concealed, with luck—but because the times were so uncertain and money so hard to come by that many men, even the wealthiest heads of great families, were deferring marriage for their sons. He himself had not made any betrothal plans or even negotiations for his second son, and he was hoping that his first son's future father-in-law would not choose this inconvenient moment to press for the wedding date . . . which he might, since his daughter was ready, had been ready for a year.

Yet how could he enlarge his household to include a son's wife and the children to follow, when it was harder every day to maintain it as it was? His sons were little help. They had passed their examinations, but so low on the list there was not much hope they would be named to official posts until he could buy the openings for them. Even with gold, with a brilliant record and with influence, it was a lucky chance for a man to set his sons' feet on the ladder that led to public office, especially in Cheng-tu, and to send them away was expensive and just as competitive.

He sighed so heavily that Hung Tu looked at him with concern and was glad, for once, when Elder Sister sent for her to run an errand, transparently devised to take her out of her father's sight. If she made him so unhappy when she was with him, she would as soon not be there.

VII

WORD BEGAN TO GO ROUND, discreetly and in the right places, that the daughter of subofficial Hsueh Yun was ready for marriage. The news stirred up some interest among the young men of the city and those older men who thought of adding a second or third lady to their households, or even a concubine.

The girl was known to be pretty and said to be well raised. The father's means were straightened and his rank not such that he could demand the highest price for an alliance with his house. It was likely to be a bargain worth looking into, certainly worth looking at.

So Hung Tu was seen in public on such occasions and in such places as she should be seen, sometimes with her father, sometimes with her brothers, sometimes with reliable older servants, but not, the curious noticed, in the company of the First Lady of the House of Hsueh or of her own mother.

Elder Sister was taking no notice of Hung Tu's coming of age to be married, except to demand her presence at inconvenient moments for trumped-up tasks and to nag at her more bitterly. She did not dare go further than this petty persecution in view of Hsueh Yun's "unseemly infatuation" for his daughter.

And that spring Second Lady was in declining health after the birth of a stillborn son.

"The ways of Heaven are just and full of wisdom," Elder Sister declared, burning sticks of incense in conspicuous places. She went on a bustling pilgrimage to the Temple of Shang Shan, above the city, where she offered rice and candles and paid a monk to strike the golden gong in gratitude for her delivery "from a too-heavy event." She did not have to define it. Everyone present understood what event would have raised Second Lady to a position of honor and dignity in that household. Perhaps, Elder Sister hinted, Hsueh Yun should take notice of the verdict of Heaven.

Second Lady made no gestures toward Heaven, and none to the world outside her gates. She never left her pavilion unless compelled to by Elder Sister's demands. After a while these ceased, on Hsueh Yun's orders, and she was left to her seclusion.

Hung Tu, sharing her roof and attending to her needs, grew conscious that her existence was becoming nonexistent to her mother; that at last the constant reproach, endured through the years, had worn down the ties between them, until this gentle, distraught, sick woman felt no emotion, no relationship with anyone except her stillborn son. Even Hsueh Yun was no longer alive to her, though she performed every act of devoted attention to him with more care than before, Hung Tu thought, watching them with aching pity.

Perhaps he did not know what he had lost. He was pressed with cares that spring. Troubles racked up round him. He spent long hours in conference with the Governor. He was working late into the nights. Something was wrong in Shu, and while he grappled with these distant demands and dangers he was blind to his nearer calamity . . . mercifully . . . yet Hung Tu felt his blindness was the deepest, most desolate bereavement.

The love between him and her mother had been the fine banner of her childhood, her secret security. Now he did not even know that her mother had gone from him.

Or did he know? Was this restless activity his retreat into seclusion? How could one be sure what older people knew, or felt, or were, barricaded from each other and particularly from their children by rigidly fixed walls?

Bowed heads, hands in sleeves, polite, prescribed gestures, carefully chosen words, always chosen by others, to express "appropriate sentiments," that was how one met one's elders. That was how she met her father, except for a few jeweled moments, unexpected as they were brief, when in the courage of her ignorance she had dared to meet him as herself. That was long ago, a small, foolhardy child, accidentally alone with him, but the father she saw then was the father she had loved and trusted all these years and for whom she was troubled now.

If people could face each other stripped of the padded quilts of prescribed behavior and start and go on from there! But some would be intolerable without those imposed restraints. Elder Sister, for instance.

Yet when did any conventional rules foil her? How was it that the meanness of the mean broke through high-built walls to devastate everything in sight, all the smiling landscape of the kind? How was it that the kind were hampered behind their own restraint?

It was a thought she often turned over, a lonely thought, until she heard her brothers discussing casually, as something they had often talked about before, "the chasm, impossible to cross," between them and the "tight world" of the elders.

They talked about it cynically, with a natural taken-for-granted resentment that astonished her. She had never dreamed that anyone except her depraved self, and certainly not any man, could be dissatisfied with the order of society, the way things were on earth. How else could they be but the established way, decreed from the beginning by Heaven? Yet her brothers spoke as though there were a choice, or could be a choice, of other ways. To them it was not a question, as it was to her, of the subjugation of half the human race, the separation of man from woman. They were in revolt against the old, against authority. They were like those mutineers who sacked the Emperor's Palace, and triumphed for a year . . . and were defeated.

She had always been, secretly of course, on the side of the mutineers. It was the brief year they enjoyed, sacking and looting the city, that made her clamor for their story and follow it raptly to the end. They were defeated, yes, but first she imagined herself among them, living in the Palace, playing with forbidden things. She did not care that they were "wicked men" whose doings were the reason why the Hsuehs "had to leave everything" and "claw their way" to Cheng-tu.

That was just the way people talked. As far as she could remember "everything" had always been here, where she was, first in the garden around her, then in the larger compound and the world beyond the wall.

She would always be glad the mutineers had their year. She saw them as a band of djinns, more than mortal, lighthearted, frisking through the Palace, dancing and cavorting to their own wild tunes. Naturally the oppressive "way of things" put an end to that. They were too free, too enchanting for their own good, these kindred of hers who had lost her or forgotten where she was. She wanted to believe they knew, but could not come for her yet because they had been defeated.

She had not thought of that childish sequence for years. It came back to her when she overheard her brothers talking together. Second Lady had fallen asleep after a restless, pain-filled night. Hung Tu left her with a servant and escaped for an hour of peace to her favorite thinking-place, a stone bench in the shade, hidden from the rest of the garden by clumps of tall bamboo.

She thought they were quarreling at first, as they used to when they were children playing along the paths. Their voices were harsh with anger. But when they came close enough for her to hear what they were saying, she realized that they were angry, not against each other, but against Hsueh Yun. They had just come from his pavilion, where things had gone badly for them.

". . . wait another twenty or thirty years . . ."

"It would take that long for 'times to improve, my sons.' "

"What does he think? That nobody ever married when the times were bad?"

"He says 'unrest,' 'bandits.' Whose fault is that? Who herded them all together and let them get organized? All they needed was a leader, and now they've got a leader. What did he expect? 'Times to improve'? Who's doing anything to make the times improve?"

"You heard him when I offered to go out there and help him. Making soothing noises, as though we were children."

"That's what he'd like us to be. A child has ears and no mouth, that's what they all want, no one to ask questions, no one to answer back. . . ."

"We might as well be castrated as live like this!"

"There are those waiting for us now who would not agree with you!"

"And how long would we all have to wait if it depended on the old bullfrog? Croak, croak, croak! 'An old man has crossed more bridges than a young man has crossed streets.' Who was talking about bridges or streets? How much money does he give us to go to the Blue Houses while we wait for women of our own? If it weren't for the clever way you pick up something now and then . . ."

"In shooting a tiger or catching a bandit, depend on your own brother."

"It's a good saying. But sometimes I wonder whether we shouldn't look into what the bandits have to offer two ambitious brothers."

"Except that their leaders are old men too."

"How old is Pockmark Chou?"

"One hears different things, and of course he has the physique of a bull, but he must be nearing thirty."

"There must be someone somewhere. . . . Or we could form our own band. . . ."

Their voices faded as they turned into another path, leaving Hung Tu startled by this glimpse into her brothers' essences, startled and curious to know more of them.

They had gone very separate ways since Honorable Tutor left. For years they never saw each other except at formal gatherings where she, and now she understood they too, had been busy with protective concealment of everything important and true, under the "appropriate" masks prescribed for the young by their elders.

She might never have discovered that Hsueh-Tai and Hsueh-Ts'an were more than official shadows, occupying certain places at certain times, if their father had not been pressed by business, and his wives, for their different reasons, unconcerned with her affairs. It fell to her brothers to exert themselves to find a suitor for her. This was Hsueh Yun's will.

It tossed them between two fires, their father's orders, which they were bound to obey, and their mother's bitter opposition to those orders, which they were also bound, on the surface at least, to respect. Their father's will came first, but their mother made life hard for them and for Hung Tu in many ingenious ways.

Left to themselves they might have enjoyed their new responsibility. They had never disliked their sister, even in her stormy childhood days. She had stung them, annoyed them, amused them, and subsided into the young girl's background of her mother's pavilion, while they went on to the world to become what they were now, handsome, dull young men, twenty and eighteen, who had finished their education, passed their examinations, and were waiting, uneasily, for their first appointments . . . and for other things too, Hsueh-Tai for his bride, Hsueh-Ts'an for his betrothal to a bride.

Both of them felt injured by their father's "abnormal attitude" toward their marriages. They were embarrassed before their friends by the long delay. Their hope now was that if they could arrange their sister's marriage for a good price, their father would be pleased and remember his duty toward them. After all, they were his sons.

"And, in the proverbs he lives by, 'have a son and everything is all right.' He should remember that."

Perhaps he would, if they did things well. It was worth a try, and it should not be hard. Their sister was fifteen, well-formed, adept in the arts of painting her face and putting up her hair. She wore her unimportant clothes with a graceful air of fashion. She could play and sing in a pleasing way. Already she attracted the attention of their friends and other young men whom they would like to call their friends, whenever she was seen. The question was to display her to them properly, to the best advantage, with the least expense, for the purse strings were grudgingly loosened. "The old buzzard, how it sticks to his fingers!" they said half admiringly.

They talked it over and decided the right place to begin was on the river, at the Dragon Festival.

VIII

THE RIVER WAS THE GREAT ARTERY for traffic, the city's floating market, where the local merchants, farmers, fishermen, peddlers, men with goods to dispose of cried and displayed their wares. It was jammed with junks, rafts, rowboats, barges, and, at this time of the year, houseboats and pleasure boats. The Dragon Festival brought everybody out, especially the young. It was their festival. But even without it there would still be crowds on the river the first fine days of spring, the best days of the year.

The Hsuehs had no houseboat of their own. They hired a punt with a boatman to pole it, comfortable cushions, an awning of embroidered cloth for shade, a hamper of cakes and sweetmeats, a container of wine. Nothing was forgotten for enjoyment.

It was all new to Hung Tu, the sun on the changing stream, the trees they drifted beneath, making unexpected patterns of shadow, the gaily painted boats like theirs, filled with friends calling out to friends, laughter, shouting, music . . . she had not imagined "going on the river with your brothers" could be such a golden time.

She was shy and embarrassed at first, but once she got over the discomfort of being stared at and appraised she settled down to enjoy herself. There was no Elder Sister with them to hurt her by malicious asides, just her brothers showing her off to the world. They were watching her smugly, signaling to each other . . . she hoped it was to each other . . . behind her carefully turned head. They seemed pleased.

There was a certain excitement in gauging the effect she made. It was a nuisance to have to remember never to look directly at anything one wanted especially to see. She was used to that, an adept at the swift oblique glance when a watcher's attention went elsewhere. Sometimes she thought women saw more than men, or at least they were more observant of what they saw. They had to work so hard collecting indirect impressions and interpreting snatches of fragments that in the end they "saw" a surprising amount of the whole situation clearly, and were able to reveal it to each other and sometimes to their men. It was a tedious strain, this "polite-looking-downward-vision," this "veiled-in-the-mist" demeanor, this crazy roundabout . . . but it was the way things were.

Her brothers were unobservant. When they were little boys they hardly saw anything that she hadn't seen already. Half the time they missed the significance of what they saw until she pointed it out. They hated that, so often she held her tongue and they missed that hummingbird, that dragonfly, that changing cloud, that mouse. When they missed something she saw, she felt shut out, as though it were she who missed it. She was lonely then, as she was now, in this boat, with them watching her.

Fortunately, though they took their duties seriously, sometimes they forgot her, busy with their own affairs, ogling pretty faces, competing with their friends. She wished they would forget her altogether, but sooner or later they remembered and showed her off to whatever spectators there happened to be. When a lull came in the traffic Hsueh-Tai was struck by an idea. He motioned to the boatman to change course and put in toward the right bank of the river. Then, casually, he asked Hung Tu to sing. She took up her guitar obediently, Hsueh-Ts'an brought out his reed flute and they began to harmonize together. It would have been enjoyable if it had been what it seemed, but they were drifting close, too close, to the landing of a rich man's house, where a group was gathered on the lawn. Hung Tu felt uncomfortable. She tried to keep it at that, just uncomfortable, but she slid to shy, to ashamed, to miserable, to angry.

The tableau was too obvious. There was some ironic applause, when Hseuh-Ts'an blew a fountain of particularly brilliant trills. He was a fine musician. Perhaps the comment she heard was well meant after all, a tribute to his skill. She wished it so, but she was aware from the looks they were giving her, and the clumsy slowing down of the boatman's pole, that she was on display to someone

43

they considered important. Even looking rigidly downward she could see robes so close that another step would bring them into the boat beside her. Green robe, white robe, gold robe, which? Or were they all important?

Her throat closed convulsively. She stopped singing. It was all she could manage to go on plucking chords and harmonizing with Hsueh-Ts'an, until at last they drifted beyond that hateful place. They picked up speed and headed back toward midstream, where there were more things to distract people's attention, where, if she were still on display, it was not so much like the laying out of a peddler's pack in front of indifferent feet.

Her brothers' friends in the passing boats stared, but they were young. Those rich robes on the bank were old men's robes. The way the old men stood was cold, stiff; if they looked at her with any warmth it was only the warmth of a moment's titillated lust. She did not believe it was that . . . even their lust was cold, burned-out. . . .

Now the punt scraped the side of a pleasure boat full of shrill-voiced girls who knew her brothers. They waved and called out greetings. Hsueh-Ts'an was pleased. He laughed and waved back, but Hsueh-Tai was annoyed and looked down at her sharply, the way he used when she was a child stepping out of her place. This time it was nothing she had done, just another of the obvious things she was not supposed to notice or to understand.

There was a great exchange of jokes and proposing of toasts, which made her thirsty to overhear. When the pleasure boat at last went on its way, she suggested they unpack the hamper, and they ate the sweetmeats and drank the heady wine. That was better. She had begun to feel weary, discouraged, set apart. The wine brought back her pleasure. It deadened self-consciousness.

Now there was a bustle of clearing the midstream channel and crowding the traffic to both sides of the river. Beating gongs and distant shouting announced the start of the Dragon procession. First came a lacquered guard boat full of soldiers, rowing so fast that it churned up a wash that rocked all the little boats, whirled some around, set others adrift. Across the river from the Hsuehs someone fell in and was fished out swearing, in a flurry of confusion.

Then came the Governor's longboat, passing slowly, painted green and purple, with a great gold dragon on its prow. Governor Wei Kao sat on a raised dais in his official robes. This was his annual appearance among the people he governed in the Emperor's name, and he was worth looking at for more than his magnificent clothes, woven for him in Cheng-tu, each year more sumptuous, to encourage the industry of the City of Silk. He was a vigorous, handsome soldier in his prime, an astute administrator, one of the best magistrates in the Empire, it was said. Hung Tu had never seen him, but she felt she knew him well from the things her father quoted and told about him daily. He was part of the Hsueh household.

Everyone stood up in the boats, waving and shouting. Hung Tu stood up too, clutching at Hsueh-Tai's arm. She forgot to look down as she stared after the Governor, and so she saw clearly, full face and frankly, a young man in the boat beyond theirs looking as frankly at her.

She should have turned her head at once, but something got into her, some excitement from the Governor passing, some wayward ripple from the river. She went on looking at him as boldly as those women in the pleasure boat had looked at her brothers, only this was different. She knew that he knew this was different, however surprised he might be.

Not more surprised than she. It was the best, most honest thing she encountered that day, and for long before it. It restored an essence she had almost lost. She would have liked to tell him in spoken words, "Thank you, for being young and true."

He smiled, he bowed toward her, he received her thought, this stranger, who was not a stranger though she had never seen him before except in dreams and daydreams, standing, smiling, looking deeply at her, while she looked deeply back.

Barges were passing, with tableaux and pageants on them. She saw none of them. Neither did he. While everyone round them shouted and waved and exclaimed, they stood in silence, exchanging essences.

Hsueh-Tai wheeled round toward her and now she looked away, hastily exclaiming something, she knew not what, about the vanishing procession. She reseated herself on her cushion. Her brothers sat down on theirs, the boatman pushed in his pole, the punt began to move forward, upstream again, then it turned and went downstream, and then upstream again, threading its way through the traffic, as everyone else was doing, until it should be time for the evening fireworks.

Wherever they went he was there, watching her from his little boat, passing, turning, returning, trailing her, sooner or later arriving where she was. Her brothers did not see him at all. He had a face they were used to, or unaware of, a blank face to them, not a rich, important face they would bother to launch her toward. Not even, she must admit, the handsomest face in the world . . . it was lopsided, there should perhaps be more space between the large eyes, more bridge to the nose. . . . She longed to know his name, but how could she ask? She sat silent. Her brothers forgot her, busy with schemes of their own.

It was the best part of the day. People were friendly, relaxed, a little tipsy, a little tired, pleased with the bets they had placed, the plans they were making, each other. The music was softer, the singing more serious, night was ahead.

Now the last time downstream, through the descending darkness, warm, drowsy, her mind full of sights and sounds, faces seen obliquely, and one face, framed in the fireworks falling over the river, this side, that side, moonlit, shadowed . . . the prize she brought back with her from the Dragon Festival.

IX

THE MOON RODE HIGH AND FULL. Second Lady was restless. Hung Tu heard her stirring and rose to join her. The divisions of day and night meant little to her mother now. The edges of things were confused. Sometimes she lay in bed all day and resisted being fed; then, if there were a moon, she would get up suddenly, dress, do her hair, put on ornaments, eat what she found, and play and sing for hours.

"Disturbing her honorable husband, Elder Sister, the household" . . . nothing stopped her. She heard no remonstrances, understood no advice. Music was all she wanted. Sometimes she held out flute or p'i-pa or gestured toward her harp.

"Harmonize with me now, never mind the hour, make music," the gentle gestures said. If they begged her to stop, she did not hear them. If they tried to take the instrument from her, she screamed and got her way. Neither Hung Tu nor the servant Fanyang who nursed her could bear Second Lady to be discovered then by anyone, especially by Elder Sister. Fortunately, so far no one who heard the music or the screaming had cared to rouse Elder Sister from the richness of her snores.

It was known in the household that Second Lady grew worse, though not, Hung Tu hoped, the nature of her illness. Fanyang asserted sturdily that her lady suffered a decline in strength after childbirth. She invented reassuring symptoms and told them round the well. Some said, "Ah, poor Second Lady," with genuine sympathy. Others disguised their pity under a lack of interest, politic to assume. The nearer they were to Elder Sister, the greater the indifference. But even these contrived at safe moments to let Hung Tu know how they felt. Some of them sent messages and little gifts of food or embroidered socks to the pavilion for Second Lady. Hung Tu and Fanyang made the most of these.

"You see," they said, "here is another peach—or an apple, or a cake—how everybody loves you! Now you must lie down—or sit up and eat this—and get well."

Sometimes Second Lady nodded, her lips said "kind, kind." Sometimes she did not hear them. The circle of her notice was narrowing.

Hung Tu thought her father knew the truth. His visits were rare and short, always in the morning, and often he sent word to know if Second Lady had passed a restful night and would be able to receive him. Hung Tu answered for her and left them together when he came. When he clapped his hands she came quickly and served him tea, and offered it to her mother if she seemed to be noticing the cup. Then Hsueh Yun would go away, heavily. It was a different step from the one she remembered through the years, departing from that house. But he said nothing to her and she could say nothing to him.

It was a long time since his sleeping mat was spread in Second Lady's pavilion, nor was it spread more often in Elder Sister's now. Fanyang said he slept alone, in a little room near his office. She said there was no woman taking Second Lady's place, but Fanyang might be lying. She would cheerfully lie to bring relief or comfort to anyone she liked. Hung Tu thought it true. She pitied her father as much as she pitied her mother. She wished that she could talk to him, not only for his sake. She needed help, advice, orders, recognition of her existence. . . .

It was a fortnight now since the Dragon Festival. She had tried to tell her mother, at first in words, and then by using music, some of the sights of the river, some of her thoughts. She composed a River Song, full of love, spring, shimmering water, boats, young, ardent lovers, and a bridegroom "eternally constant, One who knows the Sound, the Same-Heart One," using these characters from her mother's songs to lead into the subject of marriage.

Second Lady smiled politely. She patted her daughter's cheek, but her eyes were blank, her attention far away. There was no one

Hung Tu could speak to about the man on the river. Her hope was that he must know who she was. He could find out easily. He only had to contact her brothers. They were known everywhere. They would take him to her father. Then he would make his offer, and after he had gone they would send for her and tell her, "Your husband is So-and-So, who does such-and-such," and she would be properly astonished.

Perhaps he had come already. Perhaps he had sent his father, or his uncle, or some other go-between, to make the offer for him. Perhaps they were still haggling. Perhaps he was poor and could not give what they asked . . . she would marry him anyway. Perhaps they were favoring someone else, one of those old robes, who would offer more . . . she would run away, she would kill herself . . . she would take the saffron robe. Then one day he would come to the Cloud Touching Temple, and listen to her playing the reed flute and turn monk too. . . . No, they would be married, they must marry.

But why did no one tell her anything? Why was it so long? Her father came and went and was never there. Since the Dragon Festival her brothers came and went and were never there. They had washed their hands of her. Perhaps they considered one picnic on the river enough. Or perhaps they had noticed her shameless behavior. More likely they were in trouble over women or money which they must hide from their father.

He was in trouble too, with the starving hordes at the other end of the valley. There was famine and plague among them, and they were breaking loose in packs of desperate men, ready to kill for a handful of rice. They were following several leaders. The one most talked about was Pockmark Chou, a bandit chief from the North, who brought his army with him when he came and was adding hundreds to it every day. They might even march on the city, if the frightened whispers and the news told round the well were true.

That old fox, with his legend. Every day there were more stories about his growing power, his loot, his cruelty, his rough rasping wit, his playful way with torture. He got what he wanted. He

49

walked among his army of beasts and they were obedient. He kept them constantly surprised. The talk was all of his strength, his virility.

Hung Tu listened with half an ear. Her mind was full of two preoccupations, her mother's growing disorder, beginning to be thought of as madness, and her own obsession, also a madness. Her whole being was languid with first love. Every day she expected would bring news of him, at least the revelation of his name, and every night she went to her restless broken sleep no wiser.

X

SHE WAS IN THE GARDEN when the screaming began, high-pitched and terrible. As she ran toward it, sound and direction changed, so that she realized it was not her mother's voice. These inhuman awful sounds were coming from Elder Sister's pavilion.

Hurrying servants rushed past her as she hesitated in the doorway.

"What is it? Oh, what is it?"

No one answered. Then she saw Hsueh-Tai crossing the courtyard. She ran to him.

"Elder Brother!"

He turned away. She followed and caught him by the sleeve.

"Is she hurt?" He shook his head. "Then has something happened to my father?"

He pushed her aside and ran into his mother's room. Fanyang was coming out as he went in. Hung Tu seized her and shook her.

"What is it? Tell me!"

"Not now," Fanyang muttered, motioning with her head. Hung Tu looked where she pointed. Three strange men were standing inside the gate, evil-looking men, armed with knives and cudgels. They lolled against the wall, looking around them curiously, grinning, spitting, watching the running maids. One of them said something lewd.

"Bandits!"

"Hush! Keep your head down. Get out of sight. Go toward the river gate. Hide behind the boathouse. I'll come to you."

"But . . . Second Lady . . ."

"I'm going to her now. Do what I say."

Hung Tu obeyed, pushing her way through the confusion of frightened servants, running about aimlessly, whispering orders to each other or huddling together in corners, while the screaming went on . . . and on . . . and on. . . .

It was fainter from the boathouse, lost in other sounds she strained to hear, short cries, outbursts of wailing, angry voices, shouting, silence. . . .

She waited, pressed against the wall, with the bushes behind it scratching her face and arms whenever she moved, listening and hearing nothing . . . river noises . . . wind in the bamboo.

After a long time, when she was ready to come out and face whatever might be there . . . anything was better than this silence . . . Fanyang came back.

Her footsteps sounded strange on the path. She was stumbling, breathing hard and retching as she came. She rounded the corner of the boathouse and sank down on the grass, hiding her face in her sleeve. Hung Tu put an arm around her quickly and waited till the shuddering stopped.

"Now tell me."

"They're gone."

But this, apparently, made nothing better.

"Were there just those three? Why didn't someone go for help? The Governor . . . soldiers . . ."

"That's what we were afraid of, that someone would set on them before they got back. . . ."

"Fanyang, there is nothing in your breath. Make sense for me. Three bandits . . . you said they were bandits?"

"They are Pockmark Chou's men."

"Then they are certainly bandits of the worst kind and should be killed. How did they get through the gates?"

"They had a letter to your father. They . . . there is disaster to this house! They have your brother. They are holding him for ransom."

"Hsueh-Ts'an! How . . ." but she could imagine how. She heard him saying "Sometimes I wonder whether we shouldn't look into what the bandits have to offer. . . . How old is Pockmark Chou?"

So he had ridden out to offer his services, sanguine young

fool, thinking to better himself and spite his father all in one. Pock-mark Chou must have been delighted. He had found the best use to make of such a prize.

"Elder Sister sent back jewels and gold, all she had, to show good faith. . . ."

"All she had? No wonder she was screaming," Hung Tu said sar-castically, before Fanyang's next words sent her into horrified, shamed silence.

"They have cut off his right foot. They brought it with a mes-sage to the master. Since he wasn't here, Elder Sister received them . . . a present from her son, they said, and she unwrapped it in front of us all. . . ."

"Oh, no. . . ."

"If we don't send enough his left foot follows, and then his hands. And after that . . ."

"Where is my father?"

"With the Governor. Elder Sister sent for him, but she didn't dare to wait in case someone saw the messengers and set on them. They said if anything should happen to them Hsueh-Ts'an would die, a slow death, making sport for those who watched. She told them to tell Pockmark Chou the House of Hsueh sent the gold and the jewels as he had sent her son's foot, a sure warrant of the whole to follow. Elder Brother was with her. He agreed it was the best thing to be done. They left an hour ago, and Hsueh Yun has not returned yet from the Governor nor sent any word."

"But what if we send the ransom, how can we trust Pockmark Chou to release him then? What if he continues to maim him and to ask for more . . . and more . . . ?"

"Elder Brother says that there is one thing known about this Chou. He is a cruel monster, a madman, a ghoul, but he keeps his word. His whole life, his power is founded on it. When he says he will kill, he kills. When he says he will free, he frees. We must hope it is true. Elder Brother says we are lucky it is only money he wants. He might have asked for a harder thing."

"Harder?" Hung Tu could guess what Elder Brother meant. "He might have asked my father for the gates of the city. . . ."

"Yes. To leave them undefended, or to help him . . ."

"He would never do that, not even to save his son."

"That's what Elder Brother said Pockmark Chou would also know. He understands men. So he asks for what is possible and with it he can buy what he wants, even his way into the city, perhaps."

"Fanyang . . ."

"Now you must come with me to Second Lady. She is awake and restless. She knows that something has happened. I could not come for you before because I had to restrain her. She wanted to run out and stop the screaming. She thought someone was killing a baby. 'That's a mother screaming,' she said. 'I must help her.' "

"She was right," Hung Tu said. "How strange! What did you tell her?"

"Anything, everything. She does not listen. I held her down on the bed and tied her feet together. I gave her the p'i-pa to play."

"But if Elder Sister hears music now from my mother's pavilion, she will think . . ."

"Elder Sister is mercifully asleep. We have given her opium enough to keep her unconscious for hours. Now come."

Hung Tu moved gladly. "It was horrible waiting here, hiding. . . ."

"I didn't want them to see you. I didn't know what they were after. They might have wanted you too to take back with them, or . . . or . . . but they didn't hurt anyone. Just took the gold and the jewels and said they'd be back. What a day . . . what a day!"

Fanyang trotted ahead of her shakily. They crossed the deserted courtyard to Second Lady's pavilion, from which gay sounds were coming. Second Lady was singing "Spring in the Willow Trees."

How can fame and profit concern a man of genius?
Day and night I long for him to bring his lute again,
And with every cup of wine another round of music. . . .

She smiled as Hung Tu came in and put her finger to her lips.

Oh, when will the Tartar troops be conquered,
And my husband come back from the long campaign?

XI

When Hsueh Yun sent for her to come to his pavilion, Hung Tu went to him with a divided, anxious heart. Through all the strangeness of the days since Hsueh-Ts'an was captured by the bandits, she had felt alien and useless in that house, longing yet dreading to see her father, Elder Brother, Elder Sister, anyone who would tell her what was happening or turn to her for any services or help or comfort she might give, but nobody needed her, nobody came near. Even Fanyang was busy in Elder Sister's pavilion. Hung Tu stayed alone, waiting on her mother, who had gone again into the silent shadows of indifference and unknowing. The maids who brought her food knew nothing, or were forbidden or afraid to say anything. The days and nights dragged on without relief in an almost total suspension of the normal pattern of life. But now her father sent for her. Hope and perspective came back.

If he wanted to talk to her about Hsueh-Ts'an he would not have waited all these days. If it were something about Second Lady he would have come to her pavilion to see for himself how she was. No, this must be about Hung Tu, and important enough to be talked of during this crisis.

What could be important about this superfluous person that he sent for her now to come to him at once? The answer she found made her heart beat fast. It must be an offer of marriage. That was the only thing that might bring her to his mind at such a time. Marriage brought money to the bride's father, even if it weren't paid up at once. He could borrow on the payments to come, or make some arrangement . . . money, more money was needed to ransom Hsueh-Ts'an. It must be an offer of marriage, perhaps from the man on the river. There was only one way to know. She hastened across the courtyard to her father's pavilion.

She found him looking tired and ill. There was a defeated, beaten air about him she could not bear to see. Yet it was natural and certainly to be expected. Whatever Hsueh-Tai and Hsueh-Ts'an might think about the "tight world" of their elders and the chasm between them, Hsueh Yun was a father deeply concerned with his sons. The lines of grief in his face must show them that, though Hsueh-Ts'an might jeer it was grief for his lost fortune . . . not now, he would not think that now, when it was squandered on saving him.

"Daughter, I have sent for you because it is time for us to talk together."

She waited gravely for him to continue.

"Heaven sees fit to strike us with calamity."

"I know, my father," she murmured. She looked at him compassionately. "Is there news of Hsueh-Ts'an?"

"He has not been further maimed, and will not be so long as we keep our engagement to pay the ransom. He will be released when the last amount is paid."

"That is good."

He sighed.

"I am stripped of everything. I have had to sell this house and everything of value in it. I have borrowed and begged and pledged myself for payments over years."

"You have saved your second son." She was tempted by a demon of hurt memory to remind him that eighteen gifted daughters do not equal one lame son. Most certainly he would not have ransomed her, nor Elder Sister have sent the smallest, shoddiest of her jewels. . . .

"That is not all that has happened to us. Shake one branch and ten branches shake with it. I have lost my post. I am transferred to Sung Chou."

"But that is . . ." she cried out and stopped herself from continuing: the worst place in the world, where they send criminals! Instead, she went on smoothly, ". . . a heavy thing."

"Yes," he said. "Exile, after years of plenty in the City of Silk, a

56

heavy thing. I would feel it more if my Second Son's disaster had not deadened capacity for feeling somewhat. Fires and floods together halve a man's attention."

Hung Tu smiled polite appreciation of the proverb. She was not irritated, like her brothers, by her father's habit of quotation, nor did she think it insincere as they did. She understood the strengthening comfort behind an established saying. It was as though in high moments . . . or low moments, any time of sudden unbalance . . . the use of another man's words to describe the occasion brought him into line behind you, with his solution to the problem, or if he did not solve it, his endurance, his courage, his humor, his memorable, quotable comment. That was what a proverb was. If her father and other older people found it reassuring, why not? What did the sneering, jeering young men like her brothers have to offer as a substitute? Where did they turn when they were captured by the tiger, or the bandit, in the traps of their headstrong folly? To the elders they despised, and to the women, to bail them out with money, jewels, care. . . .

All the same, she hoped her father would come from the generalizations to the particular and talk to her of marriage.

To encourage him she said, "If there is something this person can do . . ."

"There is." But still he did not come to the point. "It will be a long and painful journey, almost as difficult as when we came to Shu, a terrible hardship for a crippled man."

One lame son.

"And when we arrive, the troubles are not over. It is a barren district, bleak, forbidding, frontier land, in constant skirmish with the enemy. I do not know how we will fare there, but one thing . . . it is no place for the Second Lady. I have made arrangements for her to be cared for at the Cloud Touching Temple. Fanyang will go with her and stay with her the remainder of her days." He paused. He looked at her sadly. "Fanyang tells me the sickness is so heavily upon her that she may not suffer from the change or even notice it. That will be merciful if it is true. Is it true?"

"I believe it may be," Hung Tu said. "Second Lady lives in shadow, except for moments now and then. I think she does not know us round her. If she may have her music . . ."

"That is understood. Nothing in her pavilion has been sold. Nothing that she has will be disposed of. The trouble that has come upon us is not hers, though if she were well she would share and shoulder it, as she always did. She was my peace . . . more than that, my joy. Harmonizing Reed. Her words upon the pillow lightened all my days. . . ."

There were tears in his voice. Hung Tu's eyes filled, weeping that he spoke so of her mother, as though she were long dead. It was true. She ached that she could not deny it to him.

"You have been a good daughter."

"I will always . . ."

"Yes," he said. "You will visit her and see that she is cared for, and send me your reports."

"Am I not to go with you to the North?"

"No. There are plans for you. . . ."

Now, now it came! Even in her sorrow she felt a surge of excitement, of relief. Now he would talk to her of marriage. But he seemed uneasy and reluctant to begin.

"Plans for me?" she prompted gently.

"There was a time," he said, "when your talent and your spirit alarmed me. I thought the narrow gates of marriage might not open to the best life for a poet. . . ."

(But now that I have been approached by—she would learn his name at last—with an offer of marriage for you, I have changed my mind.)

"But now that other gates are opening before you I rejoice in your fearless spirit, your knowledge, your scholarship. You will be living among accomplished singers, writers, dancers, highly esteemed for their talents and for their physical charms. You have both, my daughter, to a high degree, and as a Flower-in-the-mist . . ."

"Father!"

He faltered at that stricken cry and they faced each other, star-

58

tled into silence. Then she said defiantly, she could not help it, "Did no one, *no one,* ask for me in marriage?"

"No one. There wasn't time, child. It takes time and patience to negotiate a marriage."

Time. There was plenty of time, all these days and nights and weeks if he had loved her. If he had been even mildly curious, there was time. . . .

"Take me with you to the North," she said. "I will be useful, I will wait on Second Brother. I will be a daughter to Elder Sister. . . ."

"No," he said in a strange hard voice, "I will not take you to a land of famine, where we will live in misery, without money or influence. Such a life is not for a girl of fifteen who is beautiful and talented. Besides," he smiled at her awkwardly, "you said you wanted to be of help. You can be. The arrangement I have made for your mother depends on you. So also does the rest of the ransom. They offer us a thousand taels. . . ."

It was a handsome price, and it was all arranged. He had accepted it. He need not have discussed it with her. And no one, no one had asked for her in marriage. A thousand taels. It would take care of her mother. He said that.

What choice did she have? She would be a courtesan, a singing girl, or, as he had put it prettily, a Flower-in-the-mist. He was looking at her anxiously.

"Very well," she said, "I will 'become lost' in that Blue House. . . ."

She began to sob. He held out his sleeves. She ran to him and was folded against his shoulder.

"I will be the best, the most accomplished Flower-in-the-mist in all the Empire," she promised between her sobs.

He held her close as he used to when she was a child. Presently she lifted her head.

"Where?"

"It is the Blue House on Willow Street. The best, the most renowned . . ."

"When?"

"If a thing is to be done . . ."

He did not finish the saying this time. He held her in silence until she stopped crying. Then he put her gently from him.

"A gallant spirit will carry you farther than the swiftest horse."

"Yes," she said.

"It is better than a slow starvation."

"Yes," she said. "It is a way of life." Then she found strength to smile, and to offer him lines from Li Po:

"Journeying is hard, there are many turnings."

She had often heard her mother sing it.

"I will mount a long wind some day and break the heavy waves
And set my cloudy sail straight and bridge the deep, deep sea."

Now she heard her father catch his breath in sorrow, and to that sound she left him and her childhood in the House of Hsueh forever.

PART THREE
780 A.D.

XII

It was evening when Hung Tu went to the Blue House on Willow Street, with Fanyang behind her carrying the bundle of her belongings. They went swiftly, saying nothing until they came to the gate. Then Fanyang said, "Second Lady . . . I will take good care of her . . ." and Hung Tu answered, "I know."

The porter knew their business. He was expecting them. He took the bundle with the lute strapped to it uppermost and laid it carefully aside. Then—it was so quickly done that she did not see where they came from—he passed several moneybags to Fanyang, who as quickly stowed them in her clothes. It was the purchase price, the thousand taels that were to do so much for the House of Hsueh.

She watched the purses disappear, Fanyang too absorbed in hiding them to look at her. There were no words, no gestures of farewell. Porter showed seller out and took the merchandise to its place, in silence. Perhaps he was a mute, or, she thought wryly, a wise hoarder of words, spending them only when he must, and for such a transaction as this, small, everyday, common—to him— coins were enough.

They crossed a courtyard as large as the one she had left, with many pavilions in it, then a smaller courtyard, and another. There were sounds and shadows about them, but she saw nothing clearly in the twilight. Music, someone singing, she shut it from her ears because it hurt her to be reminded then of Second Lady. Music was an empty horror of sad contrasts lately, but while she winced, she was obscurely reassured to know it had its place here, that someone sang with feeling and skill a song she knew.

They reached the doorway of a small pavilion, where a fat woman, voluble as the porter was silent, took her from him and led her briskly inside. She chattered in half sentences with little soothing sounds as she undressed Hung Tu and wrapped her in a red silk robe. She might have been grooming a palace dog.

"There now, there now, you are ready. Are you hungry? No? Good. An empty stomach . . . better than a full one sometimes. Oil, water, wine, if he should call for it . . . there now, there now, we are ready. . . ."

She waddled out. The bamboo curtains closed behind her with a rustling snap. Hung Tu faced them, shivering in the flimsy unfamiliar robe. All was so quickly changed. A few days before Fanyang hid her from the bandits, the delicate daughter of the House of Hsueh, a jewel not to be seen. Now the same Fanyang left her in this room to face what her owner planned. . . . She must remember that she did have an owner, she was bought and paid for, she must earn the purchase price and a profit beside. She began to shake. It was cold here. She was feeling faint. There was nowhere to sit, no furniture but the day bed in the alcove and a small wooden table with the flagons on it. "Wine, if *he* should call for it." It was not for her, but she could pretend she did not understand. . . .

She dragged her feet from where they were rooted and went swiftly to unstopper the flagon and take a great swallow. It was strong, it burned her throat and stung her eyes, but it warmed her. She gulped down more, put back the stopper and went back to her standing place opposite the door. It would not be so hard . . . with a swimming head and this new warmth inside.

She did not wait long. The bamboo curtains rattled, parted, the first man came in, filling the room, the world . . . in such a lustful haste he had dropped his robe and was clawing at hers almost before he was inside the room.

She shut her eyes from that flushed, determined face. He was old, he was coarse, he was greasy, he stank of rancid sweat, but perhaps . . .

Now she was naked and he was thrusting her toward the alcove. Now he had flung her down. She struggled, silently at first, then she cried out, and felt his pride increase, his bestial joy to inflict this

64

pain . . . then she lay still, deep in the agony, the horror . . . deep . . . deep . . . deep . . . as he was deep in her.

When it was over, and he was gone and she was rid of him, the sweat of his weight, the slime between her legs, there came another man, and then a third, and a fourth near dawn, but after that the curtains parted differently, not in brutal haste.

Two girls came in. They brought hot scented towels for her face and hands. They poured sweet oil on her body, rubbing it in with skill. They gave her a steaming bowl of pungent herbs.

"Drink it, it will do you good."

"What is it?"

"I Mu. We call it 'Advantageous Mother.' It is very good for women's ills."

"This person has heard of I Mu," Hung Tu said bitterly. Her lips quivered.

"Drink. You will quickly sleep. Tomorrow brings new days."

That was no comfort to her. She began to shake as she choked the hot drink down, and then to cry.

"No, no," they said. "Lie still." They stroked her head and rubbed her neck and wiped away the hot tears as they fell. She felt the matter-of-fact compassion in their hands reaching through her skin.

"Look at us. We are well, and so will you be."

"Now look at us."

But she did not raise her eyelids. She was already sliding into a heavy sleep.

XIII

SHE WOKE CONFUSED AND STARTLED. A servant stood beside her with a bowl of tea. The sun was high, the day long begun, from the hum and bustle she could hear outside.

"Please hasten to get dressed. Elder Sister has sent me. . . ."

"Elder Sister!" Hung Tu repeated stupidly.

"Our mistress. The Lady of the House. The Lady Tall Bamboo."

"Oh, yes, yes, of course."

She swallowed the tea hurriedly and began to get up, wincing as she tried to stand.

"It will pass," the servant said, helping her. "It is the unused muscles."

Hung Tu looked at her sharply, but there was no leer in her face. She was busy with the clothes she had brought, kneeling to help draw on the socks, a richly embroidered pair with soft goatskin soles, finer than any Hung Tu had worn before. So was the robe spread out for her and the jade comb for her hair.

She wiped her face and hands with a steaming towel.

"You were washed and oiled last night," the servant said, again with no special emphasis, "so this will do for now, since we are late."

"For what?" Hung Tu thought anxiously, passing through the bamboo curtains after her. As they clicked back into place she felt her spirits lift a little to be drawing breath again outside that hateful room.

They went swiftly through the courts and across the compound. She had only time to see that it was shaded by a line of ancient willow trees and that beneath it terraced banks sloped to the river, when they reached another pavilion.

"Enter," the servant said, giving her a push.

The room was full of girls in robes like hers, facing a tall woman whose back was to Hung Tu.

"So then," she was saying in a clear cold voice, "what is the Li Chi? Together please."

"The Li Chi is the ancient book of rites," the circle muttered.

"Again, in better unison."

"The Li Chi is the ancient book of rites."

"Yes. And what does it declare? Together, slowly . . ."

"The Li Chi declares that the rules of ceremony originate in Heaven."

"Yes, and what further, Faint Moon?"

"That . . . that the movement of them reaches to Earth," a girl said hesitantly.

"Yes. And then, Red Leaves?"

"It . . . they . . ."

Nothing could have astonished Hung Tu more than this discourse on the classics at such a time in such a place. She watched, bemused, as the girl called Red Leaves twisted her hands and hung her head.

"Answer in words, not unnecessary gestures."

"Honorable Lady, I have forgotten."

"Tell her."

"They extend to all the business of life," the class chanted.

"Even to this one?" Red Leaves blurted out, adding as an afterthought, "Honorable Lady?"

"The sacred text says 'all.' It is enjoined upon us therefore, as upon every person, to apply the precept to that situation in which we find ourselves, moment by moment. If by 'this one' you refer to the business of a Flower-in-the-mist, for you and for me the correct answer must be *especially* to this one." She paused for a moment, then she added: "We have experienced disregard of the sacred precepts. Here," she held up one hand, "brutality and lust; here," she held up the other, "the frightened animal."

Hung Tu felt her essence stir with a ripple of hope. If this cool, exquisite woman of austerity and grace and these young Flowers in their smiling beauty had been sordidly raped, as she had, and were now as she saw them, then . . .

"Ceremony, which must be studied and understood, art which must be mastered and practiced, alone transform the conditions of life and death established for us under Heaven. We say of death 'there is *that*,' and we bury the corpse with art, so we must encounter lust with 'there is *that*,' and surround the acts of copulation with art, if we are to follow Tao. Now please repeat the precept."

"The rules of ceremony extend to all the business of life."

"Yes. What follows, Peach Bloom Fan?"

"They supply the channels by which we can apprehend the ways of Heaven and act as the feelings of men require," the girl nearest to Hung Tu answered placidly. She was short and plump, her hands were under control, her voice complacent. Hung Tu took a faint, unreasonable dislike to her.

"It is worthy of our notice that the rules of ceremony are not limited to the *needs* of men. The sacred text says *feelings*. This covers an extensive range. Yes. 'It was on this account that' . . . what, Fresh Berries?"

"That . . . that . . ."

"Together."

"It was on this account that the sages knew the rules of ceremony could not be dispensed with."

"Yes. Tomorrow we will explore the rules of ceremony further. We will speculate upon their meaning, and their application to our way of life. That will do for now."

There was a ragged murmur of something indistinct. Hung Tu expected to hear an abrupt: "Again. Together." None came. The teacher had turned and was sweeping toward the door, when she came face to face with Hung Tu, awkwardly bowing before her.

"Well," she said, "now tell us, what have you been taking part in here?"

"It seems to this interested person," Hung Tu said, with her hands trembling safely in her sleeves, "that she has been listening to an introduction to the classics, based on the commentaries of the

Tso Chuan, leading toward an understanding of the concept of Tao."

It was the answer which she would have given to Honorable Tutor. She knew it must be correct, but she wondered if it were wise to be giving it here, to this intimidating woman, before these others who might resent it, as Elder Brother resented her right answers long ago. But chiefly she was wondering if this were her new owner, the Lady Tall Bamboo.

"So," she was saying, "you have studied the classics."

"A little, Honorable Lady. I was tutored with my brothers."

"You will find that an advantage."

She left. A clamor of excited voices rose behind her, bewailing stupidities and sudden loss of memory, welcoming Hung Tu, answering her timid questions.

No, that was not the Lady Tall Bamboo; she was rarely seen. She would send for Hung Tu presently.

"And then you will receive your name."

That person was Second Lady, "Spark of Flint," a formidable scholar.

"And besides teaching us the classics she has charge of the First Pavilion. This is the Second Pavilion. Spring Wine looks after us. There are nine of us already, you make the tenth, but there are mats for twelve."

"We study here and eat here and live here except for special festivals, until we are more proficient."

It was too much for Hung Tu to grasp at once. She looked round helplessly.

"Your things are here."

Her bundle had been unpacked. Her clothes were gone, but her music, scrolls, brushes, inkstones, ink, her lute and little harp were carefully arranged in a chest against the wall. There were twelve of these with names brushed on them in large characters except for hers and two open, empty ones. The letters varied from elegant script to pitiful scrawl. Each girl wrote her own name, and not all knew how to use the brush. Red Leaves, for instance, whose chest stood next to hers, wrote very badly.

"You came with an inkstone," she said, smiling at Hung Tu. "That was this person's first attempt to hold the brush. And you brought instruments of music."

"Do you harmonize?"

"No." She shook her head regretfully, then she blushed and tried to look modestly indifferent, but her eyes were full of lively pride. "I dance."

There was no time for more conversation. Handclaps at the door announced the next class, and the Flowers of the Second Pavilion scrambled into line.

XIV

DANCING WAS TAUGHT by a slender girl, in green and gold like a hummingbird. She skimmed from Flower to Flower, patting at this one, pulling at that, until she was satisfied.

They stood in line before her, hands and feet in first position, heads lifted.

"What are the four factors? Together . . ."

This class, like the other, began with mastered precepts to be said in unison.

"The four factors are thought, reflection, sensibility, and intuition."

"What occurs with the proper balance of the four factors, Fragrant Plant?"

"The proper balance of the four factors can produce harmonious results worthy of being described as expressions of the harmony of Heaven and Earth."

"Well. And what must we remember next, Peach Bloom Fan?"

"The goal of a state of general harmony."

"What is that, Spring Wine?"

"It is . . . it is . . ."

"Together, tell her."

"The goal of a state of general harmony is equilibrium."

"Equilibrium. Of special interest to dancers. Continue."

"When the equilibrium of Heaven and Earth is maintained, everything then is in its proper position; all creatures are sustained."

"Well. We know the theory. Bearing in mind that we are now to see expressions of the harmony of Heaven and Earth, right hands in position. . . . *Sorrow*."

There was a fluttering of sleeves and arms.

"Stop. Take it singly, left to right, one . . . two . . . three . . ."

Hung Tu, fourth in line, closed her fingers, opened them uncertainly and let them droop, watching with relief the next girl's hand take over.

"Stop. Is there only one of you who has known Sorrow? Observe Red Leaves."

It was a simple gesture, arm and palm extended, then curled back upon itself until the tips of the fingers touched the shoulder.

"You see she keeps her fingers together. Sorrow is a single emotion, deep, curved. She unrolls the palm humbly to receive her share of it from the hand of Heaven, and then she takes it back to the person, to be endured, to be dealt with. No divisions, no distractions, no flutterings. We use the hands when emotion is important, grief, anger, hatred, fear. The fingers are for supplementary expressions, for commentary . . . fingernotes . . . we shall study them separately soon. Now then, try it again. *Sorrow.*"

A wave of arms rose, curved to the shoulders, while she moved among them, considering each.

"That is better. We are able to perceive now that some of you have been distressed by something, a bee sting perhaps, or a slight pain in the shoulder. Now try *Sympathy for Sorrow*, right hand only, going out toward the suffering of others, or of another . . . all together, one . . . stop." She sighed. "No, no. Such consolation as most of you are brandishing would drive the sufferer away. Use the wrist, use the forearm, use the mind! Copy me, if you cannot evolve a simple gesture for yourselves . . . one . . . and so . . . and so . . . now the left hand in support . . . so, and so . . . and stop. Very well, now in turn, one . . . two . . . three . . . four . . . stop. Have you learned nothing whatever about suffering?" she asked Hung Tu. "Again." Hung Tu, abashed, tried to reproduce the flashing, exquisite gesture to be copied. "And stop . . . and rest.

"We have heard from enlightened scholars that we must 'never forget to entrap the moment in the net of four lines,' whether we wield the brush or whether we are dancing. That is true, but

72

when we dance we must think of movement instead of line. So, what are the four chief movements, River Breeze?"

"The four chief movements are the outgoing, incoming, right, left."

"Yes. As dancers we express the moment and what it contains, as we entrap it in the net of movement, bearing in mind the precepts of the harmony of Heaven and Earth . . . all this, at present, with the hands alone. We are still far from adding the expressions of the feet, the body, the head."

She was using them all as she spoke, undulating before them in so beautiful a motion that Hung Tu felt faint with desire to see it continue forever. Then she stopped, smiling.

"That was a moment of *Joy*. We will approach the expression of *Joy* tomorrow. Today this person urges you to practice *Sorrow* and *Sympathy for Sorrow*, right hand only, first, then left hand supporting it. Red Leaves, Evening Breeze, and Spring Wine have understood it. They can assist their companions. Now, first position, bow, take leave. . . ." She disappeared.

The chatter broke out again, accompanied by the smell of good rich food. Servants were coming in with bowls. Hung Tu found that she was feeling faint, not from appreciation of the arts or the precepts of Heaven . . . she was hungry. She looked to see who must be waited for and deferred to, but everyone was eating. There were no elders here, no social distinctions in this pavilion. Food came and she ate it, a novel, pleasant thing, with no Elder Sister to trouble the digestion, make the bile rise in the throat, wear away thin armor. . . .

Her mind went to her mother, well on the way, she hoped, to a safe retreat near the monastery of the Cloud Touching Temple. It was too late for her recovery; still, she would be cared for there, and eat her meals in peace. Suddenly her father's face came before her . . . she thrust it savagely aside, closing her mind. She would not, could not, think of him and what she knew of him, and of all men now. She took up a handful of lichee nuts and crammed them into her mouth, as though she shouted these at least she would have and no one take them from her.

After the meal there was a lull. The Flowers . . . she was beginning to find that name quite natural . . . talked together, repeating the precepts to each other, practicing *Sorrow*. One of them
called to Red Leaves:

"Come and help me adjust my equilibrium."

Red Leaves shook her head.

"Spring Breeze, then you come."

"No. Your equilibrium will have to find its balance without me."

"Consider what will happen to the harmony of Heaven and
Earth!"

Spring Breeze laughed. She stretched out on the floor and closed
her eyes, then she opened them again, patted the space beside her
and smiled up at Hung Tu, who accepted the suggestion thank-
fully. She had craved food, now she was craving sleep, though she
had never slept without a mat before, nor so publicly. She laid her
sore, stiff body down beside Spring Breeze and pillowed her head
on her arm. Red Leaves left her seat and came to join them, lying
down on the other side. Soon they were asleep.

She woke to rustling and laughter about her, and beyond, in the
compound, running feet, music, men's voices. The traffic of the evening had begun.

Some of the Flowers were adjusting each other's robes and putting jeweled combs into their hair. Others were leaving the pavilion, summoned by a beckoning servant. They did not seem afraid.
If they were, they concealed it, as she must try to do. She got to her
feet uncertainly, looking about her for orders or directions. Spring
Breeze had disappeared. Red Leaves was in a corner, by the chests.

Presently it appeared from the talk around her that some of the
Flowers were not expected to take part in the night's activities.
Spring Wine explained it regretfully, assuring Hung Tu that in
time, when she and Partridge Sky and Yellow Dusk and . . . oh,
Red Leaves and Peach Bloom Fan were more proficient . . . smiling gently at them . . . as of course they would be, if they practiced faithfully . . . she slid toward the door and went out.

Hung Tu's heart relaxed. She was not to go back to *that room*, at least not for this night. She sat down by her chest and took her lute into her hands, to feel the comfort of the familiar wood.

Then the two attendants who had oiled and rubbed her appeared, and those Flowers still in the pavilion stripped off their robes and lay down to be rubbed and oiled. After that they drank I Mu. There was some languid laughter, some sleepy exchanges of talk. A servant collected the bowls, another rolled out sleeping mats in a far corner. The Flowers went to them but Hung Tu sat on where she was, listening to the singing in the distance, the laughter, the sudden sounds of running feet. Through the open door of the pavilion she could see the moon above a tree in the compound. She thought of the world she had left, the world that had fallen away from her so completely, under the light of this same full moon. Words welled up in her:

"How many mortals grieve
under this moon . . ."

She saw it like a loom, or a round white fan held by a ghost in silver, a great dead lady of Han.

"The moon is tranquil,
but we are sorrowing,
we are sorrowing."

She would work toward finding words to fit the vital force of the song, for she was still a poet. *"Birds from the south, birds from the north"* might come to her branches now to be welcomed there or courageously endured, as she had prophetically written when she was a child, many centuries ago, and *"at every passing wind the branches tremble"* . . . tremble and make music out of whatever came . . . whatever might come to her now, blown on the wind . . . songs to be sung and heard, the songs of a great poet. . . .

"Come and lie down," Red Leaves called to her. "Don't you know that we must sleep?"

XV

HUNG TU CROSSED THE COMPOUND toward her first meeting with the Lady Tall Bamboo in anxious uncertainty. As she followed the hurrying servant, she was trying to arrange in her mind the various things she had heard about her mistress in the last few days:

That she came from Chang-an, where she often performed before the Emperor and his court. That she was brought to Cheng-tu by the present Governor, to whom she "offered the service of towel and comb" when he was only a promising young official. That she became his favorite concubine, and even now was often summoned to the Palace to pour tea for him and to entertain his guests.

It was also said that the House on Willow Street belonged to him. Certainly his friendship and protection were a great advantage to her. It was to this House that men of importance came, the ministers, the mandarins, the merchants, and their sons, when these could wheedle gold from their fathers . . . and dodge embarrassing encounters with them. Now she began to understand why her brothers took such a lively interest in Hsueh Yun's comings and goings, especially when he might be leaving the city, and why they laughed so hard at particular proverbs, repeating them to each other derisively: "A good horse does not graze at the owner's front door," "a cunning fox keeps three escape holes," and others that seemed to her pointless. Now she understood the need they had for money, the constant strain and pressure upon them to obtain it, so that Hsueh-Ts'an went to the bandits. She brushed that memory away. It was too raw a thing, with too many sharp prongs. . . .

Blue Houses were expensive, this one especially. It was no place for the bullfrog who hopes to eat swan's meat. Bullfrogs . . . bulls . . . those four men who came to the room, were *they* rich and important in Cheng-tu? They could be. She remembered certain robes by the river. Yes, they could be. Their sons might be different perhaps and others of that generation.

She saw young men in the compound, not only at evening, but in the daytime, playing chess in corners of the courtyard, reading aloud from scrolls, reciting the classics to each other, studying for the examinations, when they would, if they were successful, "pluck a branch from the Lunar Cassia tree," becoming, like her brothers, "boughs of the Moon Cassia," in line for official appointments. Perhaps Hsueh-Tai and Hsueh-Ts'an had studied under these trees.

She remembered making ink sticks for them which she never saw them use, yet they were always needing more. Perhaps they brought them to the scholar who gave classes in brushwork every morning under a willow tree. He reminded her of Honorable Tutor the first time she noticed him, but Honorable Tutor could not have been carrying one half this man's years. It was only to a child that Honorable Tutor seemed ancient.

This man was older than any man she knew, his brushwork was old style too, and beautiful. He taught his young men for money, and the Flowers sent to him for . . . the privilege of living there, perhaps. There were many such arrangements in a Blue House.

Hung Tu was one of those who attended his class, although she was far beyond the level of the lessons. She sat in the outer circle and answered in her turn. They had started the day's recitation:

"What are the four Treasures of the Abodes of Culture?"

"The four Treasures of the Abodes of Culture are the brush, the ink, the inkstone, and the paper."

"How is character *pi* composed?"

"Character *pi* is composed of character *chu*, the bamboo, and character *yu*, the hand writing with brush . . ." she had learned this when she was still chewing with milk teeth . . . "the whole depicting a hand wielding a brush in its bamboo holder, to write or paint."

"How are brush holders made?"

Here the servant came for her and she rose, leaving another student to explain that brush holders were made of jade, quartz, gold, silver, or ivory, tipped with buttons or knobs of the same precious

77

materials, for official occasions, but that the plain bamboo handle was the most satisfactory because of its quality of lightness, which affected the balance of the brush. Balance, equilibrium, harmony of Heaven and Earth, bamboo gave man his walls, his furniture, his tools, his utensils, and more.

"The bamboo plant has the ideal qualities of the scholar and the gentleman. It represents the essence of refinement and culture. It is gentle and graceful in fair weather, strong and resilient under adverse conditions. Its suppleness, adaptability, uprightness, firmness, vigor, freshness, and even the sweet melancholy of the rustle of its leaves have been translated into qualities of mind, spirit, and character." She was going now to Lady Tall Bamboo, who might or might not have some of these qualities, who had been a famous singer of willow cotton songs. Even now, they said, when she was called on to perform them, though she had lost her voice to age, her art was still so sure, so full of subtle enchantment born of skill and excellence, that very few singers could surpass her. Men spoke of her, however casually, with a certain shift in their expressions.

Now the moment had arrived for Hung Tu to encounter her. She trembled as she stood in the doorway of the small austere pavilion, eyes correctly slanted downward, hands demurely in her sleeves.

"Come near." A hand entered the range of her narrowed vision, emerging from a silk embroidered sleeve. "Sit down there." They were face to face, the old, serene, wise peasant, grown great lady or beyond it . . . so some Buddhas looked, with humorous shrewd lips . . . and the young uncertain girl, still wrapped in angry shock.

"I would have sent for you sooner, but I was called away."

"Summoned to the Governor," Hung Tu thought. She waited.

"Have you discovered what is required of a Flower-in-the-mist?"

"Yes, Gracious Lady."

"You may call me Elder Sister."

"Yes, Elder Sister."

"If you are intelligent you will have observed no abilities are wasted here, no talents thrown away, as happens in the outer world to women, or shall we say it with a better breath, most women are not trained or encouraged to be more than lumps of unpolished jade. Their fathers, their husbands, their brothers, their sons, come to us for carved and polished stone. The arts are in our hands."

"Yes, Elder Sister."

"Now let us consider your condition. It is too late for you to become a good dancer. You should have started earlier and practiced hard and steadily. So, you have a natural grace, you can master the basic movements to attain a pleasing deportment, and that is all, in the dance. You are better grounded in music. I am told you can play the lute with proficiency, your voice is true, and you have been taught to use it agreeably, but again, it is evident you have not worked as you should."

Hung Tu bowed.

"A pity. Still, it was not for a dancer or a singer that four sacks of gold changed hands."

She was smiling as she spoke, but Hung Tu's cheeks paled with shame and rage. After so much talk about the arts, was she going to be crudely told what she was purchased for, and sent back to that room to "work as she should"?

If Tall Bamboo caught the half-formed thought or understood Hung Tu's expression, she gave no sign of it. She went smoothly on, "You have other abilities. There is something I want to show you." She took up a scroll from the table. "Unroll it, please."

Hung Tu obeyed. Then she drew in her breath, amazed. It was the copy of her first poem, "Now Alighted," inscribed "To Scholar Chang Chih-ho, from the Small Dragon Hsueh T'ao, this unworthy song."

"Honorable Tutor!"

"He gave it to me when he was recalled to Chang-an." Tall Bamboo looked at her reflectively. "Thus I have heard you spoken of by one whose essence I relied on. Chang Chih-ho came here often with his students and gave wisdom in the courtyard. He angered them with stories about you, saying he had never found any among them with your aptitude, but still they might surpass you, even the most obtuse, because your talent would be lost, wasted, when you grew up and married."

She paused. There was a silence. Hung Tu could not speak. She was struggling for composure, against a sudden rush of hot tears, a welling up of bitterness and evil breath in her mouth.

"Child, look at me. Tears have no place between us. Does not Tao reveal there is no past to weep for, no future to be feared? There is the moment only, 'to entrap in the net of four lines.' Your name here shall be Silver Hooks, after the great Wang Hsi Chih, who lived . . . When did he live?"

"Three hundred years ago, Elder Sister," Hung Tu murmured.

"Yes, and his characters were said to be like silver hooks. Let your name here recall this excellence. You will assist the old scholar in the courtyard, grind his inks, mend his brushes, and otherwise attend on him. He is to be given reverence, although he has fallen on misfortune. You will harmonize his poems, compose new songs, and play them when desired. You will also wait on any man wanting brushwork done. Do you understand? These are your special duties in this house."

"Yes, Elder Sister."

"Men come here to be refreshed, all kinds of men, for all kinds of refreshment. Poetry is a fine and strenuous way. . . ." Her voice changed, dropping in range to another, more confidential tone. "If we can catch a man's attention and keep it for an hour from business, war, promotion, we create a path for wisdom to reach and enter his essence. That is the purpose of the arts. It should be our pride that they are in our hands."

She paused expectantly.

"Yes, Elder Sister," Hung Tu said in a firmer voice.

"Then if you have understood these things and your duties in this house, you may go."

Hung Tu rose, remembering to move slowly, gracefully. She bowed and turned to the door, when the strange, harsh voice stopped her.

"Wait! This person would inquire after the health of an old and valued friend. How is Harmonizing Reed?"

"Elder Sister, she has turned her face to the shadows." Hung

Tu's voice trembled. "No one has been able to draw her back from them."

"That is sad. Will she be taking the long road to Sung Chou?"

"No, Elder Sister." (How well informed she was!) "She is to stay in the Cloud Touching Temple."

"That is well. She will be cared for, and if Heaven wills, recover. We will visit her when the times permit. I have friends there."

She motioned to the open door and Hung Tu went out. When the curtains had fallen into place again, Tall Bamboo leaned back and closed her eyes. There were orders to be given, problems to be settled, people to be dealt with, the Governor's latest directive to put into effect, yet here she was, "idling by the stream," letting her mind drift to the past in far away Chang-an, to remembered faces of friends and enemies who seemed like friends, because they had known her then, when she was young, as this child was young, the daughter of Harmonizing Reed.

"She has turned her face to the shadows." Then which, after all, fared best, the deeply envied rival who went in the red chair to marriage, or the girl left behind in the Blue House to become a concubine? Until these new words reached her she had thought Harmonizing Reed unfairly cherished by Heaven. Now she was not sure. Now it seemed that either might have traveled the way of the other and for both it would have been the same journey. "Lovely face, luckless fate." Tao for a woman, vinegar and salt, yet it had also been said, "if in Tao all things are equal, so in Tao even Man and Woman are equal." So it had been said—by some young sage in his cups, or an old sage in his dotage. She smiled wryly. What woman would have said it?

Now she must clap her hands and send for the next girl to be talked to. It was her sound habit never to see a new one until she had been deflowered in the coarse brutality of the first night. The shock of this experience was carefully arranged as the best and quickest way to achieve the five effects:

a complete break with the past;

a longing for the opposite of ignorance and lust;

respect for the training she would receive;

a bond of entrails with the others with whom she must live in the Blue House, since whatever their levels of achievement, their start there was the same, and they would be returned to that start if any needed discipline. That was the fifth effect.

Some, born and brought up in the profession, took to it naturally and were ready for work next day. Others, like this Silver Hooks, needed time and careful handling for the first shock to abate. Some, they were mostly peasants or farmers' daughters, were most at ease on the mats of lust and it was a waste of effort to teach them the arts of love. They were sent to the clients they appealed to, of which there must always be a few, even in this House, where the boors and beasts were discouraged, and if they persisted, dealt with in a number of sly ways. Limited accommodations took care of some, high prices kept out others, performances of dance and music preceding what they came for dissatisfied many, and all of them were kept ill at ease. The servants were trained to whisper of better, friendlier places, at bargain prices, down the street, where a man got what he wanted when he wanted it, without pretentious frills. The persistent were encouraged to get drunk, and if they were men of small importance tossed into the river. If they were men of rank or disposition to give trouble, they were solicitously cared for in the courtyards with remedies to make them vomit before their embarrassed friends.

In these ways, over the years, she had discouraged clods and men of coarse vibration and had gathered a group of poets, scholars, courtiers, and other distinguished men of essence able to savor the fine quality of the merchandise she offered in her House. It was considered the best House in the Province, some said in the Empire, to enter as a Flower-in-the-mist, and most girls were contented with their training there and took an honest pride in their profession.

Now and then one came who could not adapt herself. Sometimes there was scamping, cheating, infectious bitterness. Then the source of the trouble must be sold or disposed of quickly, whatever the loss in taels. Such a one was this Fragrant Plant whom she must speak to next. She sighed. It was not an easy thing to preside over a Blue House, but then it was not an easy thing to be Second Lady to a rich man either. She clapped her hands.

PART FOUR
Circa 782 A.D.

XVI

The talk that spring was all of the bandits infesting the country-side, burning, looting, killing. Farmers were driven from the land; there was no more work in the fields. Rice was famine-high. Pockmark Chou held the city in a virtual state of siege. Traffic came to an end. Even the riverboats were seized as they unloaded at the wharves beyond the city walls. No one dared go outside the gates without an escort of armed men.

The Blue House buzzed with rumors. Some said the Governor's coffers bulged with bribes from Chou, and that was why he was doing nothing to protect the city. Others said he was being recalled to the Court, or transferred, or exiled, and so he was indifferent to what happened in the Province. Others said it was known to them for a long time that the Governor faced the shadows and his mind was gone from him. These portentous things were whispered on the pillow to ears trained to forget, and they were carefully concealed from Tall Bamboo.

Then, the time being ripe, the Governor acted, leading a surprise attack through the gates at dawn to a thorough victory, as the whisperers now said they had always known he would. Had they not declared from the start that he was only waiting for the bandits to grow soft? Undisciplined and lazy from high living, they were no match for him and his well-trained troops. They fled, into the swords of more of his men, sent down the river by night to cut off retreat. It was as the whisperers said, loudly this time, hoping to be overheard where it would do them most good, Governor Wei Kao was a Tiger, smiled upon by Heaven.

There was a triumphal procession with forty heads on pikes, Pockmark Chou's the first, and a long line of slaves chained together, carrying and dragging sacks of loot.

Hung Tu stood with the others, watching the glittering show from a platform inside the fence. There went Pockmark Chou, who had ruined the House of Hsueh, mutilated her brother, beggared and exiled her father, and sent her to this Blue House . . . that purple-yellow mass, oozing upon its pike. She wished that the Hsuehs could see it now, from whatever part of their journey they were still trudging. Whenever she looked toward the mountains she thought of the long hard road to cold desolation they were traveling, and of her mother, mindless in the Temple, whose far-off walls she could see from the north end of the compound.

"There goes Pockmark Chou!"

The crowd shouted insults, spitting toward the head as it passed. She shouted too and pointed with the others, but she got no satisfaction from these gestures of vindictive hate. She was troubled and confused in her essence. Lately she caught herself at ease, even happy in snatches, certainly contented in her new way of life.

There were reasons for her well-being. She had never had a sister or a young girl to confide in, now she had many about her, sharing her meals, her studies, sleeping beside her on their narrow mats. She was beginning to be linked to some of them by ties of deepening concern.

Then she had never been encouraged to study Tao or the classics since her far-off childhood, in joking concession to a plaything. Or was it quite that? Did her father already envisage the will of Heaven for her? Then why had he not arranged for her to study further, to continue with her brushwork? Perhaps he expected Second Lady to complete her education, and Second Lady fell ill.

However it had been, she was grateful for that early, unusual training, and grateful, or at least she found it hard to feel appropriate anger, to the bandit whose wrong actions had such fine results, causing her to be entered in this place where she was encouraged to make use of every talent and taught new ones.

Here she had her Old Scholar, to whom she was not an insignificant child, patted on the head and dismissed to its toys. She was his valued assistant, and he was the great Meng Chaio, whose poems were quoted with reverence by Honorable Tutor, by her father, and even by Elder Sister on appropriate occasions

> *The thread from a fond mother's hand*
> *Is now in the jacket of her absent son*

when Hsueh-Tai or Hsueh-Ts'an went through the Outer Gates.

She had copied many lines from the "Wanderer's Song," and now she was attendant to Meng Chaio himself, expected to harmonize his poems, and even, as a matter of duty, to present him with new ones of her own. It was a privilege she would never have been accorded in the House of Hsueh. She would not have met old scholars or young poets there. If by chance she had, they would never have talked to her of their interests and their work; they would not have addressed more than formal, flowery phrases to her in her father's house. Here they sent for Silver Hooks to brush their words for them, they quoted hers to each other, they called for her to harmonize songs . . . and for other services.

There was the root of her confusion. She did not understand herself. This awakened woman's body, hers, yet strange to her, seemed willing, even eager, for more experience. The more she studied and practiced, the more it was exercised, the better it performed, with efficiency and grace. It had even found enjoyment, though not yet culmination, with certain of the men.

Surely this was against every precept taught her. Surely she disgraced the House and name of Hsueh . . . but she no longer bore it. Now she was Silver Hooks, Flower-in-the-mist, and when she contrasted the muted days of her girlhood with the burgeoning of these in the Blue House, she could not much hate Pockmark Chou. She must admit, with caution, lest there be envious Listening Ears, that she was blessed and protected of Heaven.

> *O my father, O my mother,*
> *I wander in the springtime . . .*
> *I know freedom.*

But she must put aside that half-begun poem to work on the one ordered for the Governor's Day of Celebration: "To Minister Kao upon His Victory."

> *Hail, Kao Pien!*
> *Such dazzling lightning bursts from you*

That was as far as she had gone with it. Fortunately there was still time before the Celebration. There would be processions on the river, fireworks . . . her mind went to a face . . . she exhorted it to fade. Later she might be able to linger with her memories, meanwhile she filled her mind with the first safe thought to exclude them, catching at a shining straw . . . the Flowers were to have new robes and appear before the Governor, Red Leaves told her this, to dance and to harmonize poems. It might be that hers would be chosen, if it were ready in time. It must be. But other, more clamorous poems were crowding into her essence. Everything she saw and heard this riotous, strange spring . . . the peach trees, the willow catkins growing by the riverbank, the river itself . . . sang in her, desiring to be born.

> *Peach petals are shaken by the winds of spring:*
> *silken and fragile they cling to our robes,*
> *but the yellow catkins of the willow*
> *scatter to the north, rush to the south:*
> *not attaching themselves to anything:*
> *carelessly riding the breezes of the second moon.*

"Not attaching themselves to anything." That was Tao for a Flower-in-the-mist, for any enlightened person. She must keep it so. Ride, ride with this new ferment of the entrails, harmonizing rider and horse; dance, dance with eager partners the elaborate copulation . . . but always "carelessly, on the breezes of the second moon."

Red Leaves was pulling at her sleeves, looking at her anxiously.

"How long do you think it will be before we perform before the Governor?"

"How can this person tell? One moon, two moons . . ."

"As long as that?" It was a cry of dismay. Hung Tu smiled at her.

Red Leaves stared back, lips quivering, eyes half filled with tears. Then she turned and walked away dejectedly, with no spring in her step. Hung Tu looked after her, amused.

"She has filled her essence with this dance before the Governor, dreaming that he or some great mandarin will watch her and want her for his concubine."

It was a common dream of Flowers-in-the-mist, but not of Hung Tu, nor of those few who had grown up in good society. These were yellow catkins, free, unattached, wary of the dull restrictions and daily humiliations endured by concubines in a rich man's house.

XVII

Days grew hot and languid, stress and forgetfulness of Tao rose among the Flowers rehearsing for the Governor's festival. Those teaching them grew strict and even the most favored in the pavilions did not escape the chill winds of harsh breath and disapproval.

Hung Tu, assisting at the harmonizing of her poem to the Governor, heard it sung by three pure voices, Splendor of Spring, Clear Dawn, and Cicadas Sing:

> *Hail, Kao Pien!*
> *Such dazzling lightning bursts from you*
> *that the distraught Cosmos*
> *almost ceases turning.*
> *Mountains cloak themselves in new green,*
> *the sunset is burning in new colors.*
> *After this day, both the sun and the moon*
> *must take their light from you!*

Then it was danced by fifteen Flowers under the exacting eyes of Lady Mountain Stream, whom Hung Tu still called in her mind the Hummingbird.

"Mountains cloak themselves in new green . . . massively, massively, with solid strength . . . *mountains* . . . not wavering shapes, Spring Wind. Now delicately, delicately, new green . . . no, no, *new* green. That is right, Eyes' Fascination."

Watching this magic of her words come alive, embodied in exquisite movement, Hung Tu felt she could now express *Moment of Joy* without any trouble; her essence was filled with bliss. But she had been dismissed from dancing in favor of brushwork and the composition of poems, and the greater satisfaction, for her, of watching others interpret them, like this Eyes' Fascination, a new-comer, who danced even better than Red Leaves, almost as subtly as the Hummingbird. One could not take one's eyes from her. . . .

Now the p'i-pa and the hu chin were played alone, a line of melody now. . . .

"the sunset is burning in new colors . . ."

"Burning . . . new . . . no, no, Red Leaves! You are late again. You must feel it in your essence. New colors . . . not dead, gray ones. Again . . . no, that is still not right."

Hung Tu grew perturbed as she watched Red Leaves dancing clumsily, heavily, quite unlike herself. What was the matter with her? Jealousy of Eyes' Fascination? But why was she so stupid, letting it be seen, instead of outperforming the rival?

There was no time for further reflection. A servant had appeared beside her, pulling at her sleeve.

"You are sent for to the Yellow Pavilion. Take your brush and ink."

She rose at once, excusing herself from the rehearsal and gathering up her things.

"We will continue with it tomorrow," Hummingbird said. "For now we will practice 'dazzling lightning' and 'the distraught Cosmos.' "

It was with these phrases lingering in her mind that Hung Tu crossed the courtyard and parted the bamboo curtains, to find him standing there, wistfully expectant, shyly smiling. . . . Face-from-the-River, whom she expected not to see again, or at least not here, not yet.

She said only the words that she was trained to say:

"This person is honored to offer towel and comb and to pour wine for your pleasure," kneeling as she spoke, her hands in her long sleeves.

"You!" he said, standing very still. "It is you. . . ." He laughed and after a moment she laughed too, unable to withhold it, raising glad eyes to his. It was as it had been between them on the river, but here they were alone, licensed to be together. It was now her duty to pleasure him in love. She moved toward the wine. But he had asked for brushwork. She took out the little box that held her writing tools.

Would he be pleased to tell this interested person what words should be written or would he prefer to harmonize songs and sip wine? He was moving toward her like a child sleepwalking, with his hands outstretched and one determination in his eyes. Brush and ink must wait, wine and song must wait. This that was between them could not wait.

Journeys later, his desire appeased, they whispered together on the pillow, in the ease of after-love. He talked about himself. He was tutor, he told her, to a great man's sons. He must be home before dawn. He had not intended to spend more than an afternoon hour in the Blue House. He had honestly come there to have a poem copied, "to present to the Governor at his feast of Celebration."

"You too!" she said, and caught herself in time to continue smoothly, ". . . are a poet like the others who come here to have their work inscribed. Entrust it to this person. She will take care of it."

He hesitated.

"It is included in this person's service." She lied glibly, distressed that he must already, in staying for the evening and the night, have spent more than he earned in many days of work. "If you will leave it in these careful hands, it will be ready when . . . when you come again."

"I do not know when that will be," he said awkwardly. "Perhaps not before the Celebration."

"Then it can be left with the porter and you may have it sent for."

He brightened a little. "Yes, that will be best."

They were both aware that he would come for it himself, but his face was saved. Then he forgot about face and burst out: "I wish that I could come here tomorrow and every day and every night. I wish that I could stay here forever."

"You would tire of it," she said gently. "And it is many taels, even for the rich. Next time, when you come, do not stay so long, then it will be less."

He took her by the sleeves. "Did it seem long to you?"

"Like a lightning flash across the Heavens," she quoted, "or a passing hurricane, or flowing water, or a catch of song. . . ."

"You are paid to say pretty things."

"Yes," she agreed, to tease him.

They laughed delightedly, stuffing their hands over their mouths, because about them the whole world slept.

He began to recite from his poem.

> *Go ask the river*
> *which are longer,*
> *its eastward-flowing waters*
> *or the thoughts that fill us*
> *at this parting hour.*

"This person lacks comprehension. Are you leaving the Governor or his service?"

"Oh, no," he said. "It was written for a girl I once saw on the river." Then to tease her, "I thought if I changed character 'parting' for character 'triumphant' I could give it to the Governor for his festival. It would sound quite suitable. Do you agree?"

She looked at him amazed. Was it possible he thought her so uncultured that she would not know the poem was Li Po's? One of his most famous ones?

"It has been said," she invented slyly, "by a great and ancient sage whose name eludes this ignorant person at the present time, that a song is born, like us, to have its significant hour, to be heard by those who should hear it and die at the appointed time."

"That is a true saying, if a song or a poem died, but when do words die? Does a sail fill only once, or a bird fly only once?"

She shrugged, a small dissenting gesture.

"It seems to this obtuse person that a sail bends to the wind as a bird flies on its course, toward one destination."

"A bird flies north, then south, and a ship sails to many destinations. . . ."

"Carrying new cargoes. It is a foolish image. The sage said nothing about birds or ships. He spoke of song, and the Tao of song, to live on the air and die on the air. If it is new written, for a different purpose, it is not that song."

"Take it," he said smiling. "It is yours." It was not his to give, but she said only: "Have you another for the Governor?"

"No. But perhaps I can make one, even in the short time left. You may help me. Can you harmonize a poem? I will teach you," he said grandly.

Laughter welled up in her, who harmonized poems daily with the great Meng Chaio. Such denseness would have annoyed her in any other man. In him it was endearing.

"Let us think of Governor Wei Kao on his horse."

"*Hail Kao Pien!*" she said, to start it.

He thought for a long moment, then:

"*So handsome is this Prince . . .*"

"*on his wild steed mounted,*" she shot back. He seemed astonished and doubtfully turned the line over in his mind. Then he continued:

> "*That were the Ancient, whose name*
> *he bears, alive today,*"
> "*this Prince would defeat him!*" He nodded.
> "*This Prince would outshine him!*"

"There, it is done," he said. "You see, it is not so hard. Now we have something to be sung, and with it this longer one. I will read it to you. It is badly written."

"I will copy it."

He began to read. She listened, not to the words, but to his voice, which she had often imagined and never heard before this night. It was as she had known that it would be. So was his mind and the breath of his mouth, and his body, strong, smooth-skinned, young . . . and less experienced than some she had lately known. She smiled at him.

It was near dawn when they left the pavilion at last, and she could stumble to her mat and fall into exhausted sleep. Once she was roused by sobbing and put out a groping hand to quiet Red

94

Leaves beside her, but before she found the shoulder she was reaching for she had sunk again into a heavy sleep.

In the morning it was too late to console that misery. Red Leaves' mat was empty. Spring Breeze too had gone. Now the old scholar would be waiting and she must somehow, between rehearsals and attending on him and others, find privacy and time to brush this poem by . . . she did not know his name. She looked to see if he had signed it. He had not. This was the house of no names.

It was as well that he had not, she thought, after the first moment of slight, comical dismay, for she had broken an important rule in offering her services for nothing. Her services were not hers. They belonged to Tall Bamboo. The songs she brushed for anyone but Meng Chaio were highly paid for, as they should be. This one . . . she must pretend that it was hers, part of a second poem she was making for the festival. She glanced at the words and saw at once, with a mixture of pride and compunction, that they were not as good as hers and his brushwork was atrocious. But here were two fine lines:

The trees are dark now with seed pods, and fruit
weighs down the branches. Nothing can return to an earlier state.

Still less to a state that has never been. Her eyes filled with tears. The woman who lay with Face-from-the-River, as she must continue to call him, was not the girl who had dreamed of their marriage. That girl had gone as far, as finally, as last year's river flow, bearing its rubble to the sea.

Sometimes there were gleams in the water, of jewels, lost ornaments, gold and silver trifles dropped from boats and bridges or pried loose from corpses . . . every year there were many of those.

She shivered and glanced around her. The room seemed suddenly dark, cold and damp. Hastily she folded up her own and Red Leaves' forgotten mat. Then she twisted her hair into its high smooth roll, patted her face, drew on a clean robe, and stepped into the sunlit courtyard.

XVIII

ON THE DAY the new robes were distributed, the courtyard fluttered with color, and there was a laughing bustle in the pavilions, hushed and breaking out again, and hushed. Hung Tu's heart rose high as she tried on her red gown with the gold thread woven through it and flowers embroidered on the sleeves, reflecting that *he* would see it, after the Governor's Celebration. . . . No one was to wear her new robe before then, except for this brief rehearsal.

She looked about her, bemused, exultant, filled with a new poem . . . "Trying on a Newly Finished Gown." She would send it to the Governor after she had shown it to Meng Chaio and to *him*. Face-from-the-River, Face-from-the-River . . .

> *From the center of the sun the cloth is woven,*
> *the deep-dyed, fiery crimson.*
> *And over it the mists from distant shores*
> *evoked by djinns.*

Yes, that was how it seemed. She watched the flowers trying on their veils.

> *Touched with the frost of winter fur,*
> *those veils translucent as white jade.*

Bliss welled up in her. She was writing poetry. She had come from a night of love. The whole world moved through spring, with these dancing, smiling girls . . . yet there was sadness too, this joy was tremulous with tears . . . how devise it? Perhaps by suggestion of a classic sorrow to which all sorrows might be brought . . . woven like a colored robe, worn by an immortal. . . .

Chang-o herself shines on the bridge of stars that rose
before the Weaver in the sky, when separated
from the Plowboy.

Yes, that would do. What a dance it would make, with Red Leaves or Eyes' Fascination as the Goddess. Who as the Plowboy? Evening Breeze? Spring Wine? No, it should be Red Leaves. . . . Eyes' Fascination as the Goddess, Red Leaves as the Plowboy. Then she could be as awkward and as heavy as she liked . . . as she seemed to want to be these days. Where was she? Where could she be? She should be here in the pavilion at this moment, trying on her robe.

There was no time to linger. As she crossed the courtyard to attend to her Old Scholar, she passed the dancers assembling for rehearsal in their new clothes, to be grouped harmoniously.

Nine by nine by nine again,
all colors streak the cloudy overdress.
Our senses ride with luminous colors lured.

It was only later, much later, when everyone else appeared to know it, that she learned where Red Leaves was. A fisherman brought the news to the porter at the gate. His boat was tied to the wharf below the Blue House. He was fishing there at dawn when he saw a girl, one of the Flowers, come down the path from above and stand for a while on the bank, watching the river flow. Then, his head was turned, she must have fallen, slipped, perhaps. . . .

"Jumped," the porter said. "It happens."

He did not know, he did not see, the splash aroused him. He saw her drawn under, swept away. For a moment he thought that he might follow, but . . .

"No way, no way. The current . . . before I could untie my boat . . ."

"No way," the porter agreed. "What goes in there is lost." He shrugged. "It happens."

The fisherman sighed. "No way," he repeated sadly. Then he brightened. "Give to the river, take from the river. My catch was good today. I thought . . ."

"Yes, we will purchase a fish or two, though we are glutted with them, but as a favor, because you brought the news. . . ."

Word traveled fast, by whisper, nothing was said aloud, through smiling, painted lips, no face was clouded publicly, but still the shadow fell, across the courtyard, within the pavilions . . . poor Red Leaves, the little one who danced so well, who had set her heart on appearing before the Governor. Yes, that one. But she was pregnant. I Mu had betrayed her. Finished as a dancer, maybe forever. It happened so to many, it would happen so to more. Red Leaves chose the river. No way, no way . . . the will of Heaven . . .

Hung Tu was saddened, shocked. She would have been shaken more, but she was numbed from fatigue, from the long sleepless night. She could not feel it then, as she must later. One must do one's work and go about one's way. It was a good thing she had finished the poem before she heard the news. She might not have been able to make it such a joyous thing. Now it would be danced before the Governor.

> *Blown to earth on a wind of spring*
> *a hundred flowers fall from magic gardens*
> *to edge the sleeves, to sprinkle the daring skirt.*

> *This is a style worn by immortals as they dance*
> *upon the clouds. Having nibbled the fungi of long life*
> *they dwell in the Celestial Court, in innocent revelry*
> *joyously singing, wearing such flowery robes.*

But not Red Leaves. She had not waited even to glance at hers. No past, no future, no Face-from-the-River. Poor Red Leaves.

If it happened to this person, it would be *his* child, or so she could believe, and she could still brush poems and wait on Meng Chaio. She had sometimes envied Red Leaves, Eyes' Fascination, Hummingbird, and others for their branch of the arts, exquisite grace and motion, equilibrium, the harmony of Heaven and Earth through rhythm. Dance . . . but now she thought poetry the greatest of the arts. Ungainliness of body meant nothing to a poet. Or did it, when the poet was a Flower-in-the-mist?

What happened to a Flower with a baby? What happened to the child? There were no children here. Had any of these Flowers borne children? It was impossible to ask, impossible to mention Red Leaves. The chest with the pitiful characters on it was removed. The mat was not unrolled. The Flowers in the Second Pavilion chattered as usual. Only when they drank their I Mu there was a pensive sort of silence now and then. Hung Tu was too tired, spent with lack of sleep, to ponder further. Later she would be more aware, would reproach herself . . . that sobbing in the night . . . but now, now she must sleep. Tomorrow she and all of these must rehearse again, to appear before the Governor, and she had poems to brush, her own and *his*.

> *Loveliness and compassion cannot be grasped.*
> *The turning year shakes the earth,*
> *petals drift from the flowering trees*
> *flinging a crimson pathway for satin-slippered feet,*
> *or cover the ground like frost.*

She fell asleep to his words.

XIX

THEY WENT TO THE PALACE in the Governor's barge. Not the great red and golden lacquered one that led the Spring Processions, but grand enough to satisfy Lady Tall Bamboo and awe the delighted Flowers. Hung Tu, swaying among them on her embroidered cushion, watched the sweating slaves in their new colored loincloths strain to move the heavy craft upstream. Some were rowing, some poling, some, bent double, crawled along the bank, harnessed to a tow rope. The current was swift against them, but the huge, awkward hulk moved on.

How different from the last time she was on the river, in her brothers' punt. No need to look sideways for a following face. He was not trailing them in a small green boat. There was no need for oblique pursuit and breathless, studied indifference, covering sly encouragement. He came directly to her now, staying the nights, recklessly spending all his taels. Ah, if one of them were rich, so that he could buy her from the Lady Tall Bamboo, and they could marry . . . no, for after a while he might be going back to the Blue House for what he found there now and break her heart. That was how men were, and how could a wife, any wife, compete with the glamour of the arts, especially to a poet?

It was better this way. She would see him presently, at the Governor's Palace. Those with accepted poems to be spoken would be there. His were accepted. She would hear them read and he would see her in those rich and flattering surroundings, the high-priced Flower-in-the-mist called Silver Hooks. Then he would hear her words and watch them interpreted by the best dancers in Cheng-tu . . . in the whole Province! He did not know that yet. No one had told him there would be two poems performed by the poet Hung Tu. They had spoken only of him and his work. Nor had he heard, and he might never hear, the songs composed to him during that dark, anguished time . . . long, long ago. . . .

"*Did no one ask for me in marriage?*"

"*No one, child.*"

Ah well, the ways of Heaven were strange. Who could fathom the will of the August Personage of Jade, inscrutable Dragon, holding all things in its claws, rewarding those who walked the nonassertive way with grace, with courage, and with humor. Symbol of Yang, of Cosmic Power, "stirring, leaping forth, winging across the sky," its mysterious form vaguely rendered by the spiral . . . still it was male, and could be seduced, by charm, rightly applied, lullabied by words such as poets make . . . poets like Hung Tu.

She smiled at the scene before her, all this youth, all these destinies, lacquered together, reds, golds, greens . . . suddenly she saw them all as one, stilled into one figure, essence of a woman in a little boat, trailing her fingers in . . . essence of the river, become a shallow stream.

Everything halted, silent, timeless, while the poem came:

> *Big and flat the leaves of lotus rush around*
> *the little boat that lightly rides before the breeze.*
> *The Golden Crow flies low. In the autumn evening*
> *the fish are leaping. There is a rabbit in the moon*
> *pounding an elixir to make lovers immortal.*
> *A lady trails her red sleeves in the water*
> *as she picks the delicate pink lotus.*

So it rushed out of her and so she saw the scene, and knew the immortal moment entrapped in the net of her lines. She laughed exultantly, within her mind. One must not break the stillness of the spell and send the Whole into its myriad parts . . . keep it, keep it thus, while more words came:

> *Pull up the rushy grass, disentangle the weeds*
> *and gather the water chestnuts.*
> *The willow branches dream as they dip in the water.*
> *How may we see the glimmering land beyond the source*

of the river, as we lift the grasses,
as we feather our oars in the stream?

Never had a poem flowed out of her like this. She was spent, fulfilled, released, as she was when she stumbled to her mat at dawn after copulation.

The moment broke, all things stirred from immobility to quivering life as the barge scraped the edge of the wharf and the Flowers disembarked. Servants waited on the moonlit path with lanterns to light the Lady Tall Bamboo and her attendants to the pavilion set apart for them. Here they waited, putting finishing touches to each other's hair and clothing, until they were sent for to entertain the Governor and his guests in the Great Hall.

Hung Tu, moving gracefully in her appointed place, demurely smiling, glanced obliquely right and left at the magnificence before them.

He was not in the place of honor, among those nearest to the Governor. Why should he be? These were the old men, the powerful, the rich. Her father might have been among them if he were here. In happier times he was often honored by the Governor. He would have worn his embroidered robes and sat on a gold silk cushion and watched the dancers and drunk the wine.

Her next glance went to the Governor's face. Handsome, regal, heavily mustached, Hail Kao Pien! Impressive as the Emperor himself, whom he represented. Her glance went on, searching, searching. Not in the next group, to the right, not to the left . . . ah, there he was, at the far end of the hall, among the Governor's household. Her eye traveled to those next to him, two young men in rich embroidered robes.

"Tutor to a great man's sons."

The Governor's sons!

Oh, cautious Face, now I will know you. I have only to ask: "Who is tutor to the Governor's honorable sons?" casually, of one of the concubines, this very night. . . .

Her smile widened, she gave a triumphant little laugh, and checked it, abashed, under the horrified stares of the other performers. Dutifully she set her distracted mind, her straying forces to the work at hand, and though she shifted slightly, a fraction at a time, so that she could see him without moving her head, she directed her gestures and her smiles toward the Governor.

Chang-o herself shines on the bridge of stars that rose
before the Weaver in the sky. . . .

The familiar forms swayed about her in their shimmering robes. The five musicians sat gracefully, at peace with their instruments. The sounds they gave forth were pure. Eyes' Fascination, her long sleeves flowing, her hands, her feet, her head, her lissome body all in rhythmic motion, "equilibrium of Heaven and Earth," dancing to the words she heard her own voice sing:

. . . *immortals as they dance* . . .
. . . *in the Celestial Court* . . .

how magic, how golden this hour, when her whole essence stretched toward his, in gifts, in offered words. . . .

. . . *innocent revelry,*
joyously singing, wearing such flowery robes.

The Flowers outdid themselves. When they paused there was an audible murmur of appreciation. The Governor sent them wine from his table. The Lady Tall Bamboo was gratified.

"You have done well," she said. "Now 'Hail Kao Pien.' "

Hung Tu, lifting her arms with the others, sent the words with all the strength of her essence across the Great Hall to *him*.

"Such dazzling lightning bursts from *you* . . ."

She was exalted, swept into bliss by the glories and grandeurs of her surroundings, the lights, the colors, the jewels on the robes of the listening guests, the hurrying servants bearing messages and wine . . . she was beginning to feel the effects of the wine. . . .

But she could not get near to any concubine to ask what she burned to know. It was too dangerous. There were too many jealous eyes upon her. If she were seen, if she were overheard breaking one of the first rules of the house, she would be ruined, she might be sent away. Fragrant Plant had just been sold to another Blue House for asking prying questions about a guest. Eyes' Fascination was watching her. She must wait for a better time and perhaps ask *him*.

That night when it was over and they skimmed downstream on the now swiftly going barge, gliding with the current toward their own wharf, she fingered the ornament the Governor had given her, a neckpiece of gold and silver filigree with small jade pendants . . . beautiful to wear, to look at, to touch. . . . Some of the Flowers received combs of silver and jade, some earrings and other ornaments. Eyes' Fascination's present was a jeweled fan in beaten gold leaf. But she liked her gift best and so would *he* when he saw it close to . . . oh, Face-from-the-River, very close to!

XX

THE PENDULUM OF HEAVEN swung from harmony to irritation and a vague discontent. The Flowers who had danced before the Governor had nothing now to practice for with the same absorption, while those not invited to attend the Celebration were jealous of the praise and envious of the presents the performers received.

Hung Tu found that she was tired and unable to give herself rest. Old Scholar was fractious and more exacting than she had ever known him to be. Something had disturbed his serenity. And now it seemed strange to her that he had not composed a poem for the Governor's Celebration, nor taken any part or interest in the festivities. He was the great poet, Meng Chaio. That was the trouble perhaps, that he could not offer poems in a common sheaf with others, inferiors and students. So some said. Yes, it was being whispered . . . she did not believe it. Meng Chaio had the greatness of the great, the true simplicity.

Perhaps the tongue of rumor was correct that he and the Governor were enemies, but if this were so, would he have lived, honored and at peace for many years, in the Governor's own Blue House? Unless Governor Wei Kao were also great, beyond malicious pettiness. However this might be, one thing was clear, Old Scholar was not himself. Nothing suited him, the ink, the paper, the brush, and all was Silver Hooks' fault.

He chose this time when she was dulled with fatigue to call on her to demonstrate to him and to the class the eight signs of the Golden Flower.

"Sign Chen, two short strokes, two short strokes, one long, signifying Thunder, the Arouser, life which breaks out of the depths of the earth, the beginning of movement. . . ."

"Next."

"Sign Sun, two long strokes, two short strokes. All-penetrating gentleness. . . ."

"Sign Li?"

"One long stroke, two short strokes, one long."

She brushed the lines rapidly, as well as she could, under his disapproval before so many interested witnesses of her fall from favor.

"Signifying fire, and also the principle of that which adheres to and effects rebirth. . . ."

"Next."

"Sign K'un, two short strokes, two short strokes, two short strokes, signifying the Earth, the tilled field. It receives into itself the seed of Heaven. . . ."

"The seed of Heaven . . . the seed of Heaven . . . not, remark, as some of you might think, the seed of man."

She blushed at his tone of derision.

"Continue," he said impatiently.

"Sign Ch'ien, one long stroke, one long stroke, one long stroke, signifying the Yang, which fertilizes K'un, the receptive."

"You have left out sign Tui. No doubt it does not interest you. It is easy to see where your thoughts leap."

"Sign Tui," she murmured, "signifying lake, mist, serenity."

"Now you do not show us how to write it."

"Sign Tui, two short strokes, one long stroke, one long stroke."

He grunted. "Very well, that will be enough until tomorrow. You will practice the strokes you have been given."

The Flowers and the young men rose, Hung Tu with the rest, but he signed to her to remain, to come near to him. She went apprehensively and stood before him, eyes and spirit downcast for some further reprimand. To her surprise and concern, he began to weep.

"I am an old man," he said, "an old man, about to lose the comfort of my days, an old man. . . ."

While she stood uncertainly beside him, wondering what to say, what to do, a welcome servant came to summon her to Tall Bamboo.

"Go, child," Old Scholar said, wiping his eyes on his sleeve. "Go, and forget the harsh breath of this person."

She looked at him, distressed.

"Master . . ."

He turned his head aside. The servant coughed impatiently, and after a moment's hesitation Hung Tu went away, following across the courtyard toward the Pavilion of Authority. Sometimes a summoning servant gave a summoned Flower an inkling of what to expect, but not this sour old hag, stumping on ahead, obviously pleased at the thought of trouble to come. Even her back looked pleased.

What trouble would it be? There was enough to choose from. Old Scholar obviously had something grave against her. Eyes' Fascination, a growing favorite, especially since the evening at the Governor's Palace, hated Silver Hooks and would do anything she could to damage her, partly because she had been the friend of Red Leaves, partly because their essences were inimical and never could be mixed. Peach Bloom Fan too disliked her. One of these, or someone else, might have complained of her to Tall Bamboo, about . . . well, there was one thing . . .

Probably, since Old Scholar was behaving unlike himself, he had discovered the poem she brushed among hers belonged to Face-from-the-River, and should have been highly paid for . . . that would be trouble indeed! She scratched timidly on the doorpost, watching the servant depart.

"Enter!"

Tall Bamboo received her smiling, but that meant nothing. Nor did the first ambiguous words:

"Guess, child, why I have sent for you?"

"Elder Sister, this obtuse person is at a loss . . ."

"Cast your mind back to a promise made."

Hung Tu tried to smile, to look unconcerned, as her fears took shape and grew . . . "a promise made," what could that be but the agreement between them, the rules she had undertaken to abide by?

"Come, child, you must remember, in this room . . ."

"Elder Sister . . ."

"Did I not tell you if the times permitted and if Heaven willed we would visit the Cloud Touching Temple together and pay our respects to your mother? Time permits. Heaven wills. The Governor was pleased with the efforts of his servants from this House to entertain his distinguished guests. He has sent us an escort and a litter as a mark of his favor. Well?"

"Elder Sister . . ."

"Elder Sister! Elder Sister! It is nothing but a parrot. Well, but don't stand there gaping. You must prepare yourself. We leave in an hour. . . ."

Hung Tu, swept by conflicting emotions, stammered something, anything, her confused thanks . . . she was relieved of her fear, but she was expecting Face-from-the-River daily, hourly, surely that very night . . . but then, to see Harmonizing Reed . . . and besides, what choice had she if Tall Bamboo decided to include her in the journey?

The Governor's own litter! Eyes' Fascination would be saffron-cheeked, fall into a jaundice . . . so would everyone . . . from envy! Still, it was troubling. What would *he* think if he came and found her gone? Nothing. He would return. They would have more to talk about, to laugh over. . . .

"Now then . . ."

"Yes, Elder Sister, this person will make haste."

"Take the new robe, the jewelry. Get Penny Moss to help you."

"Yes, Elder Sister." She bowed, she moved to the door.

"Do not forget brush and ink."

"No, Elder Sister."

Tall Bamboo laughed. Her eyes were flashing. She was obviously pleased to leave the Blue House and her duties there, to go on a pilgrimage.

XXI

CLOUD TOUCHING TEMPLE was a full day's climb from the city gates. The path wound through narrow canyons, over deep ravines, along great granite cliffs, treeless and stark, always a little higher, with twists and turns and unexpected vistas of the earth below, causing Hung Tu to forget the Rules of Elegant Restraint in the Company of Elders. She gasped. She cried out in delight:

"This untraveled person has never seen . . . has never been . . ."

"Wait!" Tall Bamboo said. "These are only the foothills. Wait for the high mountains." She added indulgently that those with sensitive perception were struck with awe the first time, and even when it became, as it had for her, a familiar annual affair, the experience was always impressive. It did not leave the Ch'i unchanged. On every pilgrimage the essence of the well-intentioned person was most disposed to change, "for then the Ch'i aspires toward Oneness and the Purity of Tao."

These exalted reflections put an end to conversation until the next bend in the road and the next gasp. When the palanquin, for it was more than a litter in its space and rich arrangements, grew irksome and they were stiff from its jolting, they descended to climb for a while on foot. Once when they approached a steep, precipitous place, Tall Bamboo halted to stare up at it and say:

"This is what the easiest part of the journey from Chang-an resembles. Do you remember, about the third day out . . . ?"

"This person was but a child when we came that way."

"Your mother would remember."

"I have heard her speak of it, and my father too would quote the words of Li Po."

"Can you remember them? I would like to hear."

"It seems to this forgetful person that he used to say: *Strong men died, traveling over! The earth sunk and the mountains crumbled. Lo, the road-mark high above, where the six dragons circle the sun! Lo the stream below, winding forth and winding back. The yellow crane could not fly over these mountaintops. . . .*"

"Yellow crane! He must have been journeying under another moon. . . ."

"*And the monkeys wail, unable to leap over these gorges. How the Green Mud path turns round and round! There are nine turns to each hundred steps. The traveler must climb into the very realm of stars, and gasp for breath . . . the road to Shu is more difficult to climb than the steep blue heavens.*"

"Now that is very truth, and for the well-fleshed like Li Po, larding the ground at every step . . ."

"Elder Sister, did you ever see illustrious Li Po?"

"Many times, when I was young and he was old. I knew him as you know the poet Meng Chaio, as you will come to know other poets and renowned great men. Sooner or later they all come to the Blue House. But there were more of them in Chang-an, more of everything . . . ah, that is the place for splendor, for elegance, for handsome, lusty men, and for beauties like your mother. I hope she will be well enough to talk over old times . . . ah, what times we had, when we were young together, in the House of the Great Merchant, when she played and I sang before the Emperor! To think that I shall see her tomorrow. Well, well, Harmonizing Reed . . ."

She said more, but Hung Tu's ears were closed to it. All her life she had heard that her mother came from the house of a great merchant in Chang-an, where her father met and married her. All her life she had vaguely imagined that the house of the great merchant was a house like her father's house, where her mother, not being married to the merchant, occupied a rank below his wives, above his servants, a rank called concubine. Even later, when she understood a little of what the word implied, she had never . . . it had not occurred to her . . . she had been, she was, thick, thick!

Now it was revealed to her. Now she understood what the house of that great merchant must have been . . . not the house of *a* great merchant, the House of *the* Great Merchant, and from the way Tall Bamboo referred to it, and the standards of her own establishment, it was probably the best, the most famous Blue House in Chang-an.

Her mother was a Flower-in-the-mist! Harmonizing Reed was a Blue House name, like Silver Hooks. Harmonizing Reed was trained in all the arts, like Silver Hooks. That was where and how she learned her accomplishments, where she became a skilled musician, why she performed before the Emperor, why she did not speak of this, nor of her early years, why her fragrant pillow was pleasing to her husband, and why Elder Sister hated her.

Hsueh Yun's known preference—even as a child Hung Tu was aware of it—for a second wife taken from a Blue House wounded Elder Sister where she, where any woman, would be stricken deepest. Many things were clear now. Hung Tu found herself thinking with sympathy of her father's first wife, not as she had tried to feel, with compassion for Elder Sister over the maiming of her son, but suddenly as woman to woman. Not long since she herself was reflecting that she would not marry Face-from-the-River if he asked her, because he might return to the Blue House after they were married . . . what if he had chosen, like her father, to bring his Blue House Flower to their home? Now truly Elder Sister could be thought of for the first time with compassion.

Absorbed in memories of the House of Hsueh and her childhood years, she followed Tall Bamboo into the waiting palanquin and settled her among the cushions, where presently she began fitfully to snore, leaving Hung Tu to these new reflections.

"My father's friend Li Po," she heard her brother say. Now she could guess where her father had known Li Po. If it were so, her mother must have known him too, perhaps better. She would never be encouraged to discuss it. How lonely she must have been, cut off from everything outside the gates of the House of Hsueh, from life, from music, from poetry, from performing the art she excelled in. No one listened to her play except, at times, indulgently, her husband, as a prelude to the sleeping mat.

Poor Harmonizing Reed, poor Hsueh Yun, and even poor Elder

Sister! A great weight of hatred left Hung Tu's heart. She had an impulse to shake her mistress awake, to cry out: "I am freed from something this person did not know she carried!" To laugh, to sing, to lift light hands to Heaven.

She sat still on her cushion as they jolted upward, thinking of these things, of how as a child she had not been beaten or starved or put to drudgery; of how her father had shown her affectionate courtesy, caused her to be instructed in the classics, boasted of her skills, and wept when they parted. Now that parting, remembered in the Blue House with scorn, with bitterness as a deep betrayal, showed differently. Her father, returning her to the life from which he had taken her mother, was doing all he could for her. The essence of their severance was sad, cruel, tragic perhaps, but it was not his cruelty, and it need not be tragic for one of them, for her.

The words of her present teacher, Meng Chaio, endeavoring to explain the first canon of painting, the Ch'i, the Breath or Vital Force or Spirit of Tao, returned to her. "It is something beyond the feeling of the brush and the effect of ink, because it is the moving power of Heaven, which is suddenly disclosed. But only those who are quiet can understand it."

Now she understood, or at least she understood what understanding it might resemble. Her heart went out in a rush of gratitude to Heaven and to all those preoccupied with Tao, like Meng Chaio. Then she remembered that he had spoken petulantly and wept incomprehensibly, shaken in his essence by some sudden loss of serenity, and she had been resentful and distressed. When they returned she would reassure him that his words of the first canon now were understood.

They jolted on through the darkening twilight, until at the turn of the last bend they could see the Temple gates. The coolies grunted, quickening pace. Tall Bamboo woke and began to talk.

XXII

CLOUD TOUCHING TEMPLE was not a single monastery. It was a village of halls, shrines, oratories, dormitories for priests and for nuns, guesthouses, libraries, storehouses, compounds gathered together behind a great stone wall. Flowers grew along it and on the towers and roofs, so that these ribbons of bright color in the last rays of the sun were Hung Tu's first impressions of the place where her mother now lived.

She was moved to unexpected bliss, the same small sudden delight she felt when she saw the Flowers, those other Flowers, dancing in the Governor's Palace in all their brilliancy. She prepared to descend with a high heart. Two monks were waiting for them at the gate. The litter must have been visible for a long time, winding up the path. As it came to rest, the older monk stepped forward to greet the Governor or his emissary. His eyes widened when he saw two women emerging as gracefully as their cramped limbs permitted. Hung Tu turned from helping Tall Bamboo to catch the strange expression on his face. It was one she recognized; one she often saw in the Blue House. Now Tall Bamboo looked at him, and now it was as though the light in his eyes came toward her, and when she saw it she straightened and stood before him, young. . . .

"But they are old," Hung Tu thought, amazed. "Too old to strike such fire between them, and he wears the sad-colored robe!"

She had no time for more reflection and . . . what she imagined between them might have been distortion from the waning light. The expression was gone now from both. They were stepping forward, he in silence, inviting them with gestures to pass through the gate, Tall Bamboo in silence, looking at her feet as though they might slip. Hung Tu and the younger monk followed, also in silence. It was not a moment for speech, or perhaps the rule forbade it. But that was not so, for when they reached the doorway of the guesthouse to which he conducted them, the older monk did speak:

"Tao is forever and they who possess It cannot be destroyed. You are welcome to this temple." He bowed and went away. The younger monk lingered to oversee the bundles suitably disposed and direct the bearers to their quarters. Then he too spoke:

"Tao is forever. If there is a need, rub the gong and one will come to you." He bowed and went away. Hung Tu set about making her mistress comfortable.

Presently, settled on soft cushions with a bowl of fragrant tea, Tall Bamboo stretched luxuriously.

"This aged person," she said, sighing, "comes here too infrequently. When she does, she wishes she might become a guest of the fleecy clouds, a recluse, living in these mountains, near this Temple with its myriad shrines. It is a way of life. Well, well, no visiting permitted after sundown. Tomorrow we will see my old companion and tell her that we envy her."

But in the morning when they saw her, envy could no longer be mentioned with decency. It was evident that Harmonizing Reed had gone further, deeper into the shadow.

She lay on a narrow pallet in a room so like her old pavilion that Hung Tu in the doorway stared, taken aback. All the familiar objects of her childhood were gathered round her mother in the remembered order, and to make the illusion complete, Fanyang stood among them, laughing, grunting, rubbing her hands, as though no time had passed . . . and indeed the time might be considered short, counted in moons alone, but under moons like those there was another measure. . . .

"See, she knows you, she is glad to see you," Fanyang asserted stoutly, pushing Hung Tu to the bedside, trying to attract the sick woman's attention by patting and squeezing her hands. After a while she stopped trying and the three women talked together. Then Tall Bamboo took Fanyang away with her, to offer devotions at the Shrine of Compassionate Grace, leaving Hung Tu with her mother.

Again she tried to make her presence known, speaking cheerfully, slowly, familiar words of every day, leaning over to look with love into the empty eyes. "Music," she thought, "might recall the wandering Ch'i . . ." but when she brushed the first chords, the sounds it made were so discordant she winced and put it down. It could not have been tuned for many moons. There was no one there to tune it or to play it. She glanced toward the bed. She would set it to rights, she would prepare it, as she had done so many times before for her mother, when she was a child. Only this time she must be the singer.

She sang "Now alighted on the shadowy pool," and then, thinking "perhaps a new song might arouse her," and because her own mind was filled with it, she sang the words that had come to her in the past night as she lay awake, watching the moon through the window slit, remembering the long journey upward to the wall with the blaze of flowers. . . .

"Cloud Touching Temple," she said loudly, "here, where you are living."

> *It is told of the Cloud Touching Temple*
> *that one walks only on moss,*
> *even in the wild wind, no dust is blown.*
> *It is so near to Heaven that the walls of hibiscus*
> *are level with the clouds.*
> *All is waiting for the poet and the moon.*
>
> *It is told of Cloud Touching Temple*
> *that flowers crowd the steps,*
> *float on the streams, blow into the sky*
> *across the mirror of the descending Queen . . .*
> *changing the clouds into gardens for her delight.*

She was singing only to herself, and suddenly she could not bear it. She put the p'i-pa down and covered her face with her hands. Her mind rushed from these heights, these clouds, this lonely negation of life, to warmth and youth and love, to Face-from-the-River, who sang and laughed and listened, whose ears with their perfect lobes, silk-soft to pull, heard everything immediately, however muted, the sigh, the whisper on the pillow. . . .

"How long must this one stay here, parted from you? When shall we spread the mat together . . . ?"

There was a faint rustle, a movement from the bed. She looked up, startled. Harmonizing Reed was smiling.

"Yes, yes. . . ." Hung Tu leaned over her. The gentle smile came and went, but there was no light in the eyes, no recognition. Yet she was listening to something.

Far off a monk at his devotions chanted to a flute. It was very faint.

"How could she hear that and not my singing, or Fanyang's voice raised at her ear?"

There were steps outside. Was it those she heard? But she paid no attention when Fanyang stumped in.

"Lady Tall Bamboo says she has no need of you until the sun is high. That is kind. Now we can exchange a thousand words in peace." She glanced toward the bed. "It will not disturb her. She will never hear us." Then, seeing Hung Tu's expression, she said quickly, "You must not mind it. She is not in pain, or cold, or hungry. . . ."

"That is a comfort."

"This old bundle tries . . ."

"This grateful daughter knows. But how is it she hears this and not that? When you were absent I spoke to her, I sang to her, she did not hear me, yet she was listening to something that she heard."

"The chanting perhaps. Sometimes she can still hear that."

"So far away? So faint? And not our voices, loudly beside her?"

"Now and then the voice of a man, but not always, even that is fading." Fanyang sighed. They sat in silence for a moment, then she burst out with questions. She was starved for news. What was happening in the city? What was the talk around the wells? Here there was nothing but sutras and holy chants and she did not often attend even these, since she could rarely leave her lady.

"If it weren't for pilgrims from the four quarters and visitors from the city like Tall Bamboo . . . and this time she brought you! Well, well, let these old eyes feast! She says that you dance before the Governor. She says 'it is a stork in the poultry yard.'"

"A cow licks at its calf. I am her property."

"But you danced before the Governor?"

"Oh, yes, once."

"Your poems were performed and admired. You sang and he gave you jewels?"

"He gave many gifts to poets and performers. It was his Celebration."

"Ah, ah, but yours was best of all, a neckpiece with jade pendants."

"Would you like to see it?" She searched in her sleeve and put the glistening thing into Fanyang's hands. "Here."

"Ah, ah, it is like the fountains in the Emperor's gardens in Chang-an! A fit adornment for the August Personage of Heavenly Jade Herself!" She turned it over wistfully. "It is true, then, a great future in the Governor's Palace."

"Fanyang, you have lived too long among the clouds. From here one roof resembles another. But on the streets of Cheng-tu the one-eyed can distinguish a Blue House from a Palace."

The old face before her clouded and she felt compunction.

"This person spoke from haste. Riding a tiger one cannot go on and one cannot dismount. Life is a great tiger . . . for us all." She smiled.

After a moment Fanyang smiled back. Then she repeated stoutly: "A great future." She gave the necklace back. "As the water level rises, the boat rises with it. High Lady, remember this old servant when the tide floods in."

"Be sure, be sure," Hung Tu said, touched. "If there is a special need . . . ?"

"Not yet. We are well taken care of." She glanced toward the bed, and Hung Tu understood that she was thinking, "When that one dies, what will become of this one?"

She would have liked to give reassurance, but of herself she owned nothing. She was in bond to Tall Bamboo until she could buy her freedom, as much a slave as Fanyang. She said, to change the subject:

"Is there news of Hsueh Yun? Elder Sister? Hsueh-Tai? Hsueh-Ts'an?" as though naming them brought them nearer.

"How should there be news? It is not to be expected. Perhaps some moon next year . . ."

"We must offer for them. Which monk should strike the gong?"

"Ask Tall Bamboo which monk! She comes here for one of them. . . ."

"Now whose tongue scatters that?"

Fanyang winked. "Wait until you see them together . . . a tall one . . ."

She laughed as she laughed in the old days at gossip round the well, and seeing her more cheerful, Hung Tu went away. She was troubled in her essence, she was shaken by this visit to the past. Her throat ached and tears came to her eyelids. She brushed them carefully away. The emotions of a Flower-in-the-mist must never be discerned upon the countenance, nor otherwise betrayed. She is the mirror held up to reflect a guest's mood. "Tao for the mirror is *reflection* . . . again, one, two. . . ." "Yes, noble lady, this person knows . . . nevertheless, there is sorrow. . . ." "Not for a Flower-in-the-mist."

XXIII

TALL BAMBOO WAS NOT in the guest pavilion. Hung Tu sat down to wait for her, relieved to be alone. She was never alone in the Blue House. It was pleasant in the shaded doorway, cooled by gusty breezes, pungent with sage and pine. Below, the city sweltered in midsummer heat and people moved languidly through the airless streets.

Here they were stepping briskly, pilgrims, monks in their sad-colored "feathered robes" . . . it was said that if adepts wore them rightly they could fly through the air at will . . . nuns, in the same "feathered robes" and little downy caps. They had shoes with characters on them, "in these we tread the clouds." Tall Bamboo looked wistfully at nuns. She would willingly have changed her name from Tall to Hollow Bamboo, free from the pith of self, ready to be played by the Holy One.

"Oh, that He might raise me to His lips!"

A dozen times a day she repeated, "Oh, that we might stay here forever!"

Hung Tu could not agree with her. The Temple was interesting, but they had been there for three long days and that was enough. She was impatient for the visit to be over and the litter on its way downhill, to Cheng-tu, the City of Silk, to the Blue House, to Face-from-the-River.

If *he* were here beside her, laughing, listening, if they practiced the arts together, of poetry and love, then she might sigh like Tall Bamboo to stay on this mountain forever . . . or perhaps for another moon . . . lulled to sleep by flutes and the mutter of holy words. They would take the saffron robe and chant the sutras, practice the noble eightfold way and arrive at the State of Culmination, after which there is no rebirth.

She tried to imagine no rebirth, no bewildered human strands in the Weaver's fingers, no more living, no more death, no more love . . . perhaps there might be love, but no more fire, no more lusting, no more combat on the pillow. . . . Then let it not be yet . . . not yet!

Later, when they were old. Meanwhile let Tall Bamboo come to the mountain to her monk. But, the poor old ones, Tao for him was *this,* Tao for her was *that.* Tao was for each alone, the alone to the alone. Yet the flame burned between them, however far they moved, however near they stood, the flame burned between them. She had seen it, not with Fanyang's gossip-gathering eyes but with sympathy and respect, though she found it hard to understand . . . so old, so ugly a man . . . ministering to him, yes, as she did to Meng Chaio. . . . But "a dog trying to catch mice is at none of his business." She must not be that dog. Her business was to sit by Harmonizing Reed for an hour or two each day, relieving Fanyang from her faithful attendance, to cheer the old woman, when she returned, with harmless talk and recollections of the past, to wait on Tall Bamboo and accompany her to the shrines when she desired it, and to brush whatever characters were needed.

Tall Bamboo was studying, with the help of her monk, *The Nine Steps Toward the Development of the Yang Nature,* which, she asserted, demurely smiling, were exactly those carried out in any excellent Blue House.

She went through them with Hung Tu, adding her commentary.

Step One: Correct choice of a teacher, place of residence, and associates. Securing of adequate pecuniary support.

"Nothing can be done with a Blue House too far from the center of a city or otherwise badly placed. It is also a disadvantage to invest in the wrong kind of instructor for the Flowers, and certainly the steady flow of taels is essential."

Step Two: Knowledge of the proper preparation of vessels, incense burners, and fires.

"Assuredly. They might have added to the list."

Step Three: Knowledge of the principles of Taoism and cultivation of equanimity.

"Is not this what you have been taught by Spark of Flint and the others, in music, in the dance, in the recitation of the classics?"

"Yes, Elder Sister."

Step Four: Training of the nature and laying of the foundations of character.

"Essential to the forming of a Flower apt in the profession."

Step Five: Knowledge of the times and seasons for gathering herbs and the making of elixirs.

"That also. Every good Blue House has its herb-woman. It eats into the taels to go to a Dispenser of Elixirs."

Step Six: Conservation of the body by means of medicinal herbs.

"Do we not from the very start insist upon the use of I Mu?"

Step Seven: Achievement of ability to dispatch the soul from the body at will.

"Many times these ears have heard the client say his soul left his body in bliss." She was enjoying herself, though she pretended to be serious and scolded Hung Tu for smiling. "Show reverence! Attend to the wisdom of the scholars!"

"Yes, Elder Sister."

Step Eight: Doing good works in the world.

"Now that is the same for all, in every way of life, but in the Blue House there is more opportunity to do good to a greater number."

Step Nine: Achievement of the supreme, positive self which returns to its source.

"The clear application of this precept is hidden from this person at present. No doubt it is revealed to those who master the other eight."

She smiled the sunny smile of a child indulged by doting parents in every absurdity. That was how Hung Tu perceived her expression, yet it was puzzling, because, from what she was beginning to know of Tall Bamboo, she had never been shown indulgence by earthly parents, by the gods, or by anyone but Governor Wei Kao.

"We will have a copy of these excellent precepts hung in every pavilion. Brush the characters boldly."

"Yes, Elder Sister."

She was working with a favorite brush Meng Chaio had given to her. It belonged, he said, to the painter Hsi Chih, who had thrown it away. But it was good for years yet, and she liked it the best of the three she used, especially for raveled-rope strokes, proper for drawing mountains.

When Meng Chaio gave it to her she harmonized a song about it for him and his friend Hsi Chih.

> *A bamboo handle from Yueh,*
> *fashioned to fit the artist's fingers,*
> *tufts of Hsuan sable:*
> *elegantly it once moved, under the governing mind,*
> *in a journey of mountains,*
> *a soaring of wings, or waterfalls of flowers*
> *plunging down a silken scroll.*
> *Now it is cast aside, frayed and blunt . . .*
> *no longer remembered.*
> > *Hsi Chih has a new brush in his hand.*

And Hung Tu had the old one with her on this "journey of mountains." She stroked it lovingly. Painters chose their brushes with delicate intuition. This one was sable, selected in the autumn, when the hair was neither too soft nor too stiff. How individual a matter was a brush! Some preferred fox. Meng Chaio liked mouse whiskers enfolded by sheep's wool. Others chose goat, deer, rabbit, wolf, or weasel. There were brushes made from chicken down, the hair of children, and even, some coarse ones, from the bristles on a pig's neck. She liked sable best.

Now there were hurrying steps along the path. Tall Bamboo appeared, returning from the shrine.

"Only think what this illustrious person has learned today!" she called out gaily as she approached. Hung Tu stood up respectfully to hear.

"Three scholars are here from Chang-an. All morning they have been discussing the position of the Buddha's hands. Do the fingers open or close? Well? What do you say?"

It was the tone of a tutor expecting an immediate answer. Hung Tu, astonished and amused, said hastily: "This uninstructed person has given the matter insufficient thought, but it would seem there were many positions of the Buddha's hands, with the fingers open, the fingers closed, according to what that August Being with the Voice of Heaven intended to communicate. This person has heard that there is one, with the palm outstretched, 'calling the earth to witness' to some utterance of truth, and there is another, with the fingers lightly joined, held to the breast, enjoining peace."

"Exactly. The position of the Buddha's hands depends upon the occasion. It took three minutes of a woman's attention to dispose of the matter, but those learned men and the monks and nuns here are still disputing. . . . They will arrive at nothing this moon."

She settled herself in the middle of the room on the little raised platform which, she told Hung Tu the first time that she tried it, she would like to possess for the comfort it gave to her back. It did not seem a wish beyond fulfillment to Hung Tu, who could remember three such day beds in the House of Hsueh, but Tall Bamboo seemed to think it out of reach. It was a handsome piece, with its four lacquered posts, its richly decorated sides, its delicate shape; the sort of couch Emperor Ming Huang reclined upon, surrounded by the ladies of his court, as he played the flute. The scroll hung in her father's pavilion. It was a strange couch to find in a monastery guesthouse. One wondered how it came there. Suddenly she thought "when my mother dies, her furniture, her musical instruments . . . what will become of them? Will they stay here, scattered among cells and guest rooms?" The thought disturbed her.

Tall Bamboo placed the headblock behind her neck, grunted, and said: "Now serve this person tea, and while you prepare it tell me how is Harmonizing Reed?"

"Elder Sister, she was restless. Fanyang says she passed a broken night."

"Ah, ah. She should have stayed in the House of the Great Merchant, where she had her circle of listeners and friends. Yet I remember that we envied her. Who can tell the ways of Heaven?" She took the cup of tea and began to sip it reflectively. Presently she said: "Tomorrow we must leave this place. What we came for is accomplished. You have visited your mother. I have paid my devotions. The gong was struck four times. We cannot keep the Governor's litter and his servants from him longer. Tomorrow we must leave." She sighed, she said it sadly, but Hung Tu felt her own depression lift.

Tomorrow they were going home. It was not as if she could be of any comfort to Harmonizing Reed, her coming, her going, were all one. What was left of her mother, the body without essence, would be cared for by Fanyang. It was time to consider the living. She burned to be with Face-from-the-River. The people on this mountain, monks and nuns, were old. He and she were young. Tomorrow . . . tomorrow . . .

What would she gather from these days to share with him? The sound of a distant flute, the birds that sang at night, the solemnity of chanted words, serenity, Fanyang's wrinkled face with its welcoming grin, her mother's shadow . . . that she would replace with an earlier, happier memory . . . the tall monk and Tall Bamboo. . . .

"Make music for this wearied person."

"Yes, Elder Sister."

She took the little traveling lute from its corner and sat down by the day bed. First she sang "Cloud Touching Temple" as she had sung it to her mother, then she began to improvise, slowly, words and music forming together. There were pauses, false beginnings, hesitations, but at last the poem came into its shape:

> *On the temple terrace*
> *the monks are meditating on the Surangama Sutra.*
> *The yearning sound of a flute lights the sacred words.*
> *Consider the sole reality of the true mind . . .*
> *Do the Buddha's fingers open or close?*
>
> *Remember the sermon at Benares.*
> *The best of ways is the noble eightfold way.*
> *Pursue the meditation.*
> *Right solitude! Right ecstasy!*
>
> *A cicada saddens the twilight,*
> *the nightingales sing and sing.*

They feel the bliss, the rapture
that breathes through the universe.

Let us not go to death again and again.
In the silences the flute, pure and clear as ice,
follows the falling sun.

Tall Bamboo nodded, gave little exclamations, chuckled once, and fell silent. Glancing at her sideways, Hung Tu saw that she was wiping her eyes with her sleeve. It was a moment to bend over the instrument, to tune it busily, to sing again:

The early sun dissolves the mist
that has covered the mountain.
All night I have listened to the wise,
yet failed to learn.
Dimly, darkly, the eternal pines
rise without effort from the vanishing fog.

Presently Tall Bamboo spoke.

"You are a poet, child. You have captured the essence of this Temple in these songs. Li Po himself could not do more. Sing them again, and then you must brush them out before the words disappear. You must copy them all for me."

"Elder Sister, when you harmonized your songs, did you also brush them?"

"The circumstances were different, child. This person composed only willow cotton songs, light things of the moment, to catch the ear and tickle the senses. They were created to be sung and to die, having no permanence, no value beyond the air they displaced."

"Meng Chaio and other scholars say there is much wisdom and much magic in the Wu song and in the 'cut-short poem,' the folk song, as much as in the new 'regulated forms' we try to emulate."

"That may be true, but still the popular song of the moment is not sung to last forever."

"Elder Sister, did not Li Po dispute with you concerning that? It is said by scholars that he used the Wu songs as a form to which to set new words."

"Ah, ah! *New* words. No, no, the brushing of a poem requires that the poem have the Ch'i of greatness. Painting and writing are not small Tao."

Hung Tu fell silent. Presently she murmured: "Elder Sister, there is so much to learn."

"Yes, even to sing agreeably a few light songs means neglect of brushwork, and to paint 'with the heart and hand,' making visible the invisible, means neglect of dance. To be a poet is the struggle of a lifetime. This unlettered person envies those who can express Tao in words."

"Unlettered!" Hung Tu thought, remembering the empty chatter of the women in the House of Hsueh. This extraordinary person, who looked like a peasant and often talked like one, could also look and sound like the most tutored scholar. One must remember that she had lived for many years with Governor Wei Kao, mingling with his friends. Perhaps the learned monk whom she came to the Temple to visit was one of these. It seemed likely. It would explain the Governor's litter being so readily available, and also his permission for her to leave the Blue House . . . to convey his respects and to inquire after an old mutual friend. More might never have been known or noticed by the Governor . . . or, again, his noticing might be the reason for the Blue House and the sad-colored robe.

All that was speculation and it must remain so. Meanwhile, how thankful this one was, how fortunate, that her father's choice had sent her to that Blue House and not another, that his earlier concern sent her there already well versed in the classics, so that she could take her favored place among the poets and the scholars.

Tomorrow—she stretched luxuriously, exultantly on her mat, beside Tall Bamboo, already snoring—tomorrow she would be among that challenging throng, hearing good discourse, and when the chance came, offering her work to Meng Chaio for discussion. Later these poems might be chosen for another presentation to the Governor, danced by the Flower she most hated, whose exquisite art of motion she most loved, that undulating poisonous snake with its ready fangs, that venomous Eyes' Fascination. They slept side by side now, in the First Pavilion, watchfully aware of each other, yet with respect, for each knew the other's worth. And though they hated one another they were perfectly united in expressing the entrapment of the moment's vision, and also in keeping the other carefully in view.

It was a relationship which could only be developed in a Blue House between two exceptional performers. Tomorrow they would eye one another with comfortable, familiar hate. Tomorrow she might also be eying someone more important, with love, for surely he would come to ask for her. Perhaps he had already made inquiries and gone away saddened by her absence. Or perhaps he had stayed! With Eyes' Fascination! No, she would not think of that. She would repeat her poems, she would listen to the nightingale, she would still her heart with deep and controlled breathing. "The pure men of old slept without dreams and waked without anxiety. They ate without discrimination, breathing deep breaths. For pure men draw breath from their uttermost depths; the vulgar only from their throats."

The precept did not comfort her. She would give all those pure men of old for one impure one breathing beside her from his throat.

XXIV

THE HOT LONG DAYS went by, the busy nights. There was no sign of him, no word. She dared not ask directly . . . there was no one whom she could trust. . . . The Flowers? The servants? The old porter? They would run to Tall Bamboo at once, out of loyalty or out of malice against Silver Hooks. The result would be the same. However kind, however understanding Tall Bamboo might appear at the Cloud Touching Temple, she would never tolerate a bad breach of THE RULES. Becoming enamored of a guest? Asking questions about a guest? No, no, one must go about one's work with gentle, eager smiles, as much a part of a Flower's image as her embroidered robe, and wait for news of him.

Once or twice she fancied Eyes' Fascination, Peach Bloom Fan, and others with whom she was no favorite looked at her with extra malice, as though they knew something satisfactory. If they did, they would not tell.

Where could he be? This waiting was worse than those anguished weeks in her father's house when she expected this same man, this obsession, this Face-from-the-River, to ask for her in marriage. Why must she deceive herself? She was nothing to him then and no more to him now than any little Flower in an expensive Blue House. . . . But even for *that* he should have come!

Perhaps he was ill, or dead . . . perhaps he could not afford it . . . perhaps . . .

Day after day, no word, no sign, night after night she waited, lying in other men's arms.

Oh, indeed, they all knew something, enemies and friends. There were half smiles, glances, troubled looks of compassion. Old Scholar had a strange expression, solicitous and something more. He had not recovered his good humor. Now he looked at her, and she smiled back, the demure smile of a Flower-in-the-mist, as the class in brushwork continued.

"Consider the words of Ts'ao Chih, in far antiquity. . . ."

Well, there was one more chance. If he did not come, she would see him at the Palace, if she was chosen to perform . . . if the Governor sent for them again . . . if . . .

"Painting is a moral force. When one sees pictures of the three Kings and the five Emperors . . ."

Now who could care for kings in far antiquity?

"One cannot but look at them with respect and veneration, and when one sees pictures of the Terminators, the last degenerate rulers of the Dynasty, one cannot but feel sad."

But not for that. This person's sorrow is real, is now.

Smile. Pose the brush. . . .

"When one sees pictures of rebels and usurpers of the throne, one cannot but gnash one's teeth. When one sees pictures of great sages and men of high principles, one cannot but forget one's meals."

Face-from-the-River, Face-from-the-River, all this may be true, but not for their old kings! Only for you.

"Painting is a moral force. Ku K'ai Chih, who died four hundred years ago, famous for his portraits, waited several years before brushing in the pupils of the eyes. When he was asked the reason for this delay, it is said that he replied, 'It is true that the beauty of frame and limb can be expressed independently of these delicate parts, but delicacy of character depends entirely upon them, and character must grow with the years.' Silver Hooks . . ."

"Yes, Honored Master?"

"Why do we give attention to these sayings of the Ancients on the art of painting . . ."

Why indeed?

"When we are none of us, in this circle, studying to be painters?"

"We give attention to these sayings of the Ancients on the art of painting because the art of painting and the art of brushing poems, of depicting characters in writing, are, in essence, the same. Both depend upon skill and training in fine brushwork. Both make equal use of the Six Canons, the Six Essentials, the Six Qualities, the Three Faults, and the Twelve Things to Avoid."

"The choice of words is infelicitous. Do we *make use* of the Three Faults, or the Twelve Things to Avoid? Who will correct this?"

Some hand went up, some complacent murmur put the blunder right. Hung Tu did not bother to see who it was. She was weary of these repetitions of precepts from the classics. Her mind was full of one anxiety, one enormous, all-consuming care. Face-from-the-River. Where was he? Where was he?

If she could have given her attention to anything less, it might have been to learning some of the secrets and discoveries of the art of composition, Meng Chaio's own techniques. He seldom spoke of these. Yet he was a great and honored master of the lu-shih and also the new-style four-line poem. He was starting to speak. She looked at him hopefully. Perhaps he would dismiss them and she could go to First Pavilion for a few moments' rest. No, he was exerting himself for further exposition.

"Since the nature of brush and ink does not permit correction without damage to the finished effect, it is wisdom and essential Tao for the artist to look with honesty at what is before him. If a character is ill-defined, do not set it down. Omit anything in brush-work or in life that is not *so*. Each single stroke must be a living line. No stroke may be retraced. Therefore the heart must be stilled, the eye must be open, the hand must be sure. . . ."

Hung Tu had heard it all before. When she next listened, he was saying:

"That will do for today. Tomorrow you will each bring me two lines of brushwork for discussion."

She rose to depart with the others, and, as usual, he called her back, but not to fill his pipe, to serve him tea, or to minister to his bodily desires . . . it was not often that he summoned her for these, although he could be as lusty as a young man when he was on fire . . . this time he did not seem to know what he did want, after he had motioned her to sit beside him.

Presently he cleared his throat and turned the strength of his eyes upon her. They were penetrating eyes for one so old. She often felt confused and hesitant before them. Now she looked more firmly down for safety's sake, that he might not read her thoughts and understand how far they traveled from him.

"The two poems," he said slowly, watching her, "that were composed at Cloud Touching Temple on the mountain, especially the one on the Temple terrace . . . they interest this person. Where did the poet acquire knowledge of the sutras or of the eightfold way?"

"Master, the sutras were chanted every day at the shrines and there were discussions by the monks. The poet had also heard from childhood of the noble eightfold way."

"Yes? These are not childhood's thoughts."

"Honored Master, poems do not always come from concentrated study or from deep thought . . . this poem was . . . was parrot-flash. The poet sought to reproduce the color, the persuasive sound, the essence of the Temple life. . . ."

"Ah. But the last three lines, longing for no rebirth . . . it would seem . . . child, you were not driven . . . you had no desire to assume the sad-colored robe?"

He waited for an answer, studying her face. She stared at him amazed. Now he was being rude dog chasing mice!

"Then this person was mistaken. That is a relief. There is no escape from sorrow, Silver Hooks, the illusion of sorrow, by running down another's road. Tao is Tao for us all. The Tao we are born with is the Tao we should travel. Sometimes two ways may overlap and be traveled at the same time, if there is no conflict between them, as for a poet and a Flower-in-the-mist. Sometimes the ways diverge and cannot be traveled together, as for a Flower and a nun or for a poet and a monk. Then one must make a choice, and that is a heavy thing."

He paused. She made no comment and after a moment he continued:

"Tao for a poet demands that he enter the lives of others to understand them, to re-create their essences, but he must not become entrapped by any one way too long. Tao for a Flower-in-the-mist demands that she enter the lives of others to minister to all, but she must not become entrapped into giving her heart to one. In this the poet and the Flower are alike and may travel the same road. . . ."

His voice changed suddenly.

"The heart must be stilled. . . . Silver Hooks, when the preferred is not *so,* it is better to omit him."

She was startled into looking up. The kindness in his face encouraged her to murmur:

"Then it is known? This person thought . . . this person hoped . . ."

"To cover fire with smoke and have it go unregarded? But there is nothing done under Heaven that is not known by four. Heaven knows, the Earth knows, you know, and I know."

"Tall Bamboo?"

"Assuredly, and others. But their knowledge is limited to this . . . they have seen you aflame with joy, now they see you grieve, because he has gone away."

"That is not known to this person."

It was his turn to look amazed and she regretted the revelation. To grieve because a man departs on some known, shared-in-spirit mission and to grieve because he comes no more and one does not know where he is, show different states of grief and of intimacy.

After a moment he went on:

"Well, but it is widely known . . . the Governor transferred him to the Hall of Assembled Worthies in Chang-an. He has gone, child. He left a moon ago, bearing letters from this person to the Collector and Arranger of Manuscripts at the Imperial Court. There is a new tutor to the Governor's sons."

She sat digesting this, a cold stone in her heart.

"You must forget him, Silver Hooks. Indeed, when you went on pilgrimage, this person thought, this person feared . . ." He broke off awkwardly, then he added compassionately, "You may go now. It is perhaps a day to rest."

She looked up, at the end of her endurance.

"And when you come back tomorrow, come as a poet, stepping free."

She could not answer. She could only struggle to her feet, bow, and hurry away, holding her sleeve to her eyes, hoping to hide her tears.

When she reached the First Pavilion, Eyes' Fascination was there. She said with malicious interest:

"Ah. You have seen the Lady Tall Bamboo."

Hung Tu shook her head.

"No? Well, you are to go to her pavilion."

Hung Tu poured water to bathe her face and hands. She changed her robe and smoothed her hair without giving thought to what she did, nor to Eyes' Fascination watching her, nor to the coming meeting.

He had gone. He had his choice, but he was afraid to admit that he had a choice and so he went obediently away.

The choice was not whether he would or would not obey the Governor's orders, it was whether he would or would not say farewell to her before he went . . . or was that included in the Governor's orders? That much of them he could have disobeyed.

A poet who would steal a poem of Li Po's and pass it off as his . . . was as Meng Chaio said "not *so*."

Perhaps he was replete and found it satisfactory to leave without the fatigue and the expense of a visit to the Blue House.

Perhaps he needed all his taels for the journey and for the House of the Great Merchant in Chang-an . . . and other Blue Houses along the way. . . .

Perhaps she was unjust. Perhaps even now he suffered, perhaps beneath the moon he sobbed and beat his head and called her name, as she had called his. . . .

Perhaps. But he had gone. He had gone.

Soon she too would be going through the gates of the Blue House toward another life. She knew with certainty in her frightened bones what Tall Bamboo was summoning her to hear.

How could she have forgotten so disastrously all her hard-learned wisdom? "Not attaching themselves to anything." She had written that. She had known it true. Then she had broken that and every other part of Tao for a Flower, and done so without discretion, for prying eyes to see. . . .

Now she would be sold and sent away like Fragrant Plant to a cheaper place, for drunkards and barbarians from the North and other dregs, to be used there till she died.

She would plead, and perhaps for her mother's sake . . . but Tall Bamboo was known to be implacable. Shivering, she drew her robe around her and left the room without looking back at her smiling enemy. Slowly she crossed the compound to Tall Bamboo's pavilion.

Twice before she had come there in fear and anxiety. Now, as then, Tall Bamboo received her mildly, with a smile. The edge of her fear subsided and she found herself confronted with an unexpected turn of events.

It had to do with Governor Wei Kao. There were envoys expected shortly, important officials, ambassadors from a foreign place. . . .

"Some kingdom in the North . . . barbarians with whom the Emperor has been at war, or does not wish to be at war . . . this person did not clearly receive that part of it. . . . Envoys are also on the way from Chang-an, from the Emperor Himself and His Imperial Court, to meet these ambassadors. Naturally Governor Wei Kao wishes to entertain these exalted personages. . . ."

"Naturally, Elder Sister," Hung Tu murmured.

"He desires new poems for the occasion, music, dancing, a great spectacle, all to be ready at once. . . ." She laughed wryly, indulgently. "If we close our doors and put aside the business of the house and practice from this hour with one-pointed energies, we still may not be able to arrive at the decreed achievements soon enough or well enough to please him. But we must try, and without closing our doors, since he also plans to send the visitors here."

"Yes, Elder Sister, we must try."

"We must do more, we must succeed, or incur his heavy displeasure."

"Yes, Elder Sister."

To compose new poems on demand in her present state of mind would be difficult, might be impossible, but there were old ones neither the Governor nor Tall Bamboo had seen, and the two from the visit to the Temple. . . .

In the first shock of relief that Tall Bamboo did not intend to punish her, she felt equal to almost anything, even to composing lines to strange barbarians. She looked up bravely.

"Thank you, Elder Sister," she began, but Tall Bamboo interrupted.

"Hard work is medicine for sorrow. Go and compose good poems. Send Spark of Flint to me."

XXV

THE LONG HOT DAYS of summer, the languid nights, gave way to autumn mists and then to winter cold. Changes came to the Blue House, and one for Hung Tu. It was not quite unexpected. Indeed she had worked hard to attract the Governor's attention. At first this was chiefly to annoy Eyes' Fascination, but later she began to give thought to her future. She no longer would leave it to the chance operations of Heaven. She did not intend to be caught by imprudence again.

She intended to rise as high as she could in her profession, to be as she had promised Hsueh Yun, "the best, the most accomplished Flower-in-the-mist in all the Empire." More difficult, she aspired to become known and respected as a poet and a scholar. "Small Dragon of the House of Hsueh," Silver Hooks . . . but she would shed her Blue House name when she entered the Palace. For that was the coming change, to replace Tall Bamboo as the Governor's official Hostess.

Tall Bamboo was aging, and, she explained to Hung Tu, growing inadequate for the new needs of the Shu Ya Men. Under Governor Wei Kao the entertainment of important guests had changed over the years. It was now a complicated matter.

"The peacock's tail," she said, "has too many eyes. It used to be enough to pour tea gracefully and sing the willow cotton songs. Now more is expected. The new-fangled ballet, scholarly discourses on poetry, heavy music, original songs. . . . It is beyond this person."

Moreover she was anxious to retire, not only from her duties at the Palace, but from the Blue House too.

"Another year, perhaps, and 'tall' may change to 'hollow.' There is an empty cell waiting for this emptiness."

"And a tall monk waiting . . ." Hung Tu ventured, adding quickly, "to attend upon the gate and let in pilgrims, and explain the position of the Buddha's hands."

Tall Bamboo stared at her searchingly for a moment before she decided to "skim the stream like a swallow" and ignore what lurked beneath. She continued:

"It will take two persons to replace this one." The idea pleased her. "Yes, yes, two for the one. But the Blue House can wait. It is the appointment to the Shu Ya Men that must be thought of first."

Hung Tu murmured a respectful "Indeed that must be thought of," as though she did not guess what might be coming next.

"The Governor has had the delicacy, the generosity, to consult this person and to leave the first choice in these hands."

She peered at Hung Tu, who smiled demurely and said nothing.

"After much reflection, and many discussions with Scholar Meng Chaio and others, and having observed with these dim eyes a number of considerations about many candidates . . . in short, child, you have been proposed for this high honor and accepted by the Governor."

"A great future," Fanyang said, *"a great future in the Governor's Palace."*

They must have talked it over even then, and even then she was chosen.

That was what Tall Bamboo was announcing now to Silver Hooks, a great and empty future in the Palace.

For it would be empty, with no Face-from-the-River to share it. But it would be empty with more dignity, with more importance, with more protection, and with more enjoyment, in the Governor's Palace than in any Blue House, even the good one on Willow Street.

Out of new wisdom, a new understanding of the ways of men and women, and of her own undisciplined heart, she found strength to parry the offer, to withhold acceptance at once.

"Elder Sister, was it not your opinion that Harmonizing Reed made a disastrous choice? Should she not have stayed where she was content, in the House of the Great Merchant in Chang-an?

How can this person, having the example of her mother before her, and having heard it said, not once but many times, at the Cloud Touching Temple . . ."

Tall Bamboo was taken aback. "That is a different matter," she said hastily. "Harmonizing Reed left the Blue House to be married. You are not going to the Palace as a wife or a concubine."

"This obtuse person does not understand."

"How can there be understanding if you look at the sun from the bottom of a well? Harmonizing Reed was cut off from life in the world, from the arts and from her friends. These things were her food. But is it not my complaint that there is too much rich food in the Palace?"

Still Hung Tu protested she would rather stay in the Blue House.

Tall Bamboo shrugged.

"Even if she wished, this person could not keep you here against the Governor's desire."

"Then this insignificant person will go away from Cheng-tu."

"If you were free to go, where could you go? The city is the Governor's, the Province is the Governor's. . . ."

The spirit of mischief made her say demurely:

"I will go to the Cloud Touching Temple and take the sad-colored robe, and be near . . ." she hesitated long enough for the completed thought to be received by Tall Bamboo, *be near your tall monk*. At least she thought so. There was a little frown on the old astute face . . . before she continued smoothly: "be near Fanyang and my sick mother. . . ."

Tall Bamboo seized on this at once.

"Fanyang has no need of an extra mouth, and poor Harmonizing Reed . . ." she broke off, smiling. "What is it you want, child?"

"This person has said . . . to stay here in the Blue House. . . ."

"No, that is not true. You may go now. We will talk of this again when there is truth between us. Send Eyes' Fascination to me."

Then Hung Tu was afraid. Eyes' Fascination, she knew, would not say "no" to this or to any appointment in the Palace. She turned in the doorway.

"Elder Sister, this person will do what you advise. But there is something. . . ."

"Ah, ah, now leap the ditch, child, to this friend."

But it was not easy. She hesitated. Tall Bamboo said impatiently, "Do not rub the scales under the dragon's neck. Be open and together we will see."

"Well then, Elder Sister, it has come to be apparent that external appearance and . . . and . . . and careful presentation are important . . . that is . . . if this person goes to live in the Palace, she will be among many wives and many concubines, more beautiful and younger than she. . . ."

"Some, perhaps, not many. And what is that to you? You do not go there as either."

"Yes, but, Elder Sister, who will know it?"

"Everyone who sees you work. Unpolished jade does not shine. A needle is not sharp at both ends."

Hung Tu sighed. It would be as difficult as she expected to make the older woman understand a need she had never imagined. She decided to arrive from a new direction.

"If this person could stay in the Blue House, as you did, and go to the Palace now and then . . ."

"That is impossible. The Governor has set his face against it and the work has so increased that it requires the constant presence of a well-trained official Hostess. Come to the point, child."

"Then, if there could be a robe . . ."

"There will be many robes. The Governor is generous. And jewels too."

"This person means . . ." she decided to be explicit and risk losing Tall Bamboo's support . . . "a scholar's robe, so that those who saw her, even passing by, would not confuse her with the concubines."

"A scholar's robe?" Tall Bamboo laughed heartily, rocking and fanning herself. "Peacock feathers on a hen?"

Hung Tu plunged on:

"And some sort of official title . . . to give authority. . . ."

Tall Bamboo laughed louder, choking and wiping her eyes. It

was better to loosen her mirth than to anger her. Hung Tu waited till the fit subsided. Then she smiled and said:

"Nevertheless this person will not go for less."

"Nonsense. Ask for gold, child, gold and jewels. The Governor must expect it. He will give you those, more than you expect. . . ."

"As he would to a concubine or a Flower-in-the-mist . . ."

"Eh, eh! What else?"

". . . and provoke jealousies. Elder Sister, I do not have your wisdom or your strength, and being there, underfoot and before the eye, constantly . . . no, I do not dare it. This person must have the protection, the security, of being set apart from the rest. The title, the scholar's robe, will disarm envy, and even waken pity in those who would otherwise be rivals. . . ."

Tall Bamboo considered this in silence, while Hung Tu held her breath.

"It is true," she said, at length, "that the times have greatly changed. And Governor Wei Kao . . . I will speak to him. So new, so impertinent a notion . . . He is ripe for novelties, but he may be angered, child. . . ."

"Elder Sister . . ."

"It is enough. These ears ache. . . . A scholar's robe, a title!" She chuckled. "Well, it will be a moment's talk, and then . . . we are all born the same way, we can die in a hundred ways. . . . Go to Old Scholar, here is half the morning wasted."

"Shall I send Eyes' Fascination?"

"No, there is no need." She laughed again. "A scholar's robe instead of a jeweled comb and seven jade bracelets." She jingled hers as she spoke, and waved toward the door.

Three days later she sent for Hung Tu again.

"Well," she said, "it is settled. He was startled at first, he frowned, but the moment was auspicious. He could not refrain from laughter. He has chosen a title for you, never before bestowed. . . ."

"Yes?" Hung Tu murmured eagerly.

"You are to be addressed as Nu Hsaio Shou, Female Secretary, Collector of Books. He wrote the decree at once and gave it in my presence to be posted."

"Oh, Elder Sister. . . . And the robe?"

"You are to design it yourself. And on the third day of the month, when the stars are propitious, he will send a litter for you."

"Elder Sister!"

"Elder Sister . . . Elder Sister . . . it is a green parrot. You will go far, child, with such a beginning as this."

They looked at one another, smiling, with the warmth and understanding of friends. Then Hung Tu said:

"This grateful person owes all her good fate to you."

"There is also the eye of Heaven."

"This person has often been aware of nearer eyes benevolently watching her."

"You are the daughter of an old friend and the child I did not have. Moreover, it is policy. . . . I shall expect the Governor's continued protection and patronage and many other favors to come when I think of them. Go now and vex the Flowers who aspire to be concubines, great Nu Hsaio Shou, Female Secretary, Collector of Books!" She waved dismissal. Then she added, laughing, "Do not make them so ill with envy that they cannot dance before him tomorrow. Are the poems brushed?"

Hung Tu nodded. She could not speak. She was excited and also suddenly afraid of the new life opening before her, in which she would be alone, with nothing but her wits to guide her. Still, she crossed the compound stoutly, on loud-sounding feet. She was now a scholar, as much as her two brothers, a scholar, an acknowledged poet. . . .

The moment held its sweetness. If Harmonizing Reed could know where those early songs, that early training led . . . but she could at least send word to Fanyang.

Everything seemed the same about her, nothing at all had changed, the sights and sounds, the trees, the groups in the courtyard, even the ducks by the pond . . . *golden headdress of the Mandarin drake . . . Blue and purple feathers, elegant white markings . . . serenely unaware of summer's passing . . .*

"And of mine . . ."

PART FIVE
Circa 803 A.D.

XXVI

ALL THE FEET in the Province, in the Empire, in the world, crossed Myriad Li Bridge; all the river traffic flowed beneath it. A good proportion of both were going to the Villa beside Hundred Flowers Pool. There was a willow cotton song about it.

> *By Myriad Li Bridge,*
> *Hung Tu, the poet, lives,*
> *under the loquat tree,*
> *behind closed doors . . .*

The Villa stood back from the road, enclosed in a bamboo fence, with a fishpond in the courtyard, pavilions, and a garden sloping to the riverbank. When Hung Tu sat in the shade of her favorite tree, watching the hummingbirds and the dragonflies among the flowering shrubs, the swallows, the flashing orioles along the riverbank, she might have been in the garden of her childhood. When she closed her eyes the illusion was complete. The same voice of the river, the same rush-by of feet beyond a bamboo wall. Almost she expected to hear her brothers quarreling up and down the paths or the majestic sweeping rhythm of her father's robe.

There was no news of them. But there was final word of Harmonizing Reed. One autumn day Fanyang appeared at the gates, trundling a wheelbarrow of odds and ends, among them music and the p'i-pa for Hung Tu. Harmonizing Reed had died without returning from the shadows. The gong was sounded for her twice and everything done as it should be.

Fanyang stayed to see with her own eyes that this was so, then she came down from the mountain to live with Hung Tu. As the saying went, "the foot of one traverses dangers and difficulties to unite with the foot of another to form a column of sound defense."

The arrangement suited them both. Fanyang was in the center of the glittering world. Hung Tu had a faithful servant to be her eyes and ears. The sound of that sturdy voice upraised in the courtyard was comforting. It too brought back the shapes and places of childhood. More than that, it brought important news.

It was Fanyang who gathered all the gossip of this or that dismissal or change of influence at the Palace or in the city. It was she who told Hung Tu of the willow cotton songs about her, some flattering and some not. Of the rude ones Fanyang said:

"The cicadas are grinching thus and so today."

Hung Tu laughed at the malice of the eunuchs and the concubines. She agreed: "It is the rattle of dry leaves." Once when they whispered against her too loudly, she composed a poem which she gave to her musicians to be widely sung in Cheng-tu. She called it "The Song of the Cicadas":

> *Intense, far-off is the song of the cicadas,*
> *a shimmering murmur, washed in dew.*
> *As leaves whisper together in a high wind*
> *one note resounds from every side,*
> *interminably vibrating.*
> *The persistent shrillness rings a thousand bells*
> *denying the end of summer,*
> *even as the swarms diminish.*

Only a few understood. Some, guessing it might apply to them, were gratified, thinking the poet called them "shimmering" and "washed in dew." Others thought "leaves whisper" a pleasant sound. They missed the significance of "shrillness" and "diminish." On the whole her enemies were silenced, since she appeared to be taking them into account. No doubt the words were intended to be complimentary, they said. The shrill outbursts died down. The parties at the Villa continued, with Fanyang heating the wine and Hung Tu pouring it for the Governor's guests, the poets, the scholars, the musicians, the generals, the dignitaries, all the distinguished men who came to the City of Silk.

When envoys from the North arrived she found occasion to

make discreet inquiries for news of Hsueh Yun, while Fanyang more bluntly questioned every new face at the market or the city wells, every dusty peddler who came to the Villa gates. There was no word.

The years slipped by, Governor succeeding Governor. Lesser officials came and went. The Hostess of the Shu Ya Men remained to entertain them while they were in office, to remember them when they were gone.

Governor Wei Kao had his special place in the procession of faces remembered in the night. He was the most famous, the most renowned in war and good government of the Province. He had known her father, and she had been taught to look up to him in childhood. He had taken her from the Blue House and later installed her in this Villa to protect her from the Palace intrigues, the jealousies and envies of the concubines.

His successors kept her there with modifications and minor changes in her duties and in the number and kind of her servants. One of them assigned her four musicians. One of them took away her title of Nu Hsaio Shou in the first year of his office, for her sake, he explained.

"Some newly appointed underling, eager to shoot tigers and display the skins for praise, might stumble on this title and conclude that there is in Cheng-tu some minor official, some secretary, who has been in his post too long. Then the Hostess of the Shu Ya Men might be ordered to a far-off place. It is wise not to be the bone unearthed by contending dogs. 'Nu' is a small word, easily overlooked, and when is a mistake conceded? Much harm might be done by drawing such attention to you."

Hung Tu grieved at first. She enjoyed her title, the respect and envy it brought to her, but she knew the observation was a sound one and she was grateful for Governor Yao's shrewd concern. She could still wear her robe, and it was true that no one, not even Governors, remained in office for long. Certainly none so long as she. Jealousy undid them. Every official was transferred to another Province, or recalled to the Imperial Court, or exiled to the North, like her father. How many she had seen arrive and, barely settled, depart with their women and children and household retinues, a restless river of faces, hopeful or resigned.

Some went to be rewarded, surrounded by rejoicing friends, some went alone to exile, punishment, disgrace. None might stay in the Paradise of Shu beyond an allotted time, subject to sudden change. The Emperor trusted no one too long away from the Court. Even if He had, there were, as Governor Yao said, too many officials below Him eager to shoot tigers and display each other's skins.

Terms of office varied. Governor Wei Kao held the longest in living memory, but even he was recalled before he wished to leave, and Governor Yao lasted less than two full years. Her farewell to him was still sung in Cheng-tu.

An unending line of willows borders the stream
with summer green. They trail sad branches
in the swirling waters.
The prow of your boat, dividing the wind,
breaks a feathery willow wand.
It floats away with you in mute farewell.

Another land will hold you now. . . .
Remember one who grieves for you here
under the same dim moon.

It would remind him, in that far-off place where he was, of former happiness by Hundred Flowers Pool, where life went securely on in the elegant seclusion of this Villa, where poems were harmonized among the great, such immortals as Tu Fu, Po Chui, Niu Sung-jou . . . oh, and Yen Shou and Wu Wu-ling . . . what brilliant days and nights, what revelry beside Hundred Flowers Pool! What parties and excursions, when the Loquat Gates swung wide and the heat of summer tempted restless feet to climb to the cool hills! What music and what languor in the garden when the wanderers returned!

Now another change was pending. A new Governor, Governor Tuan, would be coming to the scented pillow.

This person . . . it came to her suddenly . . . this person now was twenty-eight . . . but still beautiful and skilled in the seductive arts, and Governor Tuan must surely prove a man like other men. . . .

"Fanyang," she called, "bring the mirror and the oils."

XXVII

GOVERNOR TUAN WAS NOT like other Governors Hung Tu had known before him, magnificent large men, or if they were small, lean and wiry with imperious, fierce faces. Tigers every one. Governor Wei Kao in his golden robes rivaled the rising sun for majestic bearing. He was the true image of the Emperor, against whom she measured lesser men. Who but he could have dealt with the wars and uprisings and the raids from the North of his troubled years of office? Yet he found time for the arts and delighted to honor the poets.

It was Governor Wei Kao who took her to meet the immortal Tu Fu in his cottage outside the city, and sat in silent grace while the sick old man and the young Flower-in-the-mist, both his pensioners, living on his bounty, exchanged views on poetry and harmonized lines together. It was an evening she would never lose. It traveled on with her.

Even in the days of his twilight, after a stormy life of miseries and sickness, there was *that* in Tu Fu's songs, an immortal fire. When he sang of glory, drums beat in the blood; when he sang of simple things, the essence of his listeners wept. For the sake of this magic Governor Wei Kao suffered inconvenience, even arrogance and insults from the quarrelsome old man. But when the Governor he baited went from Cheng-tu, Tu Fu left also, and died on his wanderings.

All the Governors were patrons and protectors of the arts in some measure. Governor Yao painted landscapes and brought them to her for praise because she was trained in a knowledge of the Six Essentials and skilled in brushwork. Scholar, Poet, Painter, some combination of these qualities every Governor possessed, but Governor Tuan's essence evaded definition, at least from the image he presented to her and to the world.

His needs were not those of a man of action, though he came more often to the Villa than the lustiest before him. He came differently, and the use he chose to make of his official Hostess was unusual. Governor Wei Kao had summoned her more often to the Palace to promote the great festivals he loved to arrange for his guests. When he came to the Villa it was usually with the men he wished to honor by formal entertainment. He was always pleased if there were songs spontaneously composed for the occasion, or if any lines written by the guests were harmonized.

Other Governors followed his example, keeping, more or less, to the established pattern; some of them arranged fewer lavish festivals; some of them took more advantage of the scented pillow.

Governor Tuan came alone to the Villa, and of all the services he found there he preferred conversation. This, in itself, was not unheard of. The Villa was noted for its conversation. Governor Yao, for example, spent many hours in discussion, after or before the scented pillow, but the talk was mostly small talk, teasing little flatteries of the Blue House kind, or if he were in a grave mood, about painting. Governor Yao was a serious observer of the natural groupings of rocks, the formation of mists and clouds, and the aims of *chen* and *tzu jan*.

Governor Tuan cared for none of these things. If others dwelt upon them in his presence his eye glazed. Nor was it possible to please him with the tinkling charm bells, the flatteries of the silken tongue.

He talked of trade, "like a peddler," Fanyang said scornfully at first. Later she listened, crouched over her brazier where the sweet wine steamed, mouth open in awe, nodding agreement.

It was evident that Governor Tuan valued something Hung Tu had never thought of as a subject for conversation, nor heard mentioned by the great merchants and their sons who frequented the Blue House. These never spoke of trade, although it was the carpet beneath their feet and the source of every tael that they spent. But Governor Tuan spoke of the ebb and flow of merchandise, the scarcity of gold, the arrival and departure of ships and caravans, with love-fire in his eyes. So boatmen speak of the river. But he was Governor of Shu, second only to the Emperor in importance.

It was disconcerting, and at first she stumbled in her search for right replies, but presently she noticed two helpful and revealing things. Governor Tuan spoke to her as though to another mind concerned with the same interests. He listened with grave attention and he was always pleased if there were something to be learned, some little firsthand fact about the most common objects.

Early in their evening meetings he brought her an inkstone shaped like a lute, and when she exclaimed with pleasure at the beauty of the stone, he told her the Emperor Hsuan Tsung himself designed inkstones of many shapes and sizes, using stones of unusual color, crescent-shaped and scaled like a dragon. Then he questioned her minutely about inkstones, ink sticks, and the processes of making ink.

In the Blue House, did they add musk, camphor, pomegranate bark, or ground amber to add fragrance to the stick, improve its color, or preserve it? Did they use ten parts carbon to five parts glue or ten parts pine soot to three parts powdered jade and one part glue, which he believed gave a deeper, glossier tone? How did they make the glue? And did they dull the ink with crushed oyster shells or powdered jade?

Hung Tu told him everything she knew, all she had learned from Old Scholar and before that, when she prepared the materials for her father. She showed him how she made her own ink sticks, and how she would use the inkstone he gave her, pouring a little water into the hollow at one end, rubbing the stick on the flat area.

From ink they went to the preparation of silks and papers. Though she had lived in the City of Silk since early childhood, Hung Tu knew little about the first stages of silk, but she did know how it was best prepared for painting in the form of banners and scrolls, how to treat it with alum and glue and beat and smooth it and stretch it on a frame. She blushed to talk of such tedious trivialities to the Governor of Shu, but Governor Tuan insisted on the most precise details. In turn he told her the history of silk from early times, and how the fate of a town, of a province, of an empire might depend upon the thread from a silkworm.

"The proper use of such a thread, its wise distribution, is essential for our City of Silk."

Later they came to paper, invented many centuries before by another Governor of a Province, under the Emperor Ho Ti, a Governor named Ts'ai Lun, who made paper out of fish nets.

Hung Tu had not heard of him.

"This admiring one," Governor Tuan said, "would rather have discovered the secret of producing paper and have left that legacy to men than win a hundred battles. Although," he added, "when bandits descend from the North or rebels and usurpers stir within reach of his arm, the virtuous Governor must fight in defense of his Emperor. But consider what has been preserved for us by this fourth of the Four Treasures. Before the time of Ts'ai Lun slips of bamboo and wood were used for writing, heavy, clumsy, and inelegant. Now paper is made of many things, corn and rice stalks, cotton, mulberry, hemp, and, in Cheng-tu, silk cocoons."

Later he told Hung Tu of experiments with moss and a kind of river plant, "such as grows in the bend of the river, near Hundred Flowers Pool."

Then he organized a papermaking enterprise, setting slaves to excavate the fungus from the river bed and others to boil the water moss, then dry it and wash it in various solutions. The result was a fine quality of paper which could be made in different weights and shades, from white to blue and gray, or with mingled colors. The sheets were large, excellently formed for the seven-character line most poets preferred. He called it Hsueh T'ao paper in compliment to her, and created a special variety with pine and plum blossoms patterned through it for her use alone. He gave her a patent too and a generous share in the profits from the papermaking, so that by the time he was recalled to Chang-an, the fame of her pine-plum sheets and the poems brushed upon them had traveled far, all through the Province and even to the Red Phoenix City.

Governor Tuan would be remembered, she told him, whenever she brushed poems upon paper or walked by the riverbank. For his sake she would listen with awakened ears to the bustle in the marketplace and watch the departure of caravans with a studious eye.

She did not compose farewell lines for him. All her poems copied on his paper . . . for it should have been called Tuan T'ao paper, if he had not slanted justice aside . . . would be farewell lines to him.

Governor Tuan smiled. He gave her a silken purse well filled with gold and advised her to buy land.

"There is," he said, "a desirable spot a few li from this place, at the bend of the river in Pi-chi-Fang, where you might build a summer pavilion in the cool of a well-placed grove, and later retire there to live. Is it Li Po or is it Tu Fu who says:

> *My heart is free of care.*
> *As the peach-blossom flows down stream and is gone into*
> *the unknown,*
> *I have a world apart that is not among men."*

When she recovered from the shock of hearing him quote poetry, she said gently, "It is Li Po. Tu Fu has said:

> *I am grateful for all your kindness.*
> *After singing, I look up to heaven sighing.*
> *Our eyes are bathed in tears."*

"Ah, yes, and he has also said . . . Fanyang, fetch the wine . . . he has also said:

> *I commend you for your courteous friendship.*
> *Tomorrow there will be mountains between us,*
> *Nor you nor I knows what will come.*

I would like to think that it came to you under a roof of your own."

Fanyang returned with hot wine. They drank together. Then he said matter-of-factly, "Consult with Official Lu. He will oversee the purchase of the land and any other matters. . . ."

Then he strode toward the gate and entered his waiting litter without looking back. It was strange, she told Fanyang, over the rest of the wine . . . the Governor who made the least demands upon his Hostess gave the most thought to her welfare.

"And quoted poetry," Fanyang said. "Ah, ah! It is a scholar after all."

XXVIII

OFFICIAL LU YUAN-WEI was a man of forty, shrewd, affable, and rich. His father, his brother, and three of his sons were prosperous merchants with riverboats and caravans moving through the land. They could have founded great houses of their own, but chose instead to live together in the ancestral mansion with its sprawling waterfront and private wharves. It was the very house with the green lawns sloping to the riverbank where Hung Tu was shamed by her brothers' too obvious display of her charms. She smiled to think of her recoil from those "three old men"—no older, perhaps, than the woman now remembering them—whose scrutiny had caused her such alarm.

Official Lu was Chief Magistrate of Shu. He spent his days pronouncing judgment upon criminals and writing long reports to the Emperor, the Governor, and other magistrates. He was a better scholar than Governor Tuan, with an ear for poetry, although he could not write it well himself. He admired Hung Tu, knew many of her poems by heart, attended every public performance that she appeared in at the Palace, and now was pleased with the opportunity Governor Tuan bequeathed to him of becoming her adviser. He aspired to be her friend, her fellow poet, to hear her harmonize and sing his lines. He was a shy and somewhat lonely man.

He began the assault on friendship by taking her in his oxcart to see the land at Pi-chi-Fang. When he watched her turning in circles of delight and hurrying from grove to riverbank exclaiming "Now see this!" and "Here is the well!" and "There I will have hibiscus, and there the loquat tree . . ." he offered to lend her the amount she still needed to buy it with, so that she need not wait to lay out gardens and perhaps a small belvedere, a Song-chanting Tower, where she could sit in the cool, composing poems, or invite her friends to overlook the river, sipping wine with her while they enjoyed the view.

Then later, if she followed his advice, saving gifts and earnings and employing them with wisdom, she might build herself a little hermitage, one of those rustic rude retreats, a cottage like Tu Fu's, the ideal dwelling place for the Superior Man . . . or Woman . . . and retire there.

Hung Tu agreed with him that there should be a Song-chanting Tower there as soon as possible, and that she would use it in the manner he described, but the rest she saw with other eyes. She had no fondness for rough cottages, where the fires smoked and the thatches leaked. She had been secretly dismayed by Tu Fu's primitive surroundings. Why should great poets and Superior Beings live worse than other men?

Her retreat beside the river would be a bright jewel, complete with every lovely luxury taste and genius could devise. It might be small in size, for who wanted sprawling walls? Perfect perspective, exquisite arrangements, well-planted trees screening from the world . . . all these went through her mind the first time that she saw the land, while she was still exclaiming:

"It is higher than this person's bravest dreams! A Tower, and, as you say, some little rude hut here, beneath the trees. . . . But how can a single strand of silk make thread?"

"With money you can make the devil work the mill for you."

"That is what this person fears. An empty purse . . ."

"We will fill it."

They went back in the oxcart to the Villa and there he parted from her, since there were no orders from the Governor to entertain him, and she went in alone, to the start of a new life. It would take effort, time, long years possibly, but now she had what lately she was needing, a way of escape from the dullness closing round her, the dullness and the small gray fear that was not so small at times. There were times when the fear was a mountain.

Respect for a recluse was one thing, isolation another. Besides, she was not a recluse, but a poet behind closed doors, with no authority to open them to her friends and no power to go through them unless summoned, lived a narrowing life. Especially in these days when there was less entertainment at the Palace because of the wars and turmoil, the uprisings and famine devastating all the land. She heard of these disasters secondhand. Most news came to her these days only secondhand, through the eyes and ears of a servant, instead of happening directly around her or being heard of from the chief participants.

There were days when the only exchange of conversation with the world was an old woman's cackling "eh, eh!" over some distorted round-the-well gossip and her own indifferent replies. Sometimes the old woman was querulous or spiteful and had to be cajoled. Now that was a reversal of Tao! And after such dull days there were nights when she slept alone.

She missed the excitement of the Blue House. She missed Face-from-the-River, though she had recovered her heart. Long ago she realized he was no more to her, or to himself, than any other man. Naturally he had not loved her; why, after all, should he love her? It was not his love that she missed, it was her own. It was the fire of her craving, the color, the anguish it lent to her days and to her poetry.

Her poems now were written calmly, to order, for special occasions, or inspired by the changes in the seasons, not the changes in the blood. Nor the meditations of the spirit. She had not attained to deep wisdom. She was not upon the path to detachment. She was merely sinking into dullness, dependent for all quickening interchange of thought upon the guests the Governor sent to her for quickening. She missed the company of younger, unimportant men. And women. She missed—she smiled wryly—the give and take, the undercurrents of the Blue House.

When she was summoned to the Palace, it was pleasant to be greeted with deference by the concubines, the musicians, the eunuchs, the slaves. . . . It was less pleasant to watch ripples of excitement, of human interaction diminish and fade into formality at her approach.

She had her own four musicians, but they were only "hers" in the sense that they came to the Villa when there were important guests whom the Governor wished to honor with music. They resented this double service at the Palace and at the Villa. It was evident that they too missed the bustle, the gossip, the different levels of intrigue as much as she did.

Sometimes she thought she might return to the Blue House for a visit, then she decided against it. There was no one now whom she knew there but Spark of Flint, who ran the establishment, and Mountain Stream, who still taught the dancers. Eyes' Fascination, Peach Bloom Fan, Faint Moon, Clear Dawn, Cicadas Sing, and all the rest were dispersed and gone their ways. Old Scholar, Meng Chaio, was dead. Tall Bamboo, if she were still alive, had achieved her wish and was now a nun, chanting sutras and explaining the position of the Buddha's hands to pilgrims. . . . Now if Tall Bamboo were in the Blue House or anywhere nearer than the mountain, it would be good to visit her. But it was not wise to leave the Villa for so long a journey, nor, indeed, at all. Even to go to the market might be a mistake. She must not cheapen the image she had worked so hard to attain, the legend of her as "poet who lived behind closed doors." She had wanted a respected position, she had come to the Ya Men with a title and a robe which no one else could wear. She must not allow the curious, the envious, to see her too often.

If she had been a man with a man's Tao, she could have gone to the Blue House for companionship in those hours when she felt dull. But Tao for a woman was different. Tao for women was to pleasure men and for some it was to bear children. She had sometimes thought she might want children. But I Mu had done its work too well. When perhaps she might have had a child and kept it with her there was only emptiness.

Now she had an object of interest to fill the days. She would build a Villa of her own, where she could invite her friends without official permission, the young and the poor if she chose and exclude the rich and the old and the dull if she chose, a place where she could always go if she fell out of favor.

She began to save every tael and to look for ways of making more. Official Lu helped her. He set a new fashion in Cheng-tu. Instead of coming to the Governor's Villa, risking interference or even disapproval under another man's roof, he began to invite her to his own house, to entertain small parties. Friends who enjoyed these evenings followed his example. When the Governor did not need her she visited rich men's houses, giving lessons in brushwork to their sons, taking orders for her pine and plum-blossom paper and fees for other services. A time of bustle and prosperity began.

When the sorrowful day came that Official Lu was ordered to hang up his Magistrate's Cap and present himself to the Imperial Court to answer charges of corruption drawn up by his enemies, she had collected enough gold to begin building the retreat they had talked of on those long summer afternoons when they paced the land or sat beneath the trees where the Song-chanting Tower was to be, harmonizing lines together.

Poor Lu Yuan-wei! His lines were pale and sometimes quite ridiculous when he sang, as he loved to do, of tragic things, such as the love of Emperor Hsuan Tsung for his beautiful concubine Yang Kuei-fei, for which he plunged the Empire into ruin; or her cruel death by execution, which the heartbroken Emperor was compelled to order to save her from a more terrible death at the hands of his rebellious soldiers. Unfortunately Po Chui had written a masterpiece on the same subject, his famous "Song of the Everlasting Remorse," and his sublime words made Lu's weak ones fall to the ground more abjectly.

There were some short, inoffensive lines of his to Duke Hsin Ling, that legendary, lavish host of antiquity, which she could honestly praise, and these she decided to refer to in her farewell offering.

She joined the cortege escorting Official Lu on the first lap of his journey toward disgrace and hardship in far-off Chang-an. A few lis from the city gates, a Pavilion of Parting had been pitched by the roadside for the last hour of refreshment among friends, before the traveler must go on his lonely way over that dreaded road Li Po described, where *the earth sunk and the mountains crumbled . . . and the monkeys wail, unable to leap over these gorges. . . .*

Here she poured wine for him for the last time. Here she sang her farewell to him:

Darkness, wind, and the sorrowful snow
falling over Chun Kuan Pass,
over Jade Tomb Hill
where the ghosts of parted lovers wait.
If Hsin Ling, the Duke in I-Man, speaks of time present,
tell him that there is one who remembers
only the gracious, invincible past.

Then she embraced him, weeping, his friends stood with their sleeves to their eyes, and he wept too, helpless, ineffectual tears against his fate, against injustice . . . *pale, darkening heart, black seed, and thick juice of a well-remembered sweet-bitterness* . . . and so entered his litter and was borne away, with her words and her tribute to his words clutched in his hand.

Oh, pine and plum-blossom paper! Oh, strong and subtle brush-work! Oh, enticing upstroke. . . . Here she had written something more:

"One day Lu Yuan-wei will return to harmonize new lines with his devoted friend, in the poet's Villa at Pi-chi-Fang. Think of this sometimes."

PART SIX
810 A.D.

XXIX

GOVERNOR YEN SSU-K'UNG was in a quandary. It was the first year of his office and he was faced with an emergency for which there was no helpful or at least no complete precedent. He sat on his dais in the Pavilion of Enlightened Reflection, staring moodily at the scroll on the opposite wall.

"By the culture of the ascetic forbearances the eight meannesses vanish from the human heart and magnanimity comes in."

All very well, but how could this one be free of *fear* in the face of the impending visitation? Or be sure of not experiencing *grief*, *shame*, or *hatred*, if the worst befell? Magnanimity begets magnanimity. Let the Emperor, let his envoy, show their magnanimity first. . . .

At least he was warned, which did not usually happen. Usually these calamitous birds of prey swooped out of empty-seeming skies before one had time to adjust one's robe. This time, through the ingenuity of a friend, he knew when to expect, not what to expect, nor how to prepare for it, nor how to deal with it when it arrived, but approximately when to expect *Danger*, winding down the passes in a trail of dust, making for the city gates.

Within the waning of the moon, the message said. The man who brought it was no ordinary runner. He was a banished criminal, branded with the Golden Seal upon his right cheek. Such a one must not stop running until he was beyond the outposts of the Empire. Failure to reach the border by the date also branded on his cheek meant instant execution.

It was the quickest form of transport, and that old fox Chang Yo-yu had taken advantage of a disgraced friend's predicament to trust him with a message to another friend who might be threatened with disgrace. Binding a scarf around his wounded cheek, dusty and travel-stained, faint from his hunger and his haste, the criminal, who was also the distinguished scholar Han Yu-hai, passed the Palace guards with the remnants of his habitual dignity and the help of a signet ring.

Once in the Governor's presence he said what he had to say quickly, as soon as they were alone.

Yes, another upheaval in the Imperial Palace. Yes, of course the contriving of the eunuchs. The most powerful among them, T'u-t'u Cheng-tsui, had managed to take command of the Left Army. That was bad enough, but now he was trying for supreme command of the Imperial forces in the West . . . those fighting Wang Ch'eng-tsung.

Yes, there had been opposition to this shameful thing. Official Po Chui dared to question, in a letter addressed to the Son of Heaven, and widely circulated at the Court, whether the professional army leaders would be willing to take orders from a eunuch. He also drew attention to the ridicule such an appointment would inevitably bring upon the Empire from its enemies, especially the virile Wang.

Po Chui had disappeared. Other important officials were in serious trouble. Some were banished, like himself, for saying less than Po. It was certain that Eunuch T'u-t'u had the Emperor's ear and His protection.

Matters might change, but meanwhile complaints against Provincial Governors, including the Governor of Shu, were reaching the Capital. Examiners had been appointed, five of them eunuchs, the rest approved by eunuchs, to investigate "the climate of the Provinces" and return with their reports. Some had already set out on these congenial missions. The official on his way to the Province of Shu was Censor Yuan Chen.

"Yuan Chen! But he is Po Chui's greatest friend! He can hardly be supporting the eunuchs . . . especially . . ."

All the world was aware of Yuan Chen's reputation for lusty love affairs. Willow cotton songs commemorated his first elopement, at fifteen, with the lovely child Ying-Ying, daughter of a Warden of the northern Capital. For that he was nearly ruined. Only the intercession of Po Chui saved him then, and the glory of his songs. At that early age he was already an established poet who had passed the examinations with the highest honors. The Emperor was intrigued. He knew and liked the poems and the young poet. He ordered matters smoothed and faces saved.

There followed many other glittering entanglements, and marriage to Wei Hui Tsung, a distant relative of Governor Yen Ssu-k'ung.

"Recently dead," he mused. Aloud he said, "It is hardly the career of a eunuch."

"No, indeed. Po Chui's friend. Also the 'beloved Songbird of the Imperial Court.'"

"Then how . . . then why . . ."

Han shrugged. "The appointment was approved by Eunuch T'u-t'u. It is said that he suggested it."

Slaves entered with food and then were sent away. The Governor poured wine for his guest and urged him to eat, which he did, crouched upon his cushion like a famished beast. There was a thoughtful silence, while the Governor tactfully turned his face away.

"There are two sides to a thing and more sides to a man," Han said presently, wiping his lips. "It may be that Yuan Chen comes honorably, to investigate complaints. . . ."

"What complaints?"

"That is not known to this person, nor to Chang Yo-yu. It is known that they were made from Cheng-tu, and to the Emperor Himself."

"Now who? What enemy?"

"There are always enemies. It is also possible that an ambitious person desires to remove a rival from the indulgent glances of the Imperial Eye. When the caravan recedes, the charm of its presence fades and the value of its wares. Eunuch T'u-t'u knows this saying well."

The inflection of weary hatred with which that name was said impressed the Governor.

"It may be," he murmured.

"It may also be that the eunuchs wish Yuan Chen and those like him away from the Imperial Court while they establish their positions."

"It may be." The Governor nodded. "You have done me a great

service. This person will prepare for what may come. Now here is gold and here some pain-dispersing drugs, and food is being cooked."

"This person's thanks."

"It is nothing. You are Chang Yo-yu's friend. In happier times we would raise our cups together and spend our days in friendship and our nights in rest."

"Rest!" Han said bitterly. "They have fixed the hour of expectation and departure from the last outpost at sundown on the night of the new moon. Even if these feet run without pause they cannot get me there. I am a dead man and yet I run. Such is the terror of this hope."

"There is a ship to leave tomorrow, but progress upstream . . ."

". . . is slower than to run."

"A litter . . ."

"I am condemned to run. If I am caught riding in a litter, I can be killed . . . by those very bearers, for the reward."

"What then?"

"I will take drugs and food, if it come quickly, but not gold. I carry enough already to be robbed. Send what you choose to Chang Yo-yu. He will give it to my wife and children."

He spoke abruptly, like a man done with politeness and formal usage and all the other trappings of the living. The Governor could find no word to say of comfort, except that he would send help to his wife and be ever ready to receive him, or news of him, and to send word south to Chang Yo-yu.

Then the food came, the visitor departed on his desperate way, and the Governor retired to his dais to reflect on what he had heard, particularly to wonder which of the smiling faces round him was the enemy who had denounced him and what the denunciation was.

After a long hour of searching his memory for anything suspicious or unusual, he was still in the dark. He sighed impatiently. He must leave his curiosity unsatisfied and try instead to plan what should be done to receive Examiner Yuan Chen propitiously.

What would be the best, the proper way? Should he appear lavish, sparing nothing to entertain the Representative of the Son of Heaven? Or, in view of the new war in the West, the growing devastation, poverty, and famine in all the land except this blessed, isolated Shu, would it be more seemly to appear austere, generous in sentiment, but frugal with the Emperor's taels, even to His representative?

He sighed again. He needed an adviser. If there were someone safe to consult, but with spies and enemies around him it would not do to seem aware of the attack launched toward him. It was already dangerous enough to have closeted himself alone with a ragged messenger, and to have sat so long afterward. He glanced about him restlessly. The pavilion seemed full of unfamiliar shadows. He shivered. He drew his robe about him.

The evening hours had come. It would seem strange indeed if he were to linger here. Already there were pausing feet beyond the door among the others passing. Rustling, creaking, muffled laughter . . . all the river of Palace life, with everything it carried between its man-heaped banks of whispered curiosity.

He struck the small gong by his hand. The door opened too quickly. Servants with lights came in, and Eunuch Yin-po. It was his time of attendance, but the sight of his smooth round face, the sound of his high-pitched voice in oily greeting was unpropitious and unpleasing to the Governor.

He ordered a litter, more abruptly than he usually spoke to his officials, and heard the order relayed in that mincing voice. Then he signed to the servants that he would change his robe, and while they were hovering round him with deft touches of comb and brush and scented water for his face and hands, he thought, "Ah, yes. There is one person who will know what should be done and how to do it. One person whose life it is to entertain important guests and who must also know something of Yuan Chen."

Not for the first time he blessed the foresight of that long-ago previous Governor who had endowed the Province of Shu with an official Hostess as much respected as she was renowned. No other Governor had a jewel like her, nor one more likely to be useful now.

XXX

A BUSTLE BEGAN AT THE VILLA by Hundred Flowers Pool. Silk merchants brought silk. Silversmiths brought fretted silverware. Goldsmiths brought jeweled ornaments. Servants came from the Palace, among them lacquerers, to gild and restore the furniture. The four musicians were reinforced by three more, so that now seven instruments were heard together, rehearsing in the Pavilion of Welcome and Repose.

The dancers from the Blue House arrived to practice with the musicians. Lady Mountain Stream accompanied them, to introduce the Flowers and discuss with Hung Tu the sequence of steps and movements required for the new dances. The two met as old friends, bowing and embracing.

"Silver Hooks!"

"Mountain Stream!"

Looking at each other for the first time after so many years, each thought: "We have aged."

Then Mountain Stream: "But not so much. She is still beautiful." And Hung Tu: "More than I expected. She is no longer beautiful."

The young Flowers watching thought: "Look at these old crones!" Then in justice: "But one is not so old. Indeed, for her years she is remarkable."

"So that is the famous Hung Tu whom they hold up to us! If it weren't for the legend round her . . ."

Mountain Stream was saying that Spark of Flint sent her remembrance and that they were a little bewildered by the sudden urgency of this festival Governor Yen Ssu-k'ung was planning. The occasion for it seemed obscure, but any occasion to perform at the Palace was joyously received. Then she put her hand on one of the dancers.

"You remember Eyes' Fascination? This child has some of her

grace. Her name is Misty Grass. She has never danced at the Palace. Indeed, she has not been with us for long."

Hung Tu said: "It is a subtle name. If she dances like Eyes' Fascination, the sun of approval will cause the mist to vanish from the grass. . . ."

Misty Grass lowered her eyes demurely, but there was a slight curve of the lips which betrayed to those who were quick enough to catch it that she was not impressed with the compliment, nor in awe of the lips from which it came.

"This," Hung Tu thought, "is a Flower with no mean opinion of herself. Well, but so much the better. Neither had Eyes' Fascination. If this one is half as good, it will be exhilarating to see fine work again."

Mountain Stream named the other dancers, Floating Cloud, Twig of Spring, and Butterflies-cover-the-branches, who said earnestly:

"Gracious Lady, in honor of whom do we dance?"

Hung Tu smiled at her and then at all of them.

"Ah, yes, it should be explained, the festival for which the Governor requires our services is to celebrate a victory."

"A victory?"

"Which victory?"

"Does it matter? There are always victories. We will leave a space for the name of this one."

"Is it in times past or is it now?"

"Now, or perhaps in times to come. Listen to the music."

She clapped her hands. The musicians began to play. After a moment she stopped them. "You can hear. It must be danced in modern style."

Misty Grass shrugged, almost imperceptibly, but Hung Tu caught the arrogant young movement. She said nothing. Mountain Stream was present. She must discipline the Flowers. When she left, perhaps . . . but now she was beginning to instruct them and to sketch in preliminary motions. Hung Tu perceived that Misty Grass was indeed an equal to Eyes' Fascination. The child had poignant beauty and fresh grace . . . she reminded Hung Tu of long-forgotten Red Leaves, dancing *Peach petals shaken by the winds of spring*, only this Flower did not have that childlike joy . . . indeed she was more like Eyes' Fascination . . . Mountain Stream was right. Hung Tu looked up to nod at her, "Yes, yes, a superb performer, you are right."

After the first strangeness, they settled to work in earnest. Presently they noticed that Hung Tu took only a small part in the projected program, at least so far as she explained it to them that day. She was to harmonize two songs, one in the middle, one at the end, and though she played the opening and the closing chords of both on her old-fashioned p'i-pa, she did not sing. Their curiosity must go unsatisfied.

Once again cicadas whispered, after they returned to the Blue House:

"Her powers are waning."

"Her voice must be weakened. Naturally she would not sing."

"She knows she would suffer in comparison with younger, more attractive Flowers."

"She will make a good appearance, and I suppose we will be used to set her off."

"If it weren't for her clothes, her jewels, and the legend built around her . . ."

"If it is true that she was here with Spark of Flint and Mountain Stream, she must be as old as the mountains. . . ."

"Not necessarily. She may have been in the Second Pavilion when Spark of Flint was in the First, or when she was Second Lady to the old one, to Tall Bamboo."

"After all, it might be said of us that we are in the Blue House with Spark of Flint."

They laughed at the absurdity of this. Then Twig of Spring exclaimed:

"I do not care how old she is, so long as she writes songs as great as these."

Misty Grass surprisingly agreed. "They are good to perform. Especially 'I stood so long before the climbing rose.' Let us go through it again. Butterflies-cover-the-branches, you can sing. . . ."

"Not if I dance."

"Then I will speak the words. . . ."

> *I stood so long before the climbing rose*
> *that its scent still rises from all my garments.*
> *The stream is quiet where Sun Chu-shih lies.*
> *The birds fly east, fly west, swallow and shrike,*
> *I wander in the springtime,*
> *But Sun Chu-shih does not stir.*

"Who is Sun Chu-shih?"

"Some famous person."

"Or a lover, perhaps."

"I like the part about the birds, *fly east, fly west, swallow and shrike*, it's so easy to dance."

Mountain Stream, entering in time to overhear this, said sharply: "Nothing is easy to dance, Twig of Spring, even when you choose the most obvious lines to interpret. But it is true these words are powerful and evocative, and give us opportunity . . . let us take the second poem:

> *This magical young season banishes the clouds*
> *and wakes the land to bloom.*

"Now let me see you banishing the clouds and wakening the land, Twig of Spring. One-and-two-and . . . no, no, lower the shoulder, banish, banish . . . not swat, like killing flies . . . watch Misty Grass, and-one-and-two . . . now, wakening the land . . . *wakes the land* . . . yes, that is better. . . ."

Fish play in the river pools newly scaled in flower petals.

"Fish play. Play, not thump . . . they pass through the water, they don't divide it, they don't empty the pool, Floating Cloud. . . ."

The worldly have no knowledge of the delicate message of flowers.

"The worldly, Twig of Spring. Strut, strut arrogantly. Have you ever seen a Palace eunuch? No? Well, imagine one, and when we appear before the Governor, look around you. Only then it will be too late. Strut now. *Have no knowledge* . . . slowly, with the head, the neck, the curved arms, dimming light . . . yes, yes . . . you have a notion of it now, Butterflies-cover-the-branches. . . ."

Careless hands leave torn red blossoms scattered along the bank.

"Now that is easy, Twig of Spring. No, no, careless hands, not big clumsy ones . . . leave . . . relinquish, slowly, delicately, now the torn red blossoms . . . now scatter them . . . yes, one-and-two-and-three . . . enough."

She sighed. Her sigh said clearly, "How frustrating it is to work with clods."

Then she brightened. "There is another song with crab apples in it. The poet seems to like that fruit. This is called 'Slender Fruit Trees.'

> *Planted last year, the slender fruit trees*
> *in Wu Chun's park are already in flower.*
> *Swift with spring rain the rivers rush to the east.*
> *Joyously, through the gathering dark,*
> *the wild clear song of the oriole*
> *falls from the crab-apple tree.*
> *The dusk deepens the red tinged petals,*
> *the paler blossoms of the pear glimmer like small stars.*

"Now there are lovely, clear effects in that . . . the spring rain swelling the rivers, the rivers rushing to the east, the oriole in the tree, and the song falling . . . but the last line is the best . . . here we are pear blossoms, seen in contrast to the red blossoms of the crab apple . . . we are paler . . . practice *paling* and then glimmering like stars . . . small stars. . . . That is a wonderful sequence. Let us try it. . . ."

While her words came alive in the Blue House, Hung Tu said over and over to the small anxious Governor:

"Yes, yes, we have good things in train to give him pleasure. This person also will harmonize one of his own songs. You will see that Official Yuan Chen will greatly enjoy his visit to Cheng-tu, and will speak about it favorably to the Emperor."

But she was not as sanguine as she sounded. She knew many things about this Yuan Chen, by hearsay and from his poems. It was unlikely that he would be impressed by anything a Provincial Governor and an aging Hostess could do. Still, there was one thing . . . men were attracted by appreciation of their work, especially from the lips of fellow workers qualified to understand it.

If Tu Fu were still alive and living in Cheng-tu! But there were others, and among them this poet Hung Tu, to brush his words and manufacture special paper for them, dipped in the water of the Silk River. Oh, yes, the time he stayed here would be memorable, even to a Superior One who composed poetry at the age of nine and at fifteen occupied an official position; even to a lover who had written the poem she would harmonize at the festival of welcome: "The Vision of Yuan Chen."

> *The first time I saw her*
> *was in Yu Liang Tower;*
> *her waist was slender*
> *as the Willow Trees of Wu Chang*
> *in the spring.*
>
> *I met her*
> *and ever since*
> *my heart has longed*
> *for her.*
>
> *It was like a dream*
> *and to this day*
> *I do not know*
> *if it were more*
> *than the passing of a cloud,*
> *or a sudden gust of rain.*

It might be dangerous, considered indiscreet, to sing so intimate a song in public, yet instinct and training told her that to remind a man of past delight, when the companion who inspired him is lost or far away, does suggest . . . does invite him to turn for consolation to what is near at hand. . . . She would wait, she would see. . . . She would prepare another song, Tu Fu's tender "Cheng-tu," in case she decided not to sing "The Vision" at their first public meeting. Meanwhile it remained a secret that he was coming to Cheng-tu. Day followed day of work, of preparation. Spring was far advanced when Fanyang brought the news. Fanyang was an old and dried-up monkey, often muddled, but this thing she held straight— a caravan arriving from the South, and traveling with it an envoy from the Imperial Court.

Confirmation came from the Governor. It was indeed Official Yuan Chen. Hung Tu sent a message to the Blue House, to Lady Mountain Stream: "In the space we reserved for *Victory*, insert now the words *Yuan Chen*. Hold yourself and the Flowers ready to perform at the Palace at any time."

Then she called for Fanyang to rub her body with scented herbs and special oils and to prepare one of the new silk robes. The Governor, she knew, would send for her as soon as he could, to entertain Yuan Chen and to keep him from conference with those secret enemies. Then the Villa and all in it would be put at the poet's disposal. She lay frowning a little, wondering how it would be with so great a man, favored of the Emperor and the Eye of Heaven. She had not been faced with so important a challenge for many years.

"Fanyang, bring the Yarrow Sticks. We will consult them while we wait. A favorable oracle at this time would put heart into this person."

She tossed the sticks and they said: *T'ai. Peace. The small departs, the great approaches. Good fortune. Success.*

She tossed them again.

The sticks said: *No plain not followed by a slope. Everything on earth is subject to change. Do not complain about this truth. Enjoy the good fortune you still possess.*

"What does that mean, 'still'?"

"Ah, ah, it is a lucky oracle. *The sovereign I gives his daughter in marriage. This brings blessing and supreme good fortune.* What more could be asked?"

XXXI

THE SUMMONS FROM THE GOVERNOR CAME, and Hung Tu set forth to the Palace, as she had so often, to so many Governors; the first time slowly, in a barge dragged upstream by slaves, this time swiftly, in her own litter, with her servants trotting by it; then one small Flower among many, with her way in life to make, now the whispered-about Legend, famous and secure.

Then she was made happy with a simple robe, because it was new and new robes were rare. Now she wore one of many sumptuous robes, costing, with her jewels, as much as Tall Bamboo had paid to buy her. Then she was a child in love, hoping to steal glimpses of her lover at a distance . . . for the last time, although she did not know it. She knew nothing, not even his name. Now she could name, and number on five times the fingers of both hands, illustrious men who had been her lovers. Compared with these, the great and the gifted, and those hosts of lesser men who paid exorbitant prices for her company, Face-from-the-River was nothing.

Why did she think of him? She had not thought of him for years. Why was she going to the Palace on this summer afternoon with a shadow of the same trepidation she remembered feeling then, a sense of being on trial, of needing to please? It was unnecessary nowadays. She had only to appear and perform in her usual way to more than please. Later there might come a time . . .

Perhaps she was feeling nervous because the Governor revealed so much anxiety about this Yuan Chen, or perhaps because she knew so much about both of them.

The quick pace of the litter slowed for a procession of wheelbarrows entering the bridge ahead of them, filled with straw. On top of the straw large black pigs lay on their backs with green leaves spread upon their stomachs. They lay quietly, their eyelids sewn together so that they would not struggle to escape, nor lose the ounce or two of weight they might have lost if they were driven. What the owner trundling them through this heat might lose in weight was unimportant, like the sweat thinned from the porters carrying Hung Tu. She smiled down at the pigs as her litter passed them. Two of them reminded her of officials she had known, both eunuchs. All the pigs looked like eunuchs.

Now the litter slowed again, while a child herded a flock of ducks out of the way with a bamboo rod. The street was more crowded, more lively than usual, because the great caravan in which Yuan Chen arrived was spreading its wares in the marketplace. Soon she would have her pick of these, the jade, the copperware, the cloth. Fanyang would bring the best merchants to the Villa. Then she would buy what she needed—not for the Villa, let the Governor take care of that—everything she bought, everything she sold, everything she planned, was for her Pi-chi-Fang retreat.

She thought of it, shining in the summer sunlight, behind its grove of shady trees, with the river rushing by. Birds, flowers, fruit trees, and round the well the plant she was beginning to see with awakened eyes and growing discernment, bamboo, clusters of bamboo. *In wind, fair weather, snow, moonlight, mists or clouds, in rain, in every season, what is precious in bamboo is safely locked in by its fine knots to delight and move the beholder,* according to the precepts of right painting.

The hollow bamboo, symbol of wisdom, of the inner and outer harmony of Heaven, was the spirit she chose for Pi-chi-Fang and the essence of the life she would live there. Supported by this memory of the jewel owned and loved, and with all disturbing thoughts on lesser levels set aside, she entered the Palace proudly, borne in her litter to the Pavilion of Preparation for Right Entertainment, where the Flowers were waiting for her.

They made their graceful entrance together into the Great Hall. Presently, seated before the Governor and his guest, with a ch'in beside her and the p'i-pa balanced across her knees, she took her first sidelong, practiced glance at Official Yuan Chen, while the Flowers performed their opening lines.

Even seated, he was tall. Beside the Governor, small, deft, nervously pompous, he appeared like a large, calm dragon, with a handsome, humorous face, and what an eye! The poet's burning eye. She lowered her gaze, confused by unexpected emotion. Something like forgotten joy, something like anticipation stirred her being.

It was time to sing.

I stood so long before the climbing rose . . .

She told herself that she was moved to this astonishing disturbance of her well-balanced essence because she was performing before the great poet, friend of Po Chui, and of all those other famous scholars in the Hall of Assembled Worthies of the Academy. But it was more than this. Poets were not new to her, even the greatest. As a child she had brushed their words and heard them evoked about her. In the Blue House she was at their disposal. Many of them shared the sleeping mat with her. Po Chui himself once stayed for a month in the Villa beside Hundred Flowers Pool with her. Poets of stature listened to her songs—Tu Fu, when he was old and at the end of his singing, Meng Chaio, when he was old and grown indulgent. They heard her early gropings. Now here was Yuan Chen. Would he hear her later ones? Would he listen tonight with open ears or would he be absorbed like the Governor in watching the young dancers?

The birds fly east, fly west, swallow and shrike . . .

He would appreciate the reference. Were the shrikes not after him?

I wander in the springtime,
But Sun Chu-shih does not stir.

As the dancing and the singing ended, she looked toward him. He was smiling. The Governor too was smiling, nodding benevolently. Everything was propitious. They were pleased. She would deal with the disharmony within later. Meanwhile she tuned the strings, bending her head with grace over the instrument. It was her mother's p'i-pa, so long her responsive friend.

She began to sing Yuan Chen's own words:

The first time I saw her . . .

Her voice had never been more than true and pleasing. It lacked the depth, the range of a good singing voice, but over the years she had learned what could be done with it, through disciplined work and training, within its limitations, turning these into strength, as Tall Bamboo did with her fading voice.

The Superior One harbors gratitude. She was grateful to Tall Bamboo, to her training in the Blue House, without which she might have remained half-literate, to the goodness of Governors, without which she might have fallen upon evil times and gone the way the Flowers went, all except a few, a very few, from house to worse house, to misery, want, the river . . . whereas she . . . In gratitude she would exert herself to please this Governor, so anxious, so disturbed for his new-won place, who had said to her: "Take anything our City of Silk provides" *only save me from disgrace.* Governors too could be ruined, could go from want to exile to death. She would do what she could to charm this dangerous guest.

. . . *the passing of a cloud.*

The Flowers doing "cloud" in the background swayed in subtle grace.

. . . *sudden gust of rain.*

Now that was perfectly performed! Certainly one felt the need to shake off shimmering drops, seek the shelter of tree or pavilion, hasten toward the sun.

There was a silence, then a sign of approbation through the hall. She nodded toward the Flowers, fluttering their sleeves, rearranging themselves on their mats in a frieze of smiling grace, well-rehearsed, not a motion left to chance. They bowed modestly. Misty Grass, she observed out of a tolerant eye, was adding some gestures of her own. The child was young, with the usual ambitious dreams of pleasing the Governor. One must remember how it once had seemed to perform before him for the first time, and pretend to notice nothing . . . unless there should be a repetition inviting rebuke.

The wine arrived, the gifts, the compliments for the Flowers, and for her the expected summons to the Governor's table. Now the dangers and disharmonies within began. She would rather sing ten songs without a voice, dance without strong legs, ascend the mountain to Cloud Touching Temple without a litter, than pour wine and proffer conversation to such a one as Yuan Chen before the eyes and ears of the curious, malicious world.

Therefore she rose with every appearance of glad alacrity, in a shimmer of silvery silk shot through with golds and greens, her jade ornaments gleaming, her jeweled shoe-tips appearing and disappearing swiftly beneath her robe, to cross the distance, the time and space between them, to her waiting mat.

Seated, it was clear to her at once that for all his dignified disregard of his fatigue and the Governor's solicitous attention, the poet was at the end of his endurance, fevered from his journey across the savage mountains and the sharpness of the events which had thrust him into it, dismissed from the Emperor's Eye, though not out of His reach. No man could take himself out of the Emperor's reach while he was still alive and within the borders of the civilized world.

Poor Yuan Chen, discomfited, with anxious, bewildered eyes. Here was no haughty Censor, channel for the Emperor's displeasure, whose reports could sweep them all from their comfortable places in Shu. He had been swept from his own place in far-off Chang-an by the surge into power of the eunuchs. She had not believed until now that the Palace revolution, discussed in the marketplace, was as dangerous a menace as the Governor feared, but his fears seemed justified and he was holding to them strongly. He did not see what she did in his guest.

She saw a man uprooted, wounded, driven like a shivering bird before an official storm, like the deadly wind that blew on the House of Hsueh, destroying it forever. She had come to this encounter, prepared with the help of the precepts, to approach the Superior Man. Now she heard his cry for help uttered mutely within. She saw him afraid to lose the harmony of his forces, she saw him being swept into confusion. Her essence went out in swift support. *This person is here to do what this person can.*

She filled his cup with wine. He drank it absently. Then, constrained to courtesy, he assembled the forces of speech.

"Long ago this person first heard of the Lady of the City of Silk, whose charms and whose poetry bestowed upon the poets Tu Fu and Po Chui days lacquered with gold. Now this inferior singer has heard his words transformed, burnished with that luster, what can this person say? Let him respond in the words of the one who spoke to him first concerning Hung Tu. Tu Fu has said:

In the City of Brocade the lutes and the pipes all day make riot;
Half of the music is lost in the river breezes, and half in the clouds.
But this song should only belong to Heaven;
Among mortals how seldom can it be heard!

This person now has heard it. In more propitious times he will respond."

The effort to bow, to smile, brought lines of pain, fatigue, recent sickness, present shadow, to his face. He glanced sideways, as though he must escape from the pressures closing round him, or his essence descend to darkness, even to defeat. Yet before these curious eyes, these waiting jowls of crocodiles, these sluggish enormous fish, neutral, but ready to devour if aroused—those darting barracuda, those piranha attached to the eunuchs' service, and even this unknown Governor, who might toss him to the Destroyers if it seemed appropriate or propitious to his rule of the Province of Shu—before all these Yuan Chen must show no weakness. This she saw with concern. But the Governor did not see. He was leaning forward, waiting for the exchange of courtesies between the two poets to subside, courtesies he savored, for they reflected obliquely upon him and his hospitality, since they were exchanged at his table between his official Hostess and his honored guest. Nevertheless there were matters . . . if the moment became propitious. . . . He was not as discerning as a woman skilled in the appraisal of men. Moreover, he was afraid. He dreaded that these matters might be discussed with others before they were revealed to him. So he leaned forward, waiting, as Eunuch Yin-po waited, as the whole Court waited, attention fixed on Yuan Chen. They waited to question him. Meanwhile they watched his face.

He sweated. He turned his eyes aside in mute appeal for a way of escape from this greedy scrutiny. Hung Tu smiled at him reassuringly. There was a way of escape, a weakness even a strong man might succumb to without losing face. She filled his cup again and presently sent a servant for a stronger wine. She made amusing conversation, distracting the Governor's attention with the story of the mishaps of Ma-Sui, whirled aloft to the Moon in a feather jacket. After a while he relaxed. Soon he was smiling, watching his guest sail beyond the possibility of being questioned by Yin-po or any of those whom the Governor could only delay, not prevent from meeting him. Moreover, there would be no blame. The courteous host might not come between guest and wine.

Yuan Chen sat silent, eyes glazed. Then he lolled sideways and was gently eased to the floor.

"Look to his comfort," the Governor said loudly, "as if he were the Eye of Heaven Itself." And in lower tones, "Ask for anything you need. We must, at all costs, keep him in the Villa, contented."

She said that she would do her best to find favor with Yuan Chen. She asked for an extra keg of the Governor's best wine, and, as an afterthought, while he was in this mood, for a pair of embroidered socks she had seen, with toes of solid jade.

"Yes, yes," the Governor said indulgently. What a shrewd one it was! But he was grateful for her help in preventing Yuan Chen from talk with his enemies. Now it was possible to send him directly to the Villa to be cared for, and there the Governor controlled who came, who went.

Hung Tu was amused to trace the pattern of his thoughts. He was still afraid of Yuan Chen. She would not reassure him yet that she thought the Censor harmless, lest he regret the silks and the jewels and the lacquered furniture, some of which she had already deflected from Hundred Flowers Pool to her own Pi-chi-Fang.

She entered her litter smiling. Then she sighed. The evening had turned out strangely for one prepared to encounter the Superior Being. She had hoped, she did not know for what . . . some succor, some recognition of the needs of *her* Superior Being . . . instead she met a frightened man who leaned upon her help. It was always so. Tao and the will of Heaven . . . yet there had been a moment . . . and he was an interesting man, the most interesting who had come for a long time to Cheng-tu. There would be that to explore. . . .

While the bearers were jogging her homeward, the Governor ordered his own litter, and in it presently Yuan Chen, drunk and unresisting, was delivered to her door.

XXXII

HE SAT IN THE PAVILION for Keeping Still and Adhering to Clarity, composing a letter to Po Chui:

"After the long, hard journey, on *the terrible road to Shu,* I am moved to wish you beside me, beloved Lo-t'ien, not only for this person's well-being and joy, but for your own sake, that you might share with him this place of unexpected refreshment and ease.

"When we said our brief words of parting, with anguish and splitting apart of minds, we were dismayed at the descent of darkness and night about us. From this garden by the river, the turn of affairs, and those considerations, of which we were then so sharply aware . . ." he would not mention the triumph of the eunuchs more directly than this . . . "seem no more than shadows, drifting above the stream. The wise man continues fishing. Lo-t'ien, Lo-t'ien, how often we have sat together in your gray punt. Alas, were you constrained to sell it, as your brother told me you might be, when he overtook me on my first sad stop that night at the Shan-pei rest? I wept when he gave me your scroll. I drowned my sleeve with tears. Who but you, Lo-t'ien, would send a man twenty poems to console him on his way? Twenty new poems! Did he tell you how I wept? Kind Po Hsing-chien.

" 'No wanton words,' he said, I remember all that he said, 'no pretty rhymes. These are fraught with a serious allegory, sent in the hope that you will read them over to yourself on your journey. They may, my brother thought, help to pass the time away, and make you forget your sorrows for a while.' There were some, he added, 'that my brother felt might confirm you in the strong line you have taken and give you fresh courage.'

"Indeed, indeed they did. Each bitter night of all the bitter way I read them and now that I am here at journey's end—so far as this person knows or hopes—in the City of Silk, I read them, and they are being copied that others may enjoy the precious words I will not part with. They are being brushed on paper worthy of them, paper you have admired. You will remember those sheets of Hsueh T'ao which the old Master Tu Fu showed us, many years ago? This is where it is made . . . but of course you know that. You have been here too, perhaps at this very table, certainly beneath this solicitous roof. You saw those trees, those walks, the bend of the river, which from here I see.

"The hand brushing your words is the hand of the poet Hung Tu. You showed me once a poem of her making on a sheet of her plum-blossom paper. I glanced at it to please you, praised the paper, praised the brushwork, and closed the portals of the mind to the meaning of the poet's words. I thought no woman worthy of our serious attention. You smiled. You told me she was an accomplished Flower-in-the-mist. 'Let her follow Tao then,' I said, 'and content herself with ministering to men.' I am still of that opinion as regards the generality of women, in accordance with the precepts. But Heaven, with benevolent wisdom, has decreed exceptions to each precept, to reinforce the Truth. Needless to discuss this with Lo-t'ien, who taught this person to ponder the Book of Changes. But you were right, and this dull-witted person suffered loss. She is a poet, and her presence in the City of Silk a felicitous arrangement of the August Personage of Jade Who Dwells on the Topmost Height. It is . . ."

He broke off as a servant padded swiftly toward him.

"Elder Sister is in the garden. She says 'tell the Honored Guest that the Governor is soon expected.' "

He sat for a moment still before he rose. How hard it was to ensure any hours of concentrated thought. He had been trying for half a moon to get this letter to Po Chui brushed, so that it could start on the long journey south with the next traveler, but always some demand of the day intervened. Governor Yen Ssu-k'ung seemed determined to overwhelm his guest with attentions. Not knowing the truth about Yuan Chen's appointment as Censor to the Province of Shu, he was taking his arrival in Cheng-tu seriously.

It was serious, from the Governor's point of view. A report would have to be compiled, sooner or later, on the state of the Province of Shu under his administration, but whether it was favorable or unfavorable, if it were signed by Yuan Chen, it was likely to be disregarded by the party now in power, who would act toward the Governor of Shu as they saw fit or as they had strength to act.

For the present, since the eunuchs must be very busy consolidating their positions and reassuring the Emperor, who sometimes suffered from hindsight or things-seen-in-perspective, it was probable that there would be no drastic change in the Governorship of Shu, and for the same reasons Yuan Chen might hope for no further persecution.

The circumstances behind his appointment were not widely known. The eunuchs' supporters in Shu might have heard the story, but they would lose face if they revealed it, and as usual the Governor would be the last to be informed of Yuan Chen's precarious position.

His banishment, for it was virtually that, resulted from an episode which should have had a different outcome, as it would have, until recently, when the weakness of his protector, Chief Minister P'ei Chi, and the demoralizing rise of the eunuchs altered the right harmony and balance of the forces under Heaven.

He had clashed with a eunuch-envoy at the Government resthouse on the way from Lo-yang to Chang-an. The eunuch's men had kicked down the gate, removed Yuan Chen's horses from the stables, and threatened him and his men with bow and arrow.

Then Yuan Chen's servants turned out the eunuch's horses, restored theirs to the stables, and beat the eunuch and his attendants with stout staves. Yuan Chen looked on. He was an official Omissioner, traveling on his lawful business in the Emperor's service. The accommodations of the resthouse were intended for Government officials. The eunuch was the younger brother of a cousin of Eunuch T'u-t'u Cheng-tsui, traveling, presumably, for his private pleasure, though, as it turned out, he was helping to prepare the coming coup. Within the month Yuan Chen was relieved of his comfortable post as Omissioner in the State Chancellory and sent with indecent haste to Shu.

It was a small part, a fragment, of that endless struggle between Palace political groups and those beyond the Palace who carried on the work of the Empire in the far Provinces. It was the balance between the Within and the Without. The Governor of Shu was Without, not in the eunuchs' council. Nor was Yuan Chen. Under such circumstances, the Book of Changes recommends the Superior Man of the precepts should play his allotted part, under the Eye of Heaven, discreetly, accepting with gratitude those pleasures that come his way. The Yarrow Sticks, consulted, said: *Hsu—Waiting. The rain will come in its own time. Thus the Superior Man eats and drinks, is joyous and of good cheer. He should quietly fortify the body with food and drink and the mind with gladness and good cheer. Fate comes when it will, and thus we are ready.*

Consulted once more, they said: *Waiting. There is nothing to do but to wait until the rain falls. Nine at the beginning means: Waiting in the meadow. It furthers one to abide in what endures. No blame. The danger is not yet close. One is still waiting on the open plain.*

It was clear what the I Ching meant. Waiting on the plain was pleasant in the far-away Province of Shu. The City of Silk was hospitable. Yuan Chen liked this Governor, seeing in him more than the nervous little man alarmed for his position. There was a disarming eager friendly warmth in Yen Ssu-k'ung. Unlettered himself, no more of a poet than had been necessary to pass the examinations, he yet seemed to value poetry highly and cherish the poets who composed it. He had a fair ear for music and more than a sensual, superficial eye for the visual arts, which he seemed to savor. His performers were excellent in all the arts and he gave them his full attention. Unlike some officials Yuan Chen encountered on his travels, especially among the eunuchs, he did not sit with dulled eyes waiting to exchange perfunctory obligatory platitudes about the arts for something more important to them, news or Palace gossip. Yet Governor Yen Ssu-k'ung might be forgiven if at this time he were keenly interested in Palace gossip—understandably—but so far he had not pressed Yuan Chen for any pronouncements, opinions, or clarifications of the new situation in Chang-an.

He had talked to him with grace and charm about his own work. He had mentioned Tu Fu's sojourn in Cheng-tu and offered to take Yuan Chen to the rustic cottage, now become a literary shrine. Most commendable of all, he had installed his guest in this pavilion, in the care of Lady Hung Tu.

If he came often, once, sometimes twice, even three times a day to the pavilion, this was understandable. It was his pavilion, his Hostess, and his guest.

Yuan Chen composed his face into cheerful attention as he followed the servant to the garden where, by the pool of ornamental fish, the tea foods were already spread and Lady Hung Tu sat beside them. In the distance the seven musicians were tuning their strings and the Governor's chair could be heard arriving at the gate.

XXXIII

SUMMER WHIRLED BY in heat and dust. It seemed to Hung Tu that
she was constantly being rushed to the Palace in her litter, to ban-
quets and festivals and entertainments, or floating in the Governor's barge with her musicians about her, or wandering with the
Governor and his guests and chosen officials through the gardens
of the Villa by Hundred Flowers Pool, or harmonizing poetry with
Yuan Chen in the Pavilion of Reflection, or . . .

She watched him emerge from the guest pavilion in his red robe
with the gold ornaments, his dark head bare in the new fashion of
the Capital, shining sleekly, his step swift and sure across the grass
toward her. *Dragon appearing in the field, through him the world
attains beauty and clarity.*

A tremor of bliss, terror, anxiety . . . bliss . . . quickened her
essence like the advance of sunlight on a frosty day, spreading
warmth before it. Almost she rose, scattering teacups on the grass,
almost she ran to greet him, almost . . . the disturbing moment
passed. When she did rise, it was with her accustomed grace and the
five prescribed motions of welcome to an official.

As they stood ceremoniously bowing, she thought "strange . . ."
there was nothing about this man's body she did not know and had
not ministered to, little about the paths of his mind that she had
not discovered or surmised, but the distance between them was
fixed as far as from moon to sun.

It was true of every man to whom she offered the services
of towel and comb. What then made it so disturbing, so funda-
mentally dangerous to encounter Yuan Chen? She realized, even
as she went through the ceremonies of addressing him, seating him,
pouring out the wine, that she had inadvertently allowed him to
enter a realm no one before had discovered, still less confidently

188

strode in to disturb. She realized for the first time, as she deftly directed the servants with their trays and signaled to the musicians to begin, how sharply she had divided her two worlds. There was the river of outer life and there was the mountain of poetry, or more accurately, the dimension of poetry, of the poet's existence as a poet.

There she was alone. Once she had closed the portals and drawn about her the scholar's robe she was entitled to wear, she became poet in her own right. All day long she must minister to others, brush their words, sing their songs or offer up her own for the entertainment and approval of "guests" selected by the Governor; at night she was not free, but whenever she could withdraw into the pavilion of contemplation, within or without—at Song-chanting Tower of Pi-chi-Fang, for instance—no trace remained of Flower-in-the-mist Silver Hooks or Official Hostess Lady Hung Tu.

The two worlds overlapped only so far as the ingredients of the one provided the substance of the other. There poets met as equals, or they remained alone, *where the clouds pass and the rain does its work, and all individual beings flow into their forms,* where time is no longer a hindrance but the means of making actual what is potential.

Now into that secret place of transition to the heights where she had chosen to encounter the promptings of Heaven strolled this Yuan Chen, confident of being not only well but instantly and joyously received.

When this happened, she thought she knew; how, she was unable or unwilling to imagine; why, she hoped was evident only to herself. But he was beginning to be troubled too and to ask strange and searching questions, quoting poetry she had never heard of, lines which made no balanced sense.

He spoke of his wife and of Po Chui, his dead wife and his living friend, in tones of vehement remorse and of anger against himself and sometimes against circumstance, and even against Hung Tu, though not by name, and not explicitly. She met these gusty moods outwardly by attentive silence and redoubled efforts to please, inwardly with bewildered exultation. Fortunately for prudence' sake and the rules of right conduct, his attention was constantly diverted to the demands of ceremonial and a very full public life. He was the Governor's chosen companion. Official Yen Ssu-k'ung had taken a great fancy to the once-dreaded Censor. The merchants and magistrates of Cheng-tu also wanted to entertain Yuan Chen, and did so whenever they could. There were days and nights when he was absent from the Villa. Hung Tu took advantage of these absences to overtake her private life and also to pay visits to neglected Pi-chi-Fang. Thus far she had not invited Yuan Chen there to harmonize poems in the Song-chanting Tower. There remained one corner of the universe unassaulted by his presence or his image where she could draw breath, rest, and attend to the wisdom of the holy sages.

Now the Governor was arriving, the ceremonies of welcome began anew, the seating, the pouring of wine. Some of the turmoil and strain within lifted, for the two officials would probably exclude her from their talk and all that she must do was to attend with care to the motions of courtesy and the five hospitalities. This she could do without reflection, leaving the spirit free to ponder and observe . . . and arrive at no conclusion.

The Governor brought news. Not from the South, so long, so anxiously waited for. It was possible none would reach Cheng-tu that year. "When the first snow flies, the passes close," he said in answer to Yuan Chen's glance of inquiry, "but from the North, where the mountains are not so perilously high, there is still traffic, and sometimes roundabout word from here, from there, of friends. . . ."

He paused. There was no comment from his guest. "At this time," he continued, "the Uighurs send us tribute and their surplus horses, to be exchanged for silk."

"This person recalls the treaty with the Khan. It was my duty once to brush a letter to Ai Tangrida from the Eye of Heaven. Is the rate of exchange still fifty pieces of silk for a horse?"

"Nothing is hidden from the poet," the Governor said, lifting his wine cup courteously.

"On the contrary, it is observed that poets are *wu-i yu li*, of little use in administration," Yuan Chen said, raising his wine cup in correct response to the Governor's gesture.

"The price is still fifty pieces of silk, and here in the City of Silk we are able to pay it. They tell me there are some fine ones in the herds this year. We will look them over and make our choice. Then we will go hunting before the frost." He hesitated. "There is a man with the caravan who has inquired for Official Yuan Chen."

Po Chui! Yuan Chen thought eagerly. *Po Chui has escaped to the North. He is there on a mission. He is returning through Cheng-tu!* These possibilities ran through his mind, but if it were Po Chui, the Governor would have pronounced his name at once, and brought him to the Villa as an honored guest. Who then could it be? From the Governor's tone, no asset.

"What is the name?"

"It was understood to be Liu Ch'eng Shih."

Yuan Chen frowned.

"Liu Ch'eng Shih is indeed known to this person." He said it coldly.

There was a moment's pause, then the Governor continued easily, " 'I am cousin to the watchdog' says the fox discovered in the farmyard. 'I am cousin to the lion' says the fox discovered in the forest." He shrugged.

"It is indeed a fox, and no relative of any well-begotten beast."

"Ah," said the Governor reflectively.

"This is the nephew of Official Liu P'i."

"Ah," said the Governor again, more briskly.

"Official Liu P'i ruined this person's honored protector, Minister Wei Kuan-chih. He also persecuted Tu Fu, forcing him 'to wander ten years sick at heart.' And when he administered the district of Kiansi he was noted for exceptional severity. He removed the eyes and the livers of all who opposed him. . . . So it is said . . ." he concluded with belated caution.

But the Governor was smiling with delight.

"This person has heard of these occurrences and of others disquieting to the man of right perceptions."

There was a congenial silence, during which the two men looked at one another with complete understanding, while Hung Tu refilled their cups with wine from the brazier beside her.

"But this Liu, what shall be accorded him, seeing that his uncle is in favor with the Eye of Heaven and esteemed by Eunuch T'ut'u Cheng-tsui?"

"The Eye of Heaven will one day clear itself of mist."

"Assuredly, but while we wait for the cleansing rain to fall the prudent man will not bare his eyes and his liver prematurely to the knives."

"Therefore this person will receive Liu Ch'eng Shih," Yuan conceded reluctantly, "but may we not do him the service of setting him upon his way with speed? If he is proceeding southward to his relatives, should we not urge him to depart before the first snow flies?"

The Governor nodded. Turning to Hung Tu he began to give instructions for the reception of a second guest, when Yuan interrupted in a strange rough voice, "The cup shared by Superior Men should not be proffered to a cur." He half rose from his mat.

The Governor stared at him in bewilderment and slowly growing comprehension. Hung Tu shot him a quick glance sideways in amazement. She felt a surge of joy she had not known since she was a child, running to meet her father in the garden, *to be caught, approved, swung in the air, and as carelessly set down, aside . . . but recognized, accepted. . . .*

"At least," Yuan added, half apologetically, "not while this person still turns the jewel in his hands." He held them toward the Governor, cupped about a crucible, invisible in the air between them. It was a gesture no Flower-in-the-mist could hope to surpass.

And loved. Small Dragon of the House of Hsueh. She. This Person. This Hung Tu.

Tears rose to her eyes from the deep wells within. She felt them gather and let them fall, bowing forward deeply so that they would miss her cheeks to drip upon her dress. A Flower-in-the-mist must never weep, nor show any emotion outside the art she practiced. It was the first precept of the Blue House. "The flawed cup is tossed

aside," she heard Tall Bamboo scold daily, "onto the dung heap!"
And before that her mother's gentle admonition, "never give them
the satisfaction of your tears."

Yet here she was, publicly weeping, and the Governor, who
should have dismissed her in disgrace, looked at her indulgently,
while Yuan Chen . . . out of the corner of a glistening eye she saw
that he stared forward.

There was a strong silence.

The Governor cleared his throat.

"It would appear that our Nu Hsaio Shou," giving her that long
disused title she had thought forgotten, "is in need of rest. This
person perceives that she will be retiring from us to that jeweled
retreat she owns, into which so much effort and," he laughed gaily,
"so many pieces of valuable lacquered furniture have disappeared. . . ."

She saw Yuan Chen's astonishment at hearing her addressed as
Female Secretary, Collector of Books deepen at the mention of a
jeweled retreat of her own.

"At Pi-chi-Fang no one, not even a Governor, intrudes. Eh, eh, it
is a place for refreshment, poetry, and peace, a nest for happy song-
birds." He chuckled slyly. "A retreat for lovers. So they will say, so
they will sing, in future years."

Slowly he reversed the cup in his hands, and set it down with
finality on the table. It was the gesture of dismissal to a mandarin
of the highest rank. It was not directed to Yuan Chen, but to this
woman, silent before him, suffused in gratitude. She bowed, she
rose, she stood before him, raising her eyes and her hands in the
gesture of veneration for a great one.

She spoke the words of a new poem, born of the hour.

You see with a thousand eyes.
The leaves of the swaying bamboo gleam in the sudden rain.
They strike their roots more deeply.

She bowed again, and without a glance at Yuan Chen, left the
Governor's presence.

PART SEVEN
810–815 A.D.

XXXIV

SUNLIGHT PARTED THE BRANCHES of the bamboo grove. Shadows moved over the grass along the paths to the river, glinting in the distance. Jeweled birds flashed through the trees. The long lazy afternoon of a late spring filled the world, for the benefit, as he so evidently thought, of a small furry Personage importantly busy in the garden. He dealt with a stone. He snapped off the head of a flower. He lolled. He snorted. He rolled over.

His name was Wang Sun, Prince of Friends and Lover of Wild Grasses. When he was called by it or any other name, he sat down amazed to consider this new outrage, this indignity, this breach of Tao, this garden, this universe, unworthy to contain such as he, and ran as fast as he could another way.

Laughter followed, hurrying feet pursued. He was snatched up, scolded, cherished, borne to his destination where something seemly waited, food, drink, brush-and-brush, throw-ball, or sit-on-the-quilt-beside-her. It was more pleasurable to arrive with this little flurry and reminder of his consequence than merely to continue on his way toward her as he had been doing when she called.

He must, of course, never show pleasure, nor be dominated by another's will. It was necessary to draw up diminutive inches in disapproval, express offended dignity with a wave of the tail, look gravely aside from meeting glance-to-glance, and sniff a time or two before conceding sit-on-the-quilt-beside-her.

Hung Tu laughed at him, teased him, ruffled the tawny hair, called him outrageous names—"Small Dragon of the House of Hsueh in the Villa Pi-chi-Fang," "Great Guardian of the Threshold," "August Whiskers of the City of Silk"—while he coughed and growled indignantly.

He was a present from Yuan Chen, like the embroidered quilt, like the parrot above him, who sometimes came to her arm, like the spirited little Uighur horse in the stables, with the gold-painted hooves, like the gold carp in the ornamental pool. . . . Like everything gold and gleaming, summers, autumns, winters, springs, sun-filled days, moon-dimmed nights . . . all, all presents from Yuan Chen, the sheaf of poems, the writing brush, the shared wit, the laughter.

Now Villa Pi-chi-Fang, so remote, so still, so jealously guarded, the retreat of silence and solitude, took on the sights and sounds of a small bustling home. Servants chattered in the courtyard, horses came and went, maids drew water from the sacred well, the smell of cooking filled the air.

Hung Tu, directing events from the central pavilion, thought, "It is like the House of Hsueh." She understood the happiness her mother must have known in the early days of her marriage with Hsueh Yun. But her daughter's experience was happier. Here was no jealous Elder Sister to placate, no stepsons to endure as a reproach; here were the two companions, lovers, friends, poets working together in their snug retreat, *the same-heart ones*.

When she thought how all the years since she first acquired it, she had slowly, carefully, with the guile and determination of the miser, developed Pi-chi-Fang into this perfect shelter for them, *They cannot be parted whose hearts and minds and bodies know only each other, who have never had a dissenting thought,* she was amazed and amused. She had never connected Pi-chi-Fang with the lovers of her first childish poem, nor with any lovers. She had thought of it as the garden for her lonely retirement, the retreat for her years of decline, when she should have fallen out of favor.

Out of favor! She had walked off with the prize of the age! When Yuan Chen renounced the cares of public life to retire with the Songbird of the City of Silk, the civilized world buzzed with the story. Songs were sung in the Province of Shu and as far as remote Chang-an and even to the steps of the Emperor's Throne. When Liu Ch'eng Shih, to whom she would be ever grateful, in spite of his obnoxious character and worse connections, brought the story south over the pass to the eunuchs waiting for his report, the Palace buzzed.

On the whole Official Eunuch T'u-t'u Cheng-tsui was pleased. Here was a potential enemy for whom the Eye of Heaven still retained the weakness of a too-fond gleam neatly removed from public life, for a reason which could have no bearing upon politics.

It was, Official Liu P'i conceded, gratifying to the messenger's uncle to receive, using the language of the new group in power, *the thrust of the gelded boar,* good fortune indeed.

When the passes reopened in the spring, messenger followed messenger with gifts and commendations. Governor Yen Ssu-k'ung received a well-turned scroll praising him for his loyalty to the Eye of Heaven and his careful administration of the Province of Shu. It was accompanied by the gift of an inkstone from the hand of the Emperor Himself and a generous sum of taels. There also came in a roundabout way assurance of continuance in office. "Moons of felicitous days and nights in the City of Silk," the message said.

Yuan Chen too received an unexpected sack of taels for "salary earned in past performances" and assurances that poems flowing from his inspired brush would be placed within the range of the Eye of Heaven, Whose August Mind was gratified when men of talent decided to devote themselves with fervor and undivided attention to poetry.

This, in spite of the fact that poets were being deported, imprisoned, and executed in unprecedented numbers under the new government. Clearly not only the Eye of Heaven but the hand of the eunuchs showed to the perceptive . . . nevertheless it was agreeable to receive praise and taels without having to earn these favors in any shameful or disquieting way.

Yuan Chen hastened to send a long dutiful poem to the Emperor and bales of the finest silk to key officials. Then he turned to the enjoyment of good fortune.

Gifts and comments came from friends. Po Chui sent his *main principles of poetry* with all his work up to the time of their separation divided into four categories.

"The next time we are together we must produce all our works and criticize each other as we once planned to do. But how many years is it going to be before we meet, and where will that meeting be? What if before then something were to happen to one of us? Wei-chih, Wei-chih, you know what I am feeling as I write this."

Yuan Chen sent him a sheaf of the finest plum-blossom paper and a poem which began:

> Other people, too, have friends whom they love
> But ours was a love few friends have known.
> You were my sustenance; it mattered more
> To see you daily than to get my morning food.

It was a warm and loving answer, but the verbs were in the past tense. Hung Tu felt sorry for Po Chui. When that year no further words came from him she was not surprised.

That year! Was it possible to measure time in the Villa Pi-chi-Fang in terms of years? It would be no less impossible to measure it in terms of hours or noons or moments. It flowed like the river at the foot of the garden, with no distinctions, no divisions. To Hung Tu it seemed as though she swam through time with Yuan Chen beside her.

Continuity of bliss! How often they strolled together to the bank to stare into the water, ever changing, ever the same. If anything under the Eye of Heaven knew the essence of those days, those nights, it would be the River of Silk, the river that had flowed past the garden of her childhood in the House of Hsueh, past the Blue House, past the Villa at Hundred Flowers Pool.

> Go ask the river
> which are longer,
> its eastward-flowing waters
> or the thoughts that fill us
> at this parting hour.

The river was still flowing eastward. Until it reversed to flow westward she would not remember the last line.

XXXV

"WEI-CHIH, WEI-CHIH, it is three years since I saw you and almost two years since I had a letter from you. Is life so long that we can afford such estrangements as this?"

Po Chui wrote from his exile at Kiukiang. The eunuchs were well entrenched. There seemed no likelihood that any who had opposed their rise to power would return from banishment.

"I am in good health," Po Chui wrote. "All the members of my household are also well, and my brother arrived here last summer. How many times we have remembered together his last sight of you!

"Here on the river it is rather cooler than is general in the South and there is not much malaria. Poisonous snakes and troublesome insects do of course exist; but there are not very many of them. The fish of the P'en River are particularly fat and the river wine is excellent. Most of the other things one gets to eat and drink are pretty much the same as in the North. I have now a large number of mouths to provide for. I have begun by telling you of these matters thinking that as you have had no news of me for so long you must be feeling anxious.

"The night that I began this letter I was sitting in my cottage under a window that looks out onto the mountains. I let my brush run on as it would, setting down my thoughts at random, as they occurred to me. Now as I make ready to seal up the letter I find that the dawn has almost come. Looking out I see one or two monks, some sitting, some asleep. From above comes the sad cry of the mountain monkeys, and from below the twittering of the valley birds. Friend of all my life, ten thousand leagues away, thoughts of our days together in the world's dusty arena rise before me and blot out the scene. I again address you in verse:

Long ago I sealed up a letter that I had written to you at night
Behind the Hall of Golden Bells, as day was coming in the sky.
Tonight again I seal a letter, in a hut on the Lu Shan
Sitting at the first tinge of dawn, by a lamp that still burns.
The bird in its coop, the monkey in its cage are still not dead;
Though the years pass, they yet may meet somewhere in the world
of men.

"Wei-chih, Wei-chih! I wonder if you know all that is in my heart tonight? Lo-t'ien bows his head."

Yuan Chen answered this gently, compassionately, telling his suffering friend that he had found written on a wall in the Governor's Palace a poem by Po Chui, which had been brushed there by a Flower who had never forgotten him. "Her name appears to be A-juan." He added that he was studying the *Lotus of the Good Law* in between writing the parts of a long poem which he hoped might become the material for this new art of the dance which was beginning to emerge. Did Po Chui have an opportunity to see the new versions of *Rainbow Skirts and Feather Jackets*, especially the Middle or Clapped Prelude, when the dancers began to revolve like whirling snow?

Then he reminded Po Chui of the saying of his old Dhyana Master, Wei-k'uan, that "on the plane of Assembled Occasions one cannot escape from the secret laws of predestination. Existence is the state when 'occasions' are assembled; non-Existence is when they are scattered. There is therefore no separation. It appears probable that even now we loiter by the riverside, waiting for the moon to rise."

But it was with Hung Tu that Yuan Chen loitered by the banks of the River of Silk, and once again there came, that year, no further word from his exiled friend, and once again Hung Tu felt sorry for Po Chui, even while her own heart exulted at the circumstances which caused his despair.

"Irresistible Man," she wrote,

Irresistible man, most honored on the scroll of the East Hall,
At last we understand each other.

Today, face to face, each reads the other's heart.
See how the world makes itself new!
Every branch of the willow grove ends with a torch
In a blaze of sudden green.

She also was working on a sequence for a possible ballet, stringing together elements of happiness which made up her day.

First there were the things she saw about her, the living things which shared it with her. Wang Sun, for instance . . .

> *Pampered and perfumed, vigilant*
> *at the lacquered entrance, the petted dog*
> *responds to every move of its master.*

Its master. There was no question in Wang Sun's mind about this or any other matter of importance. He belonged to HIM, however many times HE gave away the Prince of Friends and Lover of Wild Grasses to lesser folk, to HER. She too belonged to HIM, as could be observed with half an eye and was only seemly. Why then all the wasted motion? Let the Master appear and shine on his world.

Whenever the small impetuous golden frame said this, so obviously, Hung Tu, shaken with amused delight, would pick him up and hug him, to his fury.

Then there were the things about her that she used, the new writing brush. When Yuan Chen gave it to her, she remembered the one Hsi Chih had thrown away, Old Scholar Meng Chaio's earlier gift to her, and how she had cherished it. She sought the old poem she had written for Meng Chaio, and began to rework the lines for inclusion in this Sequence of Happy Living at Pi-chi-Fang.

> *A bamboo handle from Yueh*
> *fashioned to fit the artist's fingers;*
> *tufts of Hsuan sable:*
> *elegantly it once moved*
> *under the governing mind*
> *in a journey of mountains,*

> *a soaring of wings, or waterfalls*
> *of flowers plunging down*
> *a silken scroll.*

With slight changes from the original it could be used. She would go on to describe the virtues of the new brush. She put it aside to consider the next verse about the little horse Yuan Chen had given her, which she rode beside him on so many festive occasions, hunting, exploring the countryside, or crossing the morning meadows for exercise.

> *Arching neck and fiery eye,*
> *white ears, a coat of roan,*
> *tireless pacer on gilded hooves*
> *outdistancing the wind.*

The parrot squawked above her head, "me too, me too." She smiled. "Well then, you too, why not? You are here in the garden this auspicious time." She began to trace tentative words in the air with the point of her brush, then, frowning, she set down two lines on the paper:

> *a bird reared with human beings,*
> *used to a cage of love.*

It was as far as she could get with it. There was another bird to be dealt with first, the swallow that had flown to his hand and refused to leave. How they laughed at the efforts it made to sing, the chirpings and scoldings it gave to the world, protesting that here was a poet. But then he listened gravely.

> *The bird that came to hand, he tenderly loved.*
> *Its song enchanted him.*

Remembering the movements of those strong, suggestive hands over the small, trembling body of the bird, she put down the brush. Her own body was shaking like the bird's. The lines of the next offering came to her:

> *Held throughout the night*
> *the gleaming peerless pearl,*
> *in the hand of the loving, appreciative one.*

Yes, it was like that; yes, it would always be. The brilliant, the beautiful head on the pillow. *The same-heart one.* Yuan Chen. Suddenly the smiling, incongruous figure of Lady Tall Bamboo appeared in her mind. She wondered if it had been like this for her and her monk in the Cloud Touching Temple, remembering that strange long-ago journey toward the crossroads of Tao. She hoped so. In her present languorous state of happiness she wished all lovers everywhere, past and present, a measure of this happiness.

A gleam of gold flashed in the pool. Fish too must be in the offering.

> *Carp swam in the pool all summer,*
> *dreaming the days away,*
> *eluding the threaded hook.*

And the falcon:

> *Proud, turning head, glittering eyes,*
> *fierce talons, dagger sharp . . .*

She was not satisfied with that verse. But Yuan Chen loved the falcon which the Governor had given him and often took it with him on his wrist when he walked with her, so it must have its honored place in the sheaf of offerings. So too must the framework about them in the garden, loquat trees, clumps of tall bamboo.

> *A shadowy pattern on the Hall of Jade,*
> *lithe and tenacious trees,*
> *yielding, yet strong, a living barrier to cold.*

And there was the mirror, his latest gift to her:

> *The polished metal mirror of the Hua Chuang*
> *gleamed like new gold in its veils of silk,*
> *as golden as the waxing moon*

on the fifteenth night
of the harvest month.

He gave it to her for the Dragon Festival which that year was more resplendent than any she could remember, even those elaborate processions of her first Governor, Wei Kao. At Dragon Festivals she thought of him, sometimes she heard of him, serving the Emperor in far-off places or in the Capital itself, but he never returned to Cheng-tu.

She took up the mirror and looked into it, smiling. Daily it showed her the face of her new happiness. She would gather together the ingredients of that happiness in this sheaf of verses and make of it a glittering procession of gratitude toward Yuan Chen, as memorable, as rich, as Governor Wei Kao's progress down the river in his lacquered barge.

It might be the sequence would be sung or even expanded into the new form of art coming across the borders from India and Tibet. There had always been stories-in-dancing and some Taoist unrolling-of-flowing-forward-events, as well as the shorter song sequences performed in Blue Houses, but the presentations now being talked of in the Capital were different from these.

For one thing they no longer depicted ordinary men and women, or even extraordinary men and women, the heroes and beauties of antiquity. The Jade Emperor and the Queen of Heaven were the principal characters of these new "ballets" and the lesser characters were djinns and fairies. It was no longer acceptable to sing of the triumphs and defeats of human life. She was not sure the change was for the better, but it was interesting.

Suddenly she remembered the mutineers of her childish fantasy, when she supposed them to be djinns, dancing in the Emperor's Palace for a year before they were defeated. She gave a delighted little laugh. Nowadays she could laugh when she pleased, or scold, or cry . . . she was mistress of her household, of her life.

If she had known, if she had been able to guess, as a child in the garden of the House of Hsueh, what existence beyond those walls might ultimately bring. . . .

There was a coming to life of the garden about her . . . Yuan Chen returning from the Governor's Palace. Hastily she swept the writing things under a silk. It was not time for him to be shown the sequence yet. When Tao brought the hour they would unroll the Scroll of Happiness at Pi-chi-Fang and look at it together.

XXXVI

THE YEAR OF THE FIRST BALLET in the City of Silk was also the year of the great local scandal, the one emerging from the other. It began auspiciously with rumors from the Capital that the reign of the eunuchs was drawing to a close, and while it would not be prudent for the Superior Man to take open notice of rumors prematurely, still these were heartening.

As runner after runner arrived from Chang-an with official reports to the Governor and unofficial confirmation of the news in them to Yuan Chen from his rejoicing friends, it appeared that the eunuchs' long-time chief protector, Minister Li Chi-fu, had offended the Eye of Heaven and was banished to a minor post in an eastern Province with an insalubrious climate. Following this relief to the spirits of the good, this overdue righting of the balances of justice, Chief Eunuch T'u-t'u Cheng-tsui had been stripped of his offices as Commander in Chief of the Western Forces, General of the Left Army of the Holy Plan, and Commissioner for Diffusing Comfort, in charge of the torture of prisoners and the requisitioning of commodities, to be relegated to a lowly rank with insignificant duties and no power over others in the City Arsenal.

It was now possible for Po Chui to send Yuan Chen his poem against T'u-t'u Cheng-tsui.

In the morning I climbed the Tzu-ko Peak,
In the evening I lodged in the village under the hill.
The Elder of the village was pleased that I had come
And in my honor opened a jar of wine.
We raised our cups but before we began to drink
Some rough soldiers pushed in at the gate,
Dressed in brown, carrying knife and axe,
Ten or more hustling into the room.

They helped themselves to the wine we were going to drink,
They snatched away the food we were going to eat.
My host made way and stood at the back of the room
With his hands in his sleeves, as though they were honored guests.
In the yard was a tree that the old man had planted
Thirty years ago with his own hand.
They said it must go, and he did not dare refuse;
They took their axes, they felled it at the root.
They said they had come to collect wood for building
And were workers attached to the Army of the Holy Plan.
Ah, be careful! The less you say the better;
Our Eunuch General, the hsuan-wei-shih, stands in high favor.

Now he had fallen. It came too late for hundreds of important men, thousands of lesser men, murdered or maimed and broken, and for their families, scattered, destitute, to the four ends of the Empire. Still, it had come at last, and over all the land the spring festivals took on sharper notes of rejoicing.

In Cheng-tu the Governor decided to stage a complete ballet in the Palace, in honor of his friend Yuan Chen, whom it was now not only safe but politic to honor, and whom, moreover, he had grown to love. Yuan Chen had been working on a long "Notation of the Rainbow Ballet" for over a year, with Hung Tu's help. It was only fitting that it should be performed.

Hung Tu would not appear in it. She had given no public performances since her retirement with the poet to Pi-chi-Fang. The Tao of her life had shifted completely from Flower-in-the-mist and official Hostess to "Elder Sister" in her own household, with all the functions of a wife and companionship in the arts besides, the most complete relationship any woman could have with any man. For this one must be an exceptional woman, beauty, poet, scholar, trained performer, great artist, attached to as great a man.

She began to realize how complete her retirement was when the plans for the ballet went forward and she had no part in them as a performer, either dancing or singing. The rehearsals were in the Palace and the Blue House, with only now and then smaller groups meeting in the Villa by Hundred Flowers Pool. There she went with Yuan Chen, welcomed prettily by the new Hostess, one of the Palace concubines, not always the same woman, for the Governor had never refilled Hung Tu's exceptional office.

After she left her litter or dismounted from her horse at the gate, she was led into the familiar courtyard, seated with courtesy upon a guest mat, called "Honored Lady," served with heated wine or tea or fruit or whatever delicacy was at hand, and left to her thoughts, while the Hostess resumed the more important duty of attending to the needs of Yuan Chen and the Governor if he were present, which he often was.

Now and then someone would ask Hung Tu's opinion as Misty Grass and the others went through the complicated graceful steps, or the singers sang the sequences she and Yuan Chen had composed. Sometimes her opinion was accepted, sometimes disregarded, but always she was listened to with deference. It was strange to sit in these pavilions at the Villa by Hundred Flowers Pool as a guest, watching another serve from the familiar set of dishes, hearing the musicians accompany another voice. Often she caught herself looking about her for old Fanyang, dead these many moons. Often she checked herself in the act of supplying some small courtesy the moment required. But for the most part she sat entranced, absorbed in the complexities and beauties of the new art.

Ah, if there had been ballet in the House on Willow Street in the days of her training there! This Misty Grass who danced more like a flame than mist, these Flowers who sang in the new notation, how fortunate they were. But none as fortunate as she, whose mat was spread each night beside the poet in whose honor all was set in motion, the composer, the performer who would himself represent the Jade Emperor of Heaven.

Yuan Chen spent his days rehearsing, sometimes returning late into the night. But they woke together on the pillow, and those hours they must spend apart she was working on her own surprise offering to him, the Sequence of Happy Living at the Villa Pi-chi-Fang. The Governor ordered its performance on the evening of the ballet, to precede it, as a demonstration of the perfection of the old, classic forms which would further heighten the effect of the new.

She would be sole performer. Almost she welcomed the time Yuan Chen spent away from Pi-chi-Fang, for then she could rehearse undisturbed, sitting in her Song-chanting Tower beside the flowing river, with Wang Sun at her feet waiting resignedly for his god to return. She was using her mother's ancient p'i-pa, probably for its last public appearance. It was becoming very frail, but there was no instrument like it for purity of tone, delicacy, strength. There was a depth, intensity of singing line sustaining the faintest half note . . . often she wondered about the unknown man who had made it and passed to his ancestors. Were there others of his making in the world? How and where did her mother acquire it? A present from the Emperor, perhaps?

There was no one now alive to tell. She turned it in her hands, watching the texture of the wood respond to light and shade. Then a string snapped and the ends flew up to sting her hands. Wang Sun barked disapprovingly.

She was dismayed. Certainly if it were going to break it was better that it did so now, unobserved except by a dog and a parrot, than later at the Palace in the middle of a performance, but there was no spare string at Pi-chi-Fang with which to replace it. She remembered that the musicians kept musical supplies at the Villa by Hundred Flowers Pool. She would send a servant there to see . . . no, she would go herself, to be sure of bringing back the right one. There would still be time to practice before Yuan Chen could return from the Palace, where the ballet was rehearsing.

She ordered two horses, her own and another, and with a servant following, set out across the meadow by the short cut to the Villa. She rode astride as the women polo players rode, robe falling loosely over her embroidered leggings. The fiery little Uighur snorted and bounded forward, racing the winds. This was what they both loved, but lately riding had been neglected. When the ballet was over, they would start on their excursions again.

She reached the gates of the Villa, dismounted, flung the reins to the servant and ran inside, crossing the courtyard with swift steps, intent on quickly finding what she had come for and returning home before Yuan Chen could get there. It would be, she thought, in the Pavilion of Repose, in a certain lacquered box. She went directly toward it, thrusting the curtains aside.

There, on the mat she occupied for twenty years, the mat where she and Yuan Chen first embraced, she saw them, Yuan Chen and Misty Grass, in the act of love.

Saw him . . . saw him . . . caught up the first thing to hand, a pair of embroidered socks . . . hit him across the head with them. The jade on the toes broke and flew about the room as she struck and struck again. She threw them aside to pommel with her fist, to scratch with her long nails.

Sounds were coming from her mouth. Hands were upon her, wrenching her away from the astounded, indignant man, the cowering girl. Then the Governor was in the room, attendants, servants, aghast at what they saw before them, such a breach of Tao, such a blasphemy against the Eye of Heaven, whose representative this great man was.

No one knew what to do next, but Hung Tu thrust aside the restraining hands as she had thrust aside the curtains and turning, with a complete absence of proper forms of address to anyone in that room, that place, that universe, went swiftly to the gate, mounted Uigha and rode away.

Many saw them pass, the mettlesome little horse with the golden hooves, the jeweled trappings, carrying the well-known, proud figure of the Poet, the Songbird of the City of Silk, and the lumbering beast behind, carrying a servant whose mouth seemed to be open in an O of horror and astonishment. They greeted no one. They passed the turning to Pi-chi-Fang, they rode along the river path to the North Gate of the city, they turned toward the mountains, they began the long, steep climb to Cloud Touching Temple, climbing in silence through the afternoon, with no sound but the stones sliding beneath the hooves of the laboring beasts.

As twilight fell they arrived at the monastery. Now Hung Tu turned at the jangling of the bell, as the servant after a moment of hesitation, rang it. She stretched out her hands to him in a gesture of farewell, of gratitude for services.

"Take the horses back," she said. "Go home, good Fu Yang, after you have rested and received refreshment. The moon is high tonight. Do not stay until morning, lest you incur the wrath of authority."

"Lady," he stammered, "lady . . . this person . . ."

She stretched her hands to him again, in formal dismissal, as the gates swung open to receive her.

He watched her passing through them, his lady.

"She will need clothes. She will need money. She will need . . ." he knew not what. His lady . . . forever disgraced . . . who might be executed . . . banished . . . branded . . . he knew not what. He was only a servant, knowing nothing. He lifted his free hand to his eyes, the other held the reins. He wept the tears she had not shed.

Below, among the lights of the city, the cicadas grinched.

"Is it true?"

"She struck him?"

"Repeatedly."

"Across the face."

"This person is amazed."

"In the Governor's presence?"

"In front of the world?"

"Oh, what will happen next?"

Behind him, in the guest room of the monastery, his lady . . . his lady . . . hid herself.

Slowly the tired beasts went down the track to the City of Silk, to Pi-chi-Fang.

XXXVII

NOTHING HAD CHANGED in the guest room of the monastery. Here was the raised platform in the middle of the room with its four lacquered posts, a little the worse for wear since Tall Bamboo admired it as a day bed, comfortable to her back. Nothing had changed. *Everything had changed.*

The monk still chanted in the distance to his flute. The gong still hummed, the mutter of sutras rose, the nuns went by in their downy caps, everything was the same. *Nothing was the same.*

"Stilling the heart," the young monk said . . . the tall monk was not there, that was not the same . . . "as the Ch'i of Tao permeates the whole universe, so the Ch'i must fill the stillness of the heart-mind and the whole being."

"This person is stilling the heart," she repeated dutifully.

How absurd it was! How could the heart be stilled? There was no heart there to be stilled. *Nothing was there to be stilled. Everything was stilled.*

What would they do to her? Would she take the saffron robe? Be permitted to? What did it matter what they did. *Everything was changed.*

"Tao is forever," they said, "it is necessary to eat," when they brought the bowl.

"It is necessary to eat," she said, and left the food untouched.

"Tao is forever," they said, "now night is come. It is the will of Heaven that we sleep."

"Tao is forever," she said, and sat upright upon the mat, eyes wide. *Nothing was the same.*

Through the night they came.

"Tao is forever. Now lie down. Drink this. Let the hands of healing smooth your head."

The hands of healing might come, might go. *Everything was changed.*

In the City of Silk the cicadas grinched.

In the Blue House Misty Grass exulted. Had she not displaced the Legend of Cheng-tu. Did she not appear, in public, as the Queen of Heaven, opposite the Jade Emperor of Heaven? Surely now the Governor would give her all that had once belonged to disgraced Hung Tu. But the Governor showed no sign of understanding this. After the ballet might be a better time to approach him. She set herself to wait.

In the Palace, seated with Yuan Chen in the Pavilion of Enlightened Reflection, the Governor expressed his regret, his consternation at the insult proffered to his honored guest, his now-long-held-in-esteem friend, and this in the City of Silk over which Official Yen Ssu-k'ung presided.

"This person's face is forever dimmed. There will be restitution, public apology, and whatever punishment the offended Representative of the Eye of Heaven desires for the impious."

Yuan Chen demurred. Apology, if Governor Yen Ssu-k'ung's honor as a host required it, but not a public one.

"This person would find it painful to experience." He looked at the Governor ruefully. "This person would prefer to remember the Songbird of Pi-chi-Fang in happier ways."

The Governor received his statement with an appreciative movement of the hands and eyes. "The generosity of the Representative of the Eye of Heaven confounds us, but let it be as Yuan Chen has said."

He busied himself with pouring wine. They were alone, as far as it was possible to be sure of solitude in the Palace. Invisible eyes and ears were everywhere.

Yuan Chen sighed.

"Five years is a long time to set aside for one short moment of forgotten Tao. Moreover the fault sprang from no indifference." Then he asked in a different tone, "How is she now?"

"Facing the shadows. They tell me that she does not eat or sleep, nor utters a sentiment that is her own. They fear for her, lest she should not return from that Dark Place to which she is gone."

Yuan Chen stirred restlessly.

"She was composing a tribute to be offered before the ballet of the Jade Emperor and the Queen of Heaven. It was called the Sequence of Happy Living at the Villa Pi-chi-Fang. I believe it would have pleased you."

"This person will never hear it."

"That is probable."

"Unless . . . let it be sent to me. Let that be the only penalty suffered by the Songbird."

"It shall be so, and a written apology, when she returns from the shadows."

"This person will be far."

"It is the will of Heaven."

They began to discuss the latest news from the Palace, especially the recent summons to Yuan Chen to return to Chang-an before the passes closed, and the probable fate of the Governor, who had also been ordered to hold himself in readiness in case his presence should be desired in Chang-an.

"I will inform myself of the situation," Yuan Chen assured him, "with all discretion and dispatch, and send word at once by a trusted mouth. Meanwhile a message of this kind appears to be fortunate. When evil is designed, it befalls without warning."

The Governor brightened.

"That is true, but this person would prefer to remain in the Province of Shu."

Yuan Chen laughed. The Governor interpreted the laughter aright.

He sighed.

"It is true, I have been here longer than any other Governor except Official Wei Kao. To and fro goes the Way. The Superior Man lends grace to his feet. Coming and going is without blame. But still Official Yen Ssu-k'ung would rather stay in Shu."

In the garden at Pi-chi-Fang a small brown dog, bereft of both his gods, refused to eat.

XXXVIII

THE NIGHT OF THE BALLET came and went, unparalleled for brilliance in living memory, the cicadas said. Departing Official Yuan Chen, in whose honor it was held, played the Jade Emperor of Heaven with exceptional grace. The dancing, the wine, the food, the costumes, the gifts were superb, yet something appeared to be lacking.

Minds strayed from the spectacle. Thoughts went to the absent one, without whom, for the present generation and perhaps in living memory too, no gathering at the Palace seemed complete. Nothing was said, her name was not pronounced as the night wore on, but there were yawns, a shuffling of feet, and a certain dullness of countenance among a few, for whom some ingredient of habitual enchantment seemed to be missing.

There was curiosity. How did she fare in her mountain cell? For the perceptive there was the interesting study of the Queen of Heaven's face, the young dancer, Misty Grass. At the height of success she was looking puzzled. Showered with rich presents, generously applauded, presented to the Court by Yuan Chen himself, she still looked disappointed, as though she hoped for something more. What more could there be for a Flower-in-the-mist? Unless . . . unless she had hoped for an appointment such as the Official Hostess of the Shu Ya Men once held . . . still held, for all the cicadas could discover. Surely even in these degenerate days of the decline of excellence, no one, however talented, could hope to take the place of the disgraced Songbird of Cheng-tu? Disgraced or not, there was only one Hung Tu.

Whatever the ins and outs of expectation might have been, Misty Grass went back to the Blue House with jewels, expensive silks, and a well-filled purse from the Governor. Yuan Chen prepared to depart with a caravan, one of the most imposing ever to set forth from Shu . . . forty camels laden with silk, spices, and other rare commodities, five with plum-blossom paper, also horses, carriers, way-clearers, slaves, and provisions.

He too bore away gifts and possessions gathered over his five years in the City of Silk. But there was no farewell poem among them, no parting word, no sign from the recluse of Cloud Touching Temple, no garland from the garden at Pi-chi-Fang. Hung Tu still faced the shadows. It was the Governor who escorted Yuan Chen on the first lap of his way and took leave of him in the Pavilion of Parting pitched by the city gates.

The two friends embraced, the Governor with tears in his small mournful eyes, Yuan Chen less sadly, but with more emotion than he expected to feel. Then he entered his litter and was borne away on the first part of the road to the Capital.

Did she watch? Did she know?

What would befall her now? Would she take the saffron robe? He turned the idea over. It pleased him, but he did not think it probable. Even if she should desire such an ending to her years . . . and he would like her to desire it since it would mean no other man enjoyed his jeweled bowl . . . the Governor or those succeeding Yen Ssu-k'ung would be against it. Cheng-tu without its Legend, its Songbird, its Hostess, would be sadly diminished.

When she returned from the shadows . . . He sighed. He smiled. How strange for a woman trained as a Flower-in-the-mist to be so moved to despair over the simple, ordinary, daily occurrence of the coupling of a client with another Flower. The training of any Blue House . . . but with these it was different. They both knew that. With these the service of towel and comb was an expression of a deeper dimension of unity . . . why else did he take such pains to conceal his traffic with Misty Grass from Hung Tu, and even, in a sense, from himself.

Five years was too long a time to be restricted to one bowl, however beautiful, and a woman, older . . . how much older? He had never been able precisely to discover, but at least ten years.

It was perhaps good that the foolish catastrophe happened, making parting easier, so that now he could set forth to the Capital with less regret and no despair.

Some regret there must be, a sense of loss. One did not lightly leave such a woman . . . more than the woman, the life, the experience, the *Sequence of Happy Living at the Villa Pi-chi-Fang.*

He was going to advancement, to emergence from retirement into official life, to a friend who loved him with a depth no woman could hope to achieve or even comprehend . . . he would have believed this once.

Po Chui would be waiting, to take him to some restful place after the journey, some cool, enchanted cottage by the river, where they would spend long hours in a drifting boat, or on the hillside under pine trees . . . somewhere comfortable, already being prepared for him with loving care and joy. The only other creature to manifest such joy at his appearance was a small brown dog. Perhaps he should have carried Wang Sun away with him, but what could one do with a dog on such a journey as this? He would not survive the hardships, and if he did, what would his life be in Chang-an? He was better off where he was. When Hung Tu emerged from the shadows . . . There it was, again, it all returned to that. . . .

He would think of Po Chui. Of the news they would discuss together, the poems to be read and exchanged, the laughter. Meanwhile . . . he reached for the flask of rice wine. He would drink himself to sleep.

XXXIX

MANY MOONS LATER a runner reached him from Governor Yen Ssu-k'ung, who had not yet received his summons to leave Shu and remained in nervous expectation of it, which spoiled his days and nights "in our Cheng-tu."

He gave the latest news of the City of Silk, among it that he had lately refused permission to the Songbird to take the saffron robe and had ordered her return to Pi-chi-Fang, from where, when she regained her strength, he intended to reinstate her in the Villa by Hundred Flowers Pool. He enclosed the promised *Sequence of Happy Living at the Villa Pi-chi-Fang*, to which new lines had been added at the close of every verse, purporting to be apology or admission of mistake, instead they breathed reproach, conveyed a poignant sadness, new accusation and complaint.

Yuan Chen smiled. He sighed. Ah, she was indomitable, unique. He showed the verses to Po Chui, whose time of triumph it was. They read them together in the summer house they shared before they would be separated again, Po Chui to his new post as Governor of Chung-chou, a hundred miles below Chung-king, Yuan Chen to his appointment as Head of the Han Lin Academy. It was separation, but to Po Chui not the painful abandonment Yuan Chen's five years in the City of Silk had meant to the friend abandoned. It was Hung Tu's turn to experience that grief. Po Chui could afford to be generous. He genuinely admired Hung Tu. It was he who had first endeavored to interest Yuan Chen in her poetry.

He examined with an ungrudging eye the long poem which Yuan Chen told him had once been called *Sequence of Happy Living at the Villa Pi-chi-Fang*, and was now *Apology Offered to Official Yuan Chen.*

The first part of the first verse was brushed in a gold-brown ink. "The color of the dog's coat," Yuan Chen said. The second part was brushed in dull dark gray. "The color of grief," Po Chui said. He read the lines aloud.

> *Pampered and perfumed, vigilant*
> *at the lacquered entrance, the petted dog*
> *responds to every move of its master.*
> *One jealous growl, one snap at the favorite,*
> *and it is banished from the master's side,*
> *from the comfort of the folded quilts.*

The next verse was brushed in yellow ink, the color of a bamboo stalk. The second part in rusty brown.

> *A bamboo handle from Yueh*
> *fashioned to fit the artist's fingers;*
> *tufts of Hsuan sable:*
> *elegantly it once moved*
> *under the governing mind*
> *in a journey of mountains,*
> *a soaring of wings, or waterfalls*
> *of flowers plunging down*
> *a silken scroll.*
> *Now frayed and blunt, it is laid by,*
> *no longer remembered.*
> *Yuan Chen has a new brush in his hand.*

The next was written in gold, like the hooves of the little Uighur.

> *Arching neck and fiery eye,*
> *white ears, a coat of roan,*
> *tireless pacer on gilded hooves*
> *outdistancing the wind.*
> *Startled at the flutter of a robe,*
> *bewildered at a face but newly come,*
> *the rider thrown . . .*
> *never again stabled in the special stall.*

The next was in green with strokes of red.

Distractedly flying high over the Lung Hsi marshes,
over the waste of reeds, rushes, swampy ground;
a bird reared with human beings,
used to a cage of love.
Because it spoke loose words it did not understand,
exiled from the world it knows.
It cannot long survive.

The next was in silver.

The bird that came to hand he tenderly loved.
Its song enchanted him,
but building its nest on a column of coral
the bird spatters drops of mud on the rosy surface.
Driven off, the nest destroyed,
uttering piteous cries she circles in air.

The next was in ivory.

No longer treasured by the lapidary
the lustrous pearl he once called peerless:
he has found a sparkling gem,
one of many such.
It will amuse him for a day,
but because of a shadow, a fancied flaw,
he has forgotten the pearl
that once adorned his hand.

The next was in red and gold.

Once carp swam in the pool all summer,
dreaming the days away, eluding the threaded hook.
It was a cherished lily that the red-gold fish
dragged under the water.

The next was in brown and gray.

Proud, turning head, glittering eyes,
fierce talons, dagger sharp.

One flight, one capture
on a mission of its own . . .
never more will the Prince permit
the falcon to perch upon his wrist.

The next was in green and brown.

A shadowy pattern on the Hall of Jade,
lithe and tenacious trees,
yielding, yet strong, a living barrier to cold:
the slender leaves ward off the summer heat:
but new growth shakes the old foundation stones,
the bamboo is uprooted, cast aside.

The last was in leaden silver.

The polished metal mirror of the Hua Chuang
gleams like new gold in its veils of silk,
as golden as the waxing moon
on the fifteenth night
of the harvest month.
Yet, untended for a span, the mirror
of the "transformation-tidy-up box"
neglected, unpolished, the moulded figures
around the rim blurred, the lion dog handle
dark with dust,
is torn from the box,
and nothing in its place.

It was evident that Hung Tu had returned from the shadows with none of her poetic force or her subtle wit impaired, whatever else might be damaged or amiss.

"One thing puzzles this person," Po Chui said, turning his intelligent questioning face to his friend, when they had sat in silence for a while. "Why does the abandoned one apologize to the abandoner? Why are these reproaches called apology?"

Yuan Chen did not enlighten him. He did not care to be reminded of that flying jade, those scratching nails.

"It is a story," he said evasively, "for another day. But she is talented. . . ."

"In everything she undertakes," Po Chui assented. "I well remember . . ."

But Yuan Chen did not desire to hear, to consider, another man's remembrance of Hung Tu. He changed the talk to their new appointments, and where and how they might expect to be meeting next.

Po Chui smiled as he watched his pensive, anxious face. Lis away, in the far North, a small brown dog in a garden looked with the same expression toward the gate. The goddess indeed had returned, smelling and looking the same, yet not the same. Where, oh where was HE?

PART EIGHT
817–819 A.D.

XL

THE PROVINCE OF SHU fell upon evil days after Governor Yen Ssu-k'ung took his reluctant leave of the City of Silk. He left on a misty autumn day, the last that he could travel in safety before the passes closed. Hung Tu accompanied him to the Pavilion of Parting, erected by Myriad Mile Bridge. She gave him a farewell poem:

As I wait alone on Myriad Mile Bridge
I remember the sweet songs of the ancient poets . . .
but even Hsi Ho, who spoke so clearly of the woes of love,
cannot heal my sadness . . . as I wait in the gentle rain
beside the tethered fishing boats.

They embraced for a long moment, the Governor trembling and in tears. Then he entered his litter and was borne away from the friend he esteemed and the place that he loved.

He was lucky to depart when he did, before the troubles of the next two years began. There was first a drought, such as no one could remember since the far-off days of Governor Wei Kao's early years in office. Then the rice crop failed, and starving men roamed the fields, looting, burning, killing, and dying where they crawled, where they fell, in the irrigation ditches, along the roads, for the crows and scavengers to eat.

Cattle were torn apart alive, devoured raw, farmers were wounded trying to defend their homes, others abandoned what they could not carry and fled to the crowded city, where they roamed the streets, slept in doorways, stole what they could, died where they lay down, and were hauled away and flung outside the walls.

Prices for food soared beyond the reach of all but the very rich. Householders cowered behind barred gates. Whispers spread of horrors, cannibalism, human-eating bandits organized to attack the city. Caravans went heavily guarded and even so were often looted. Two of the riverboats sank trying to reach the southern wharf with food supplies. No one left the city without an armed escort and then only in daylight and never far. It was an evil time.

Hung Tu paid little attention to the growing disorders, or, indeed, to anything about her, until one morning the household at Pi-chi-Fang was roused by a terrible screaming. It filled the air with an agony unbearable to hear. Servants ran through the grounds, searching the bushes. Some went straight to the stables. There they found Uigha, backed against the darkest corner of his stall, trembling with terror, eyes wild. It was not he who screamed. Two horses were down, legs torn off, bellies ripped, large strips of skin hanging loose. The servants beat the quivering carcasses to death. Horses, dogs, cats, and, it was rumored, children, now were food for any who could get to them. Famished human beasts must have tunneled for many days to make these openings to the stable to fall upon this meat.

It was time to move from Pi-chi-Fang to the Villa by Hundred Flowers Pool, farther from the city walls and what lurked beyond them, to the patrolled part of the city. Hung Tu, riding Uigha and clutching Wang Sun to the saddle, hurried them to comparative safety. The shock of their danger, the bloody shambles in the stable roused her from the listless indifference in which she passed her days, wearing out the tedious hours of a life from which the fire had departed. Now she was confronted with forgotten sights and sounds of her childhood and forced to take notice of them.

Then it was Pockmark Chou who terrorized the countryside. Now the leader's name was Famished Fox. The whispered rumors, the cruelties, the horrors were the same. The only difference between those far-off days and these she encountered now was that then a strong Governor took matters into his capable hands, scattered the bandits, executed Pockmark Chou, restored order and cleaned up the ruined countryside, whereas now a weak official, unable or unwilling to come to any decisions or to take any responsibility except for his own skin and property, an interim governor, waiting for his successor, cowered behind the Palace gates with a stockpile of food, hoping for matters to right themselves without his interference.

Fortunately the army was still there, led by an able General, who had managed so far to protect the city. How long he could do so without help and better support from the Governor was a matter for anxiety.

Hung Tu pondered the situation now that she was made aware of it. General Cheng-Wei-Chou was too young to remember the times of Governor Wei Kao and his tactics against the bandits. She sent for him.

It was still an honor to be summoned to the Songbird of Cheng-tu, one that had gotten rarer through the years and was almost nonexistent at this time. There was still entertainment at the Villa by Hundred Flowers Pool for the Palace guests when the Governor desired it, but this Governor was too much of a poltroon to desire anything beyond the safety of his own sleek hide. The young officer put on his best robe and presented himself with curiosity and respect at the Villa gates.

The respect deepened when he heard what the Lady Hung Tu had to say.

"It is indeed an excellent suggestion," he said thoughtfully, "and one which might succeed now as then, but this person is hampered and deterred by a restriction which Governor Wei Kao did not suffer, nor impose upon others. My orders are never to be more than a hundred yards from the Palace gates."

They looked at one another. Then she said:

"If the disorders continue and the bandits become bolder, there will be no security within the Palace gates."

"True, but the Governor hopes that reinforcements will arrive with the new Governor."

"New Governor?"

"Official Liu P'i."

Hung Tu drew in her breath at that dreaded name.

"The last runner to arrive, three weeks ago, said that he was already on his way with a considerable army. He will deal with the bandits as he proceeds."

"One begins almost to pity them," Hung Tu murmured.

"When he reaches the Capital, the Governor and his household will depart, taking this person with them to protect their passage."

"Take this person also."

The young officer smiled. "Indeed, if it depended upon one inspired choice, this person would take the Lady Hung Tu with him everywhere forever."

He looked at her with such devotion that Hung Tu was startled. She had seen the same expression in Wang Sun's honest eyes turned toward Yuan Chen. She closed her own for a moment, against that memory. When she opened them again, she was looking at a little bronze object clumsily held out to her. She took it from him, since that was what the young man seemed to want her to do, and turned it about in her hands. It was a dragon, sturdily shaped, with quaint originality and excellent tool work. It had a smooth pleasant feeling. She started to hand it back.

"Gracious Lady, confer happiness upon this clumsy craftsman and keep it."

"Is it of your making? It is beautiful."

"This person has long wanted to give it to the Songbird of Cheng-tu."

She looked astonished.

"When I was a sickly, pain-filled child, my mother soothed me to sleep with certain songs, 'Now Alighted,' 'Under This Moon,' 'In My Garden,' and there was one she used to dance for me when we were alone. She told me stories. . . ."

"Dance?"

"Yes, it was called 'Trying on a Newly Finished Gown.' "

"Who was your mother?" Hung Tu asked, knowing the answer must be a Flower from the Blue House on Willow Street, long years ago, to know that song.

"She was called Spring Breeze, and she referred to Lady Hung Tu as Silver Hooks."

"Spring Breeze! I do remember her, a dancer of exquisite grace. . . ."

"The grace remains."

"Where is she now?"

"In Chang-an, in the house of Official Wei. My mother is Third Lady."

"And she remembers!" Hung Tu said after a moment's silence.

"She is forever saying that there are no songs like those, no dances like those, no poets like those of the time when she was in Cheng-tu with Silver Hooks. She remembers best the Year of the Horse. . . ."

"The Year of the Horse! That was when this person first came to the House on Willow Street."

"My mother also."

Hung Tu put the dragon gently down on the table in front of her. She clapped her hands for servants to serve tea.

"When I was young," the young man said, following the dragon with his eyes from her hands to its resting place, "I wanted to be a craftsman in metals and to spend my life making useless pleasing things."

"Useless?"

"Not armor, not plows, not utensils, except perhaps a bowl, well-shaped and right to the hands."

"And dragons, like this one."

"Yes."

"Why did you not follow such a harmonious Tao?"

"My father . . . " he broke off. "It is necessary for a son to make his earthly way. My father presented me to the Emperor, and when I had successfully passed the examinations, I was appointed to serve under General Wei Kao. . . ."

"Governor Wei Kao?"

"Yes, he is my father's cousin. Everyone was pleased, except my mother. She did not agree with my father that I should be in the army. She wanted me to carve beautiful things, to be a poet, a musician, a painter. It was the only time I heard my father address her in anger and contempt. This person suffered to hear the love between them damaged on his account. I told my father I would be a great general, I told my mother I would keep those things she had taught me in my heart, and I destroyed all my metal pieces and un-finished works . . . except this."

"Why did you destroy them?"

He shrugged. "All except this," he repeated, taking up the dragon. "This I kept, not knowing why, but Heaven is wise. It was so that I could give it to Beauty . . . to the Queen of Heaven. . . ."

He paused, confused. Her expression warned him that he had blundered. He recalled the Scandalous Episode and that other Queen of Heaven. He cursed his stupid tongue.

"I mean . . ."

She interrupted him.

"General Cheng-Wei-Chou, this person is honored to offer towel and comb and to pour wine for your pleasure." It was the custom-ary Blue House salutation, to which she added, smiling at him, "and if it please you to unroll your mat tonight . . ." she let the sentence trail, looking past his joy, over his shoulder, with a strange expression . . . later he thought it a mixture of defiance and still-angry pride, directed not at him . . . "at Yuan Chen," he decided.

At the moment he could only stammer his delight, as awkwardly as the boy who made the dragon, not as the man he was, the success-ful rising general.

That night and after nights the mat was spread for him where Yuan Chen had lain, and many others, but only Yuan Chen and he by invitation from her, and even Yuan Chen in the beginning was the Governor's guest.

It was beneficial to them both, enchantment for him, and for her friendly warmth, some sort of small reassurance, furthering her re-covery.

After a few pleasant days, she gave him a poem to send to his mother: "Answering Lady Wei."

Do not compare bean flowers with Ching Shen jade.
Bean flowers have fragrance.
Will there ever be any like those in the Year of the Horse,
The breeze blowing on freshly turned earth,
shaking the vines, scattering royal pollen
in the burning country sun?

XLI

As Official Liu P'i neared the city to become its new Governor, the countryside was filled with a pall of smoke. It was rumored that he was burning all he could not loot, and killing or taking prisoner everyone who could not escape his path, whether they were bandits or the remnants of honest men, farmers, peasants, women, children.

It was his method of subduing a Province that was out of hand. He made ashes of everything, and men were forced to begin again, living like rats and swine in the devastated countryside, forbidden to build themselves the most primitive shelters, while they hastened to cultivate such crops as he might designate, with nothing to work with but their hands.

"The dead are better off than those he spares," Cheng-Wei-Chou said. "He keeps his prisoners for his own entertainment later. We are already enlarging the torture chambers."

"Then who farms the land?"

"Those who displease him in Cheng-tu, or arbitrarily, those he selects at random. It may be anyone. And if they do not produce an abundant crop he removes their livers, slowly." He broke off. "Let us not talk of this. We will hear and see enough horrors when he arrives." Another thought came to him. "Would it not be a propitious time for you to visit the monks at Cloud Touching Temple?"

"On the contrary. I have received a communication from our cloistered Governor to hold myself ready to entertain Official Liu P'i 'to the utmost of this person's ability.' "

Cheng-Wei-Chou put his hands to his eyes for a moment, as though to rub out that vision.

"Let us not give way to anxiety," Hung Tu said, smiling. "I understand the Coming One's basic interests lie in another direction."

"He uses both eunuchs and concubines. He delights in giving pain, in degrading whatever is in front of him."

"It is in the hands of Heaven. While we wait for this enigmatic Personage to come among us, let us occupy our remaining hours in pleasant and creative ways. There is a poem I would like to harmonize with General Cheng-Wei-Chou."

But he was not to be diverted. He looked at her with anguish. A sound, half groan, half grunt, escaped him.

Was it possible, she thought, amazed, that he did indeed suffer, did indeed experience more than an agreeable comb-and-towel companionship with this old person, whom he knew to be at least his mother's age? Was it possible for him, or any man, to feel . . .

She touched him gently on the shoulder. He groaned again, he said in a strange, husky voice something that sounded like the first lines of a familiar poem, and yet she could not place the lines.

> *Those in Beauty from their birth*
> *whose Tao it is to disturb the atmosphere*
> *and rearrange the entrails*
> *of the sentient*
> *have the strong obligation . . .*

"What is that?"

"It is the first part of a poem that this . . . this late-comer . . . is making in honor of Lady Hung Tu."

It was touching, it was ridiculous. Alas, the fires were long since dead that could have responded to such words. Fortunately silence seemed to be sufficient acknowledgment. He was gathering his composure to take leave.

"Stay in the Inner Court," he said, bowing to her. "This person will put a notice on the gates, with the Governor's seal, and station men beside it and do what else can be done to protect this place of jeweled memory. If it is clearly shown and understood that the Villa at Hundred Flowers Pool belongs to That One already, Governor Liu P'i will probably not allow it to be looted. As for Pi-chi-Fang . . ." He looked at her sadly.

"Pi-chi-Fang has receded somewhat from this person's life and thought," Hung Tu assured him gently, "to the extent that what may happen there can no longer be the deep affliction that once it would have been."

He understood the allusion and not for the first time thought with indignation of that inferior man—however great a poet he might be—who could treasure lightly and carelessly betray this woman.

As though the thought of Yuan Chen, in any form, had power to arouse him, Wang Sun came waddling from the shadows to sniff suspiciously at the thinker's boots. Hung Tu picked him up. He was an old dog now, no longer resentful of attention. Holding him in the crook of her right arm, she said as an afterthought:

"If there should be a need to save the helpless small one from cruelty, tell me, in time to kill him."

He promised. He took himself away to oversee the enlargement of the torture rooms for those less fortunate than a dog, those whom he would be unable to kill when Official Liu P'i came to his pleasures. He was still a day's march away, judging from the nearest, newest fires.

XLII

IN SPITE OF ALL that the people of Cheng-tu had heard about the new Governor and had been able to observe for themselves during the weeks of his progression toward them, no one was prepared for the horrible sights and sounds of his entry into the city. He arrived at noon on a hot day of that scorching summer, riding at the head of his troops, a small, yellow-faced, unsmiling man on a dusty-coated horse.

Behind him five hundred soldiers marched, most of them with pikes, and on the pikes they brandished human remains, heads, arms, legs, entrails, general hunks of bloody flesh, which they shook off at the doors and gates of houses and sloughed off on the road for the prisoners to stumble over in their bare feet, women, children, emaciated, wounded men, bound together with ropes, whose faces showed no sign of sentient humanity.

They walked among the fragments of their dead with no change of expression in their sunken eyes. Now and then one died in the torturing rope and was dragged on by the rest. Now and then a chain swung by a soldier, almost carelessly, blotted out the features of another, dragged on by the shuffling figures bound to it, screaming, faceless, unable to sag anywhere but forward.

It took two hours for the long slow mass to reach the Governor's Palace, where it camped, soldiers to the right, prisoners to the left, Palace officials, headed by the departing Governor, drawn up in the center, bowing, hands in the sleeves of their best robes of state, to welcome Official Liu P'i.

All that afternoon and far into the night the householders of Cheng-tu cleaned and scraped their walls and gates of human fragments and filth and tried to sweep the muddy, oozing road of some of it. Slaves ran with blood-spattered wheelbarrows and baskets to and from the city walls, emptying their contents to the glutted crows. Everything in Cheng-tu stank. The smell reached even those barricaded behind closed doors.

It was not an auspicious beginning to the new Governor's rule. Many cursed the frightened, inefficient man delivering up his people to Liu P'i before departing for the safety of the Capital, where he would be too far away to see or hear what happened to the friends he was abandoning.

But not without some inkling of their fate and some unpleasing memories. Liu P'i would see to that, was even now attending to it in his way. Rumor said that what went on in the Palace was worse than what went on in the streets, and Liu P'i would not allow the ex-Governor to depart until he had witnessed the bulk of it, "so that he might render a true account to the Eye of Heaven of those wise and humane methods by which the Province of Shu was being restored to that good order which it had recently been found to have abandoned . . ." a phrase not calculated to reassure the man under whose administration this abandonment took place, especially as the wise and humane methods included the rape and torture of his favorite concubines and the deportation as agricultural laborers of most of his best servants.

These things reached Hung Tu's ears through the gossip of the guards at her gate, who heard them when they changed shifts and told them to the servants. Hung Tu spent the first three days after the Governor's arrival in the Pavilion of Rest and Reflection in the Inner Court, trying to calm the frightened servants and to keep Wang Sun from barking.

That was impossible. When the first whiff of human carrion reached him he began to bark, a high-pitched, outraged yelp that could not be stopped for more than a few moments, until he grew so hoarse it was inaudible, a whispered bark that shook the whole of his frail old body on Hung Tu's knees. He barked, without food or sleep for a day and a night, and died in a convulsion on the evening of the second day.

Hung Tu would have liked to take his body to Pi-chi-Fang for burial in the garden there, but she did not care to ask and no one cared to tell her what was happening in that place. He was buried in a neglected corner of the garden, by a clump of bamboo which would soon obliterate the traces of his grave.

Now there was nothing to do but wait for the almost certain summons to the new Governor or for his arrival at his Villa gate. What arrived first was an agitated servant with a message from Cheng-Wei-Chou.

"He says 'Farewell, Honored Lady.' He is to depart at dawn. He says he does not come to the beloved presence, because he is," the brow puckered to remember the strange word, "he is soiled. He will return when the years have cleansed him. He says farewell."

Hung Tu answered: "You will tell him that this person understands the message and you will take him the answer I will give you when you have fed and rested."

She went to her ink and brush. Oblivious of all but the anguish of the friend who felt he might not come to her, she composed his farewell poem.

> *The sacred mountain is blurred in the rain,*
> *the river dark.*
> *Weeping we climb to watch our friends depart.*
> *A thousand horsemen are riding to the East,*
> *Before them the flags flutter, two by two.*
> *We lift our wide sleeves to wave them on*
> *and dry our eyes on the silk.*
> *Lo Fu stands alone on the stony peak above us,*
> *she has no tears as she gazes at the vanishing column.*

She read it over and sat for a moment thinking. Then she rose and went to the red lacquered box in the Pavilion of Repose and took a sheet of plum-blossom paper from it. Onto this she copied another, more intimate poem, written to another man, who never saw it and now would never see it. She changed the inscription. She would call it "To Speed a Parting Friend."

> *The lotus is pale on black water,*
> *the moonlight is cold,*
> *the hills wear shrouds of mist.*

Not now, not now does our parting begin . . .
as long as the road that stretches to the frontier
the dread of this moment was deep in my heart.

It was written to Yuan Chen, but Cheng-Wei-Chou had earned it. She was grateful to him for many things, not least that his love and his shame before evil restored her to a belief in the dignity of Tao.

She gave the servant two gold pieces and told him to do what he could for his master's comfort, and particularly to tell him—she repeated it—that she understood his message.

Then she sat down to wait, in the room where she had first entertained Governor Wei Kao and all the other eminent men who followed him; where she had first loved Yuan Chen and later surprised him with Misty Grass; where she had responded as best she could to this honest young man's strange devotion, and where she now decided, when the moment of trial arrived, to utter her first "No!" to a Governor or his guest.

She laughed. She raised her hands in a sudden gesture the walls of this Villa had witnessed and must surely remember, would always remember. . . .

Curved about a crucible invisible in the air.

And the words that went with it:

"The cup shared by Superior Men should not be proffered to a cur."

Her eyes filled with tears. Nor would it be. Taken by force, perhaps. Broken, destroyed, perhaps. But never proffered to any of the House of Liu.

Nor, from this time on, to curs.

XLIII

WHEN THE MEANING of the evasive, polite message his official Hostess of the Shu Ya Men delivered to him by a servant, at the gate of his own Villa, penetrated the Governor's astounded, outraged mind, he returned to the Palace in silence and outward composure.

Within the hour those who had witnessed the insult were dead or dying, Fu Yang, the servant, slowly, in Hung Tu's presence, so that she might observe his agony and he might clearly understand on whose account his death was to be longer and more cruel than the rest, lasting indeed, half the night.

These preliminaries ended, she was brought to the Great Hall of the Palace and there stripped before Liu P'i and his guards. He looked her up and down disdainfully before he made a gesture of refusal, of disgust.

This was to be his version of the No. It was to be his No, not hers. In the course of time and the orderly pursuit of his duty to the Eye of Heaven, he had examined Hostess Hung Tu and found her unfit for duty. Therefore, taking into consideration the long years of her service to the city and . . . any flowery phrases here would do, about the compassionate mercies of the Eye of Heaven . . . he had decided to release her from her appointment and remove her from Shu.

Exile, he thought, looking her up and down. Anything else might stir up trouble. It was not an ordinary Flower-in-the-mist. It was a Legend. And she had friends among the hotheaded poets around the Emperor. Branding, mutilation, torture might become known to one of these, resented and reported to the Ears of Heaven.

Such a risk outweighed the momentary spasm of pleasure it would bring him. He was sated, for the time being, with orgasms of pain inflicted in keener ways upon younger bodies. He could afford to let the old broadtail go, counting on the hazards of the road, the lusts of bestial serfs she would encounter, unprotected, to punish her.

A man of his eminence . . . Liu P'i . . . defied by this. . . .

One admired the look in the old hag's eyes. It might have been enjoyable to put out those two eyes, slowly, and do some other things . . . but . . .

Not politic. It would not further his plans to attract extra attention to himself from the Capital just now, while his projects were developing.

"You are banished," he shouted at her. "You deserve to be flogged and branded on both cheeks like any other common criminal, but because you purveyors of filth have to make your living out of your looks, and yours are faded enough as it is . . ." he let the spiteful sentence trail.

"Do any of you want her?"

Prudently the guards shook their heads and spat between their feet.

"Then throw her out. Twelve hours to be gone from the city. Death if she returns. Or if she fails to report to the Governor of Kaifeng within five moons."

This was impossible. Everybody knew it. He repeated, "Within five moons."

He turned away. For the first time the nude, still figure stirred. She was looking about for her clothes. They had disappeared. The guards guffawed. A servant, one of the old Palace slaves, hesitated, then seeing that they were closing in on her to turn her naked into the streets, tore off his ragged robe and flung it in her direction. He made the gesture as contemptuous, as violent as he could, but it was still a brave one. Fortunately Liu P'i's back was turned. He was preparing to leave the room. And the guards were tired from their long day's work. He was allowed to be charitable, and she was allowed to wrap the robe about her and move unmolested to the gates.

Once in the streets she ran in her bare feet, her disheveled hair pulled partly about her face, hiding the emptied eyes. Even so she had looked at Cloud Touching Temple, lost, detached, removed, within the shadows. Her frantic body bore her forward.

No one interfered with her. Those few abroad in the city had their own tragic horrors to attend to. She reached the Villa by Hundred Flowers Pool and rushed inside. The place was deserted. Silent . . . silent. The slaves, the guards, the . . . everyone, dead or worse. On account of her. If she had not allowed herself the luxury of pride. . . .

It might have come to the same in the end, but it was still her decision, her setting-in-motion, her act . . . arising from her love for Yuan Chen. . . . For this they had died in torment, for this poor faithful good Fu Yang . . . she shut her eyes, pressing her hands upon them, but the vision formed upon her eyelids. It was a memory she would not be able to dispel.

"Fu Yang, it is over! You are now at peace! But for me . . . for those alive, it is not yet ended. . . . I will have the gong sounded for you . . ." she babbled in a hoarse whisper, not knowing what she said, or where she went, roaming the empty pavilions, running to the garden and back to the Pavilion of Rest and Reflection. Nothing in the Villa had been looted, nothing touched. It was Liu P'i's Villa, clearly posted. Who would dare? Everything was in its place, even her jewels, even the lacquered box with the taels in it and Yuan Chen's poems among her writing things.

What should she try to take, what leave? The bulk of her possessions was still at Pi-chi-Fang, hidden in many places, if it had not been discovered, stolen, or burned. She dared not venture there to see, but she had here some hoarded taels, some jewels, enough to take her to Kaifeng if she decided to make the hopeless attempt and set out for it instead of dropping where she stood, to wait for death.

Twelve hours. First she must sleep. But if she slept she would surely not awake in time to leave the city before dark. The sun was high in the heavens now. If she slept she might not awake before the hours of grace were over. She had not slept for . . . never mind how long, what hours . . . she must forbid herself to sleep.

She must make ready, must start toward the Northern Route now. Once outside the city gates, and several lis from the city limits, a safe distance . . . if there was such a thing as safety . . . she might find some sheltered place for the night. It would be cold in the mountains. She shivered. She faltered. She knew nothing of the Northern Route, beyond the first few lis of it, which she had ridden on hunting parties with Governor Yen Ssu-k'ung and Yuan Chen.

Ridden! Horses! She drew on her plainest robe, twisted her hair into a knot, and went hesitantly to the stable. Supposing there should still be . . .

She opened the door. A warm smell of horse dung flowed toward her. In the darkness she could hear them stamping, snorting, rustling. They were still there. Then her eyes grew accustomed to the darkness, she could see them, Uigha and the mare pushing forward. Hungry, thirsty, frightened, nuzzling for reassurance. Before she had time to pat them, a man came out of the shadows with a rope in his hands. She turned in terror, but he whispered, "Hush," and stepped into the light.

It was a face she dimly remembered, not a cruel, not a vicious face . . . she groped for where, for whom. . . .

He said, "No harm. The horses." And then, "We did not know you would return. We need the horses. We are going now."

She looked over his shoulder and saw two other faces peering through the stable door. He moved toward Uigha. She stepped between them.

"Where are you going?" she asked sharply.

He shrugged.

"Out of the city?"

He did not answer. He was twisting the rope in his hands.

"To the South, to Chang-an? To the North? I am going to the North. You may come with me and take care of the horses. I will pay you."

He came nearer. She saw the wound on his cheek still oozing into a bloody rag. The others pressed behind him. All of them she saw now were branded. Desperate, outcast men, they could kill her, they could ransack the place for the money she had stupidly mentioned, they could take the horses. . . . There was nothing to prevent them, but . . . he was still standing, facing her in silence.

Then he said, "Come. Now you have seen. Get what you need, Elder Sister . . . but make haste."

She hesitated. If she left them now . . .

"We will wait," he said, correctly reading her thought, "the time it takes to water these. Then we will go, and take them with us. We need them. We are going North. You may come, if you can keep up with our march."

PART NINE

823–824 A.D.

XLIV

Frontier life is known to be harsh
yet reality is worse than dread.
These delicate songs are wasted on cattle.
The herds of Lung T'ou, unmoved, browse as before.
Hung Tu tunes her lute, her brow dark, humiliated.

Lawless hordes gallop on the endless plains,
Bivouac fires call others to join their brutal ranks.
What can she hope for, condemned to this barbarous land?
Frightened, she shrinks from the emptiness
beyond the Pine Forest.

He stared at the poem, addressed to no one in particular, and then at the more personal one on another scroll, addressed to him: "For Cheng-Wei-Chou, the Water Clock."

The water clock drips the minutes away
drop by heavy drop.
The lamp goes out. There is no more oil.
The shadows seem to fly between the walls
of the garden,
crossing and recrossing in the moonlight.
A night bird cries.
I look from my casement into the brightness
of the moon.
The night will never end . . . will never end.
Oh, unbearable to be alone in life!
Desolation penetrates my very depths.

Below this she had written: "Send help to me if you can. I am at the turn of the Yellow River near Loyang, by the third bridge on the road to Kaifeng. I fall upon evil days."

It was dated the third moon of the fourth year of the first Governorship of Official Liu P'i in the Province of Shu. A year ago. She was
still alive after four years of exile. But it had taken twelve long
months for the scrolls to reach him, and already she had fallen upon
evil days. She might die before help could arrive. Even traveling
with utmost rapidity upon a good swift horse and suffering no
delays from floods or storms or turbulent conditions, it would take
eight moons at least to arrive at the gate of Loyang.

"How was the Honored Lady when you left her?"

But the messenger knew nothing. He had the scrolls fourth-hand
from a camel driver who was returning North and could not deliver
them. When he received the reward he expected, more than he expected, two gold pieces, he departed, and Cheng-Wei-Chou stood
watching with unobservant eyes. His vision turned inward, northward, to that bend in the Yellow River near Loyang. He sighed.

On the table lay another package which the fellow had left with
him, relieved to be rid of it. This one was addressed to "Official
Yuan Chen, Governor of T'ung Chou in Eastern Shansi, or if he
has been recalled from thence, he may be heard of at the Han Lin
Academy in Chang-an. He will reward the bearer."

The camel driver could not read, and even if he knew what was
said in those firm and beautiful strokes, he could not push on now
to Chang-an. He must stay with his caravan.

"He will reward the bearer," Chen-Wei-Chou said tonelessly.
"Well, but this person has attended to the matter for him."

He swept the packet into his sleeve. Still holding the two small
scrolls in his clenched hand, as though some determined thief might
snatch them from him, he passed through the doorway into the
courtyard of the Governor's Palace. Stepping carefully between the
mounds of heaped-up rubble and mud and worse things they concealed, he made his way to the Great Hall.

He did not look about him, he kept his eyes fixed on the door to
which he was bound, yet even so his essence suffered depression at
the knowledge of what he must see if he glanced aside.

He found the new Governor, his kinsman, venerable Official Wei
Kao, seated in the massive stone chair used on state occasions in

Cheng-tu. It was the only piece of furniture in this part of the Palace that had not been smashed or carried off as loot. It was too heavy, but there were dents here and there which showed that somebody had swung an axe against it. Senseless, senseless.

The Governor sat hunched over, staring at the floor, with a strange expression on his face. He had not looked so hopeless, so defeated, so despairing, in the worst of the bloodiest fighting when the issue was still undecided. Now that he had won, and the traitor Liu P'i was dead, and it was over, except for the clearing up . . . that must be it, the clearing up, the desolation, the blackened ruin of the countryside, was afflicting him.

As though he caught the essence of this thought, the Governor spoke:

"When this person came here first, the Province of Shu was a fertile and perfumed garden, and Cheng-tu the capital of Paradise. Now no one of his own will would set foot here. It is all to do again." He put his sleeve to his eyes, and Cheng-Wei-Chou looked swiftly away. If the old Tiger himself, the legendary hero of a hundred battles, to whom the Eye of Heaven turned when danger threatened the Empire . . . if Governor Wei Kao wept, then there was cause for grief. But that much any man could see who looked at the City of Silk, remembering what it had been.

"There is news of an old friend," he said gently, touching the hand clenched on the chair. It relaxed. It opened to take the scrolls. The Governor smiled

"Cheng-Wei-Chou," he said. The three words held a caress. He began to read. His eyes lightened. The grim expression left his face. For a moment he was in the vigor of his prime and all about him beauty and splendor.

"Hao, hao, hao, it is good. She will return to pour our wine and gladden these halls again."

" 'One morning T'ien Ch'eng Tzu slew the Prince of Ch'i and stole his kingdom,' " Cheng-Wei-Chou quoted sadly, "then it was said, 'the past will not return.' "

"It was also said, 'When water runs down from a high place to a low one, the current is irresistible. The feet can walk, let them walk, the hands can hold, let them hold.' If the Songbird of Shu returns, the spirit returns to Cheng-tu. All we need is men to rebuild the city and work the lands, and the rich men and merchants follow."

He closed his eyes, fatigued at the thought of all that must be done.

"One brushstroke at a time the painting grows," Cheng-Wei-Chou said encouragingly. "It was in this person's mind to supplicate a favor."

"It has been amply earned by one who fought as twenty tigers with claws of sharpened gold. What can this impoverished person in the ruins of this city award him?"

"Leave to travel northward for a year, or as long as it may take to ride to Loyang and return."

"This person can see nothing against it, except that you are needed here."

"But men are also needed, and perhaps could be brought back from the North, fugitives in hiding, and peasants greedy for a strip of land. . . ."

The Governor looked at him for a moment, then he smiled.

"The Master said: 'Heaven helps the man who is devoted; men help the man who is true.' "

"Words cannot express thoughts completely," Cheng-Wei-Chou muttered, unable to meet that smile. "Is it true that for a banished criminal to return one step of all her steps without a written pardon from the Supreme Ruler of Men is to invite swift death?"

"It is true. But to wait for such a pardon to arrive might also mean sure death to one who has 'fallen upon evil days.' Moreover, it should be remembered, if the deposed Official Liu P'i, who pronounced the sentence upon her, represented the Eye of Heaven at that time, so Governor Wei Kao, who revokes it, represents the Eye of Heaven at this time."

He drew himself up a little in the battered old chair.

"It is indeed fortunate for her and for all . . ." Cheng-Wei-Chou began. The Governor swept this aside.

"The Seal of Shu should be enough on an official script, until the Imperial Decree of Confirmation reaches us."

"Will there be confirmation?"

"This person believes so. Consider . . . it must rejoice the Eye of Heaven to observe that a delicate woman, at the height of the traitor's power, when strong men—even young generals—trembled before him and ran to do his will . . . knew the Evil One for what he was and dared to oppose him, losing all except her life . . ."

"And alas we are not certain of that yet. . . ."

". . . out of her devotion to the Throne."

"It is indeed an example of gratifying loyalty!"

Both men smiled, knowing that devotion to the Emperor was probably not uppermost in Hung Tu's mind at the time of her banishment. There was a silence while they contemplated the simple beauty of this tableau.

"If indeed the attention of the Emperor were directed to such a scene . . ."

"This person believes the Eye of Heaven may be guided to glance toward it."

"By whom?"

"By Yuan Chen."

There was a silence. Cheng-Wei-Chou frowned, but the Governor continued firmly: "Yuan Chen is much in favor at this troubled hour. When we left Chang-an he was at the Court. He is an old admirer of the Songbird. If word should reach him now of her predicament, he would intercede for her and might obtain not only confirmation of pardon, but even an award of taels, which she must sorely need."

"Has Yuan Chen indeed such influence, or is it from his own wide mouth, or perhaps the cicadas sing . . . ?"

The Governor did not answer this outburst of spite directly.

"If this person could find some pretext to write to Yuan Chen, on behalf of the Songbird, in such a way that if it were intercepted by his enemies it would do no harm to him or to her, through mention of the proscribed name. . . ."

"There is such a pretext," Cheng-Wei-Chou said crossly. He searched in his sleeve for the package and held it out between them. "This arrived with the other. It is addressed to him. No need to name the name of a criminal. . . . Yuan Chen must know that script."

He was looking both sullen and sheepish, and the Governor guessed that he had not intended to forward the package unopened, or perhaps at all, to Yuan Chen.

He turned it over thoughtfully.

"If it contains new songs," he said, not looking at Cheng-Wei-Chou, "we might be tempted to depart from the ways of right behavior and open it, lest immortal words be lost to enlightened men, yet . . ." now he did glance up, sideways, like a shrewd old bird, ". . . it might give us pain to read them. I own this person would be chagrined to find them better than the ones addressed to him, and if they were worse, he would be chagrined that the poet's powers were failing. But they drop from the Hand of Heaven on her behalf. I will send them to Yuan Chen in such a way that he may spread them before the Eye of Heaven. . . . But why are the feet rooted and the mind lost in mists of conjecture? The morning is quite gone by."

Cheng-Wei-Chou muttered something, eyes lowered, abashed to be understood.

"Collect what is needed for the journey. Take twenty men and ten horses. Take what provisions there are, and as many taels as this person's purse can spare. Take a litter, if one remains in this desolate place. Tell the soldiers you are going in search of men to work the land. Round up what you can on the way home, but first ride day and night to the place where she is. Bring back the Songbird of Shu to the City of Silk. . . ."

They embraced, and as they held each other's sleeves, the old Tiger said huskily, "You will be sorely missed from your place. Make haste, make haste to return." He drew himself up to give blessing. "The course of him who acts, taking Heaven as his guide, and holding himself, in all things, to Simplicity, is that of the *yang* in its fullness. The deeds of such a man are requited by Heaven and Earth."

They embraced again in silence, and Cheng-Wei-Chou went away.

XLV

News drifted and sifted to the North. It came with the slow caravans and the feet of patient runners. It rode on the bitter winds, it
fell with the snow, it shouted through the forests and whispered in
the currents of the river: "He is dead! That One! Impiety is punished! He is dead! That One! Impiety is punished!"

Twos and threes of frightened men crept into the countryside.
Their demented leader was dead. Now every man's hand was
against them. They did not pronounce his Name, lest mention of
the powerful demon bring worse evil upon them from the shadows
where he lurked. His madness had turned against the Eye of
Heaven. Such blasphemy was punished. They had seen him killed.
They had fallen with his fall, and now those few who had not died
around him in the last stronghold of his Palace or been captured to
work the blackened lands destroyed at his command were crouch-
ing in ditches or crawling in the woods, trying to prolong doomed
lives.

The news surged over and past them, stirring the world as it went.
Restless beasts sniffed the air. They lowed. They pawed the ground.
Men lifted their heads.

Some said: "Hibernating creatures begin to move. Wild geese are
heard. It is the start of spring."

Others brought out pitch pipes to play the Five Notes of the
Elements. Women said: "A unicorn went by." Monks in the Tem-
ples chanted "The Seven Beginnings and the Eight Breaths regain
their proper places."

All the earth was relieved.

Word reached the bend in the river where the strange woman
lived who doctored hurts and told old tales and now and then would
sing in a faded voice, moving the hearts of passers-by for small cop-

per coins or handfuls of rice or a stick of firewood. She too felt the stir in the air and knew the ways of extremity had changed.

"A unicorn went by."

Eighteen months had come and gone since her cry for help went South. Either Cheng-Wei-Chou was dead, or he had grown indifferent . . . and Yuan Chen . . . but perhaps her words had never reached them. There were a hundred ways for them to be lost. The camel driver might have met with misfortune, or left them behind at a resting place, or tossed them aside at the very start perhaps. She lay awake night after night, seeing the scroll and the package lying in the mud or trodden underfoot or . . . then she wept, quietly, not to wake whatever creature shared her sleeping mat.

Yet now the airs had changed. Something was different, new. Thoughts must be turned toward her. Help must be on its way. She felt it was so, in her essence, a wordless certainty. It came as she was brewing *ma pien ts'ao* to give to a sick man for the chill disease, the one forever recurring that came out of the forests here and rose from the river.

"You must learn to make it yourself if you want your man to live," she told his woman. "Come close. Now watch how it is done. Cook one liang of ginseng in two bowls of water. Not river water. You must take it from a spring. Boil it to half-away, then he must drink all down and go into a sweat. . . ."

She looked into the woman's stupid, staring eyes . . . what use. She listened to the sick man's breathing. He would die. She thought: "A little longer and I will not be found here; no, I will not be found here at the rise of sun."

There were many ways of dying. Better the bruised and bleeding feet, the hunger, the cold, the fears, the . . . whatever lay in wait upon the road to Shu . . . than slowly withering here in the squalor of the world.

She would set out, she would go, step by step by step. . . .

But if she left this place who, if any searched, would find her? She must stay.

Oh desolate! The night will never end.

254

Over and over as she thought these things, despair ran through her depths.

But men were already working at her Villa Pi-chi-Fang, rebuilding the ruined tower, restoring the ravaged grounds. In far-off Chang-an a poet read to an Emperor. And horsemen were riding toward her, not many lis away.

XLVI

THERE WAS A STIR in the hamlet when the horsemen arrived, led by a gaunt general flourishing a sword and shouting hoarsely for news of a personage never heard of there. Then someone remembered the crone at the bend of the river.

It appeared that she, whom they had taken for their needs and beaten . . . worse things came to mind, but it was not a moment for remembrance, nor safe to slink away . . . might be an important one, even a great lady.

They went with him to her hut, to show the way. No one saw the meeting. He went in alone. It was dark inside. Those who strained to listen heard no sound. But it could not have been auspicious, the gaping crowd surmised, for when he emerged his brow was clouded. He looked at them with loathing. There were whips and chains in his eyes and they drew back, afraid.

He went to his saddle pack and brought out a long soft cloak, such a glitter of silk as no one in Loyang ever saw before. Presently she emerged, shrouded in its folds, and no one could see her face. She entered the rich litter, borne by two strong horses, and so they went away, the general riding beside it, his hand on the silken tassel that kept the curtains closed.

In Cheng-tu Governor Wei Kao prepared a reception for his friend in the rebuilt wing of the Palace.

In far-off Chang-an the poet read:

The last rose mallow has shed its petals.
Autumn withers the hills of Shu.
A messenger brings words of tenderness,
words of postponement.
He cannot come yet, but he will come . . .

Women know little of the inflexible rules of power.
Night after night one climbs the hill to wait.

Another spring has gone. The green of rushes
spreads along rivulets choked with petals.
Careless of brightness, forsaken in the moon
thousands of clansmen are grieving.
Raised sleeves hide desolate tears.
There is one who does not come through the Ch'in Pass.

"It has a sweet, singing cadence," the Eye of Heaven said. Yuan
Chen read on.

Poems are written in various shapes,
their messages clear,
but these are songs of love
diaphanous and free:
remembering flowers when days darken,
weaving moonlight into night's obscurities,
knowing that drooping willows
wake in the morning to dance.

During years, I have guarded these songs,
precious, as white jade is precious,
secretly cherished.
They are yours now . . .
They were always yours and mine . . .
but now I am fragile, I cannot protect them.
Keep them for your children.
They will learn from them
to what heights love ascends.

His voice faltered. He put his sleeve to his eyes.

POEMS BY HUNG TU

Adapted by Mary Kennedy

1. DELICATE FLOWERS FADE

Delicate flowers fade in a day or two.
Loveliness and compassion cannot be grasped.
The turning year shakes the earth,
petals drift from the flowering trees
flinging a crimson pathway for satin-slippered feet,
or cover the ground like frost.

The blossoms have fallen from the tree
where we met to say goodbye . . .
to have a final supper together.
Then it was that late bloom lingered in the air,
reluctant to leave us.
A few petals scattered along the grass
making a bright design, as the thin tissue
of a pleated green gown is bordered in yellow.
All that is exquisite and frail is evanescent . . .
perfume dispelled, cannot be recalled.
No ghosts of these torn buds will haunt us!

The swallow extravagantly lines her nest with petals,
with butterfly movement petals flutter above the bridge.
They fall where the carp lurk under the water weeds.
The fish strike at them, they disappear in small whirlpools.
Dampened by dew, they cling to the curtains,
They are blown on the wind to deck the bamboo shades.
They shimmer in sun. They wilt under rain.
They swim on careless currents of air.

They enrich the woven medallions on the robe
of the courtesan singing to her lover.
They fall into the upraised cup of the poet
as they assail the pagoda.
Into the poet's enameled cup falls the rarest flower of all,
a drift of scarlet petals drenched in pale wine.

As a dream melts away, they mingle with the yellow catkin of the
                                                                willow,
the mimosa, the acacia, the plum blossom, the peach,
the locusts, the artemesia, the hua ping hua.
Bees ruthlessly despoil them,
with a tumult of laughter the children scatter them.
They fall into rain puddles,
they are lost in the storm.

As the beauty's jade hairpins slip from her wind-blown hair . . .
as birds must go south when the storms of autumn buffet them
in a gale of ending . . . they vanish, they disappear like early snow.
Into the dim ground they are pressed by jeweled slippers.
Attendants spend days sweeping piles of lost flowers
from the terraces, from stepping stones and grass . . .
pools of color splashed into the shadows.

All summer fragrant court was held in walled pleasure grounds,
yet plants devotedly tended by the gardeners
escaped to sow themselves along the way,
dodging the turning wheels of chariots, catching the light.
Who would choose among flowers in garden or meadow or ditch?
Luscious blooms gathered in gardens
wither as soon in loving hands,
and fastened in shining hair, die amorously.
Cast into the mud, they are still to be pitied.

Summer has left and the vases are empty.
The trees are dark now with seed pods, and fruit
weighs down the branches. Nothing can return to an earlier state.
The gently falling flowers will never return to the bough.
Beauty's girdle slipped awry . . . it was first loosened.
When fragrance is lost, what more is there to lose?
Wearily she binds a garland on her brow,
or circles her waist in an airy deceit.
Do not throw away flowers when the dancing is finished,
hold them against loneliness,
let them fade with youth into the approaching dark.

Let them stay where they have fallen
on the steps, on the path into the garden.
This color is balm for one abandoned
who wakes in night and walks in the rustling leaves.

2. NOW ALIGHTED ON THE SHADOWY POOL

Now alighted on the shadowy pool
two birds float together on the green water.
They rest as one, they move as one,
they cannot be parted,
whose hearts and minds and bodies
know only each other,
who have never had a dissenting thought.
Even the leaves and the rushes
cling together, bending above them.
Happy birds, happy birds.

3. IN MY GARDEN

In my garden
the Wu t'ung tree is tall,
roots in the earth, head in the sky.
O, for the eyes of an Emperor
to see the phoenix!

In my garden
the Wu t'ung tree is tall,
birds from the south,
birds from the north
are nesting there.
At every passing wind the branches tremble.

4. UNDER THIS MOON

Under this moon many hearts are grieving.
The moon is serene
as a lady of Han at her loom,
holding the shuttle in her white fingers.
She is a tranquil ghost in silver,
but we are sorrowing, we are sorrowing!

5. HAIL, KAO PIEN!

Hail, Kao Pien!
Such dazzling lightning bursts from you
that the distraught Cosmos
almost ceases turning.
Mountains cloak themselves in new green,
the sunset is burning in new colors.
After this day, both the sun and the moon
must take their light from you!

6. PEACH PETALS ARE SHAKEN

Peach petals are shaken by the winds of spring:
silken and fragile they cling to our robes,
but the yellow catkins of the willow
scatter to the north, rush to the south:
not attaching themselves to anything,
carelessly riding the breezes of the second moon.

7. SO HANDSOME IS THIS PRINCE

So handsome is this Prince
on his wild steed mounted,
that were the Ancient, whose name
he bears, alive today,
this Prince would defeat him!
This Prince would outshine him!

8. FROM THE CENTER OF THE SUN

From the center of the sun the cloth is woven,
the deep-dyed, fiery crimson.
And over it the mists from distant shores
evoked by djinns.
Touched with the frost of winter fur,
these veils translucent as white jade.
Chang-o herself shines on the bridge of wings that rises
between the Weaver in the sky and the Herdboy
over a river of stars.

Nine by nine by nine again,
all colors streak the cloudy overdress.
Our senses ride with luminous colors lured.

Blown to earth on a wind of spring
a hundred flowers fall from magic gardens
to edge the sleeves, to sprinkle the daring skirt.

This is a style worn by immortals as they dance
upon the clouds. Having nibbled the fungi of long life
they dwell in the Celestial Court, in innocent revelry
joyously singing, wearing robes like this.

9. BIG AND FLAT THE LEAVES OF LOTUS

Big and flat the leaves of lotus rush around
the little boat that lightly rides before the breeze.
The Golden Crow flies low. In the autumn evening
the fish are leaping. There is a rabbit in the moon
pounding an elixir to make lovers immortal.
A lady trails her red sleeves in the water
as she picks the delicate pink lotus.

10. PULL UP THE RUSHY GRASS

Pull up the rushy grass, disentangle the weeds
and garner the water chestnuts.
The willow branches dream as they dip in the water.
How may we see the glimmering land beyond the source
of the river, as we lift the grasses,
as we feather our oars in the stream?

11. IT IS TOLD OF THE CLOUD TOUCHING TEMPLE

It is told of the Cloud Touching Temple
that one walks only on moss,
even in the wild wind, no dust is blown.
It is so near to Heaven that the walls of hibiscus
are level with the clouds.
All is waiting for the poet and the moon.

It is told of Cloud Touching Temple
that flowers crowd the steps,
float on the streams, blow into the sky
across the mirror of the descending Queen . . .
changing the clouds into gardens for her delight.

12. A BAMBOO HANDLE FROM YUEH

A bamboo handle from Yueh
fashioned to fit the artist's fingers;
tufts of Hsuan sable:
elegantly it once moved
under the governing mind
in a journey of mountains,
a soaring of wings, or waterfalls
of flowers plunging down
a silken scroll.
Now frayed and blunt, it is laid by,
no longer remembered.
Yuan Chen has a new brush in his hand.

13. ON THE TEMPLE TERRACE

On the temple terrace
the monks are meditating on the Surangama Sutra.
The yearning sound of a flute lights the sacred words.
Consider the sole reality of the true mind . . .
Do the Buddha's fingers open or close?

Remember the sermon at Benares.
The best of ways is the noble eightfold way.
Pursue the meditation.
Right solitude! Right ecstasy!

A cicada saddens the twilight,
the nightingales sing and sing.
They feel the bliss, the rapture
that breathes through the universe.

Let us not go to death again and again.
In the silences the flute, pure and clear as ice,
follows the falling sun.

14. THE GOLDEN HEADDRESS

The golden headdress of the Mandarin drake
gleams in long grass near the marble steps.
A duck is nesting nearby in a green hollow.
Blue and purple feathers, elegant white markings,
shine in the pride of fine weather . . .
they are serenely unaware of summer's passing.

15. THE SONG OF THE CICADAS

Intense, far-off is the song of the cicadas,
a shimmering murmur, washed in dew.
As leaves whisper together in a high wind
one note resounds from every side,
interminably vibrating.
The persistent shrillness rings a thousand bells
denying the end of summer,
even as the swarms diminish.

16. FAREWELL TO OFFICIAL YAO

An unending line of willows borders the stream
with summer green. They trail sad branches
in the swirling waters.
The prow of your boat, dividing the wind,
breaks a feathery willow wand.
It floats away with you in mute farewell.

Another land will hold you now. . . .
Remember one who grieves for you here
under the same dim moon.

17. PARTING FROM LU YUAN-WEI

Darkness, wind, and the sorrowful snow
falling over Chun Kuan Pass,
over Jade Tomb Hill
where the ghosts of parted lovers wait.
If Hsin Ling, the Duke in I-Man, speaks of time present,
tell him that there is one who remembers
only the gracious, invincible past.

18. FROM HSIANG CH'UN, DEEP IN THE
SOUTHERN DESERT

From Hsiang Ch'un, deep in the southern desert,
has come a runner in black to Ch'u Shui
with lichee nuts, renowned for excellence:
brittle red shell, pale darkening heart, black seed,
and thick juice of a well-remembered sweet-bitterness,
like a taste of Jasper Lake.

19. I STOOD SO LONG

I stood so long before the climbing rose
that its scent still rises from all my garments.
The stream is quiet where Sun Chu-shih lies.
The birds fly east, fly west, swallow and shrike,
I wander in the springtime,
But Sun Chu-shih does not stir.

20. THIS MAGICAL YOUNG SEASON

This magical young season banishes the clouds
and wakes the land to bloom.
Fish play in the river pools
catching new scales from the small petals on the surface of the water.
The worldly have no knowledge of the delicate message of flowers;
Careless hands leave torn red blossoms scattered along the bank.

21. THE SLENDER FRUIT TREES

Planted last year, the slender fruit trees
in Wu Chun's park are already in flower.
Swift with spring rain the rivers rush to the east.
Joyously, through the gathering dark,
the wild clear song of the oriole
falls from the crab-apple tree.
The dusk deepens the red tinged petals,
the paler blossoms of the pear glimmer like small stars.

22. THE LEAVES OF THE SOUTHERN BAMBOO

The leaves of the southern bamboo gleam as bright as frost in the
southern rain.
They strike their roots more deeply.
Long ago Ch'in sages, when they had drunk too much pale wine,
were sheltered by them:
and poor forsaken ladies of Chun's court hid their tears in bamboo
shade.
Our empty hearts are restored as we look at these admirable
shadows.
These slender trees, aged, but ageless . . .
Unyielding, unbending.

272

23. SAD WORDS TO YUAN CHEN

Pampered and perfumed, vigilant
at the lacquered entrance, the petted dog
responds to every move of its master . . .
one jealous growl, one snap at the favorite,
it is banished from the master's side,
from the comfort of the folded quilts.

A bamboo handle from Yueh
fashioned to fit the artist's fingers;
tufts of Hsuan sable:
elegantly it once moved
under the governing mind
in a journey of mountains,
a soaring of wings, or waterfalls
of flowers plunging down
a silken scroll.
Now frayed and blunt, it is laid by,
no longer remembered.
Yuan Chen has a new brush in his hand.

Arching neck and fiery eye,
white ears, a coat of roan,
tireless pacer on gilded hooves
outdistancing the wind:
yet startled at the flutter of a robe,
bewildered at a face but newly come,
the rider thrown . . .
Never again stabled in the special stall.

Distractedly flying high over the Lung Hsi marshes,
over the waste of reeds, rushes, swampy ground;
a bird reared with human beings,
used to a cage of love.
Because it spoke loose words it did not understand,
exiled from the world it knows
and cannot long survive.

He tenderly loved the bird that came to hand,
Her song enchanted him:
but building her nest on a column of coral
the bird splatters drops of mud on the rosy surface.
Driven off and the nest destroyed,
uttering piteous cries she circles in air.

No longer treasured by the lapidary
the lustrous pearl he once called peerless:
He has found a sparkling gem,
one of many such,
and amuses himself for a day.
Because of a shadow, a fancied flaw,
he has forgotten the pearl
that once adorned his hand.

Once carp swam in the pool all summer,
dreaming the days away, eluding the threaded hook.
It was a cherished lily that the red-gold fish
dragged under the water.

Proud, pivoting head, glittering eyes,
fierce talons, dagger sharp.
One flight, one capture
on a mission of its own . . .
never more will the Prince permit
the falcon to perch upon his wrist.

A shadowy pattern on the Hall of Jade,
lithe and tenacious trees,
pliant, yet strong, a living barrier to cold:
interlacing leaves ward off the summer heat:
but new growth shakes the old foundation stones,
the bamboo is uprooted, cast aside.

The polished metal mirror of the Hua Chuang
gleamed like new gold in its veils of silk,
as golden as the waxing moon on the fifteenth night

of the harvest month.
Yet, untended for a span, the mirror
of the "transformation-tidy-up-box"
neglected, unpolished, the moulded figures
around the rim indistinct, the lion dog handle
dark with dust,
is torn from the box,
and nothing in its place!

24. DO NOT COMPARE BEAN FLOWERS

Do not compare bean flowers with Ching Shen jade.
Bean flowers have fragrance.
Will there ever be any like those in the Year of the Horse,
the breeze blowing on freshly turned earth,
shaking the vines, scattering royal pollen
in the burning country sun?

25. AS I WAIT ALONE

As I wait alone on Myriad Mile Bridge
I remember the sweet songs of the ancient poets . . .
but even Hsi Ho, who spoke so clearly of the woes of love,
cannot heal my sadness . . . as I wait in the gentle rain
beside the tethered fishing boats.

26. FAREWELL TO CHENG-WEI-CHOU

The sacred mountain is blurred in the rain,
the river dark.
Weeping we climb to watch our friends depart.
A thousand horsemen are riding to the East.
Before them the flags flutter two by two.
We lift our wide sleeves to wave them on
and dry our eyes on the silk.
Lo Fu stands alone on the stony peak above us,
she has no tears as she gazes at the vanishing column.

27. THE LOTUS IS PALE ON BLACK WATER

The lotus is pale on black water,
the moonlight is cold,
the hills wear shrouds of mist.
Not now, not now does our parting begin . . .
as long as the road that stretches to the frontier
the dread of this moment was deep in my heart.

28. FRONTIER LIFE IS KNOWN TO BE HARSH

Frontier life is known to be harsh
yet reality is worse than dread.
These delicate songs are wasted on cattle.
The herds of Lung T'ou, unmoved, browse as before.
Hung Tu tunes her lute, her brow dark, humiliated.

Lawless hordes gallop on the endless plains.
Bivouac fires call others to join their brutal ranks.
What can she hope for, condemned to this barbarous land?
Frightened, she shrinks from the emptiness
beyond the Pine Forest.

29. FOR CHENG-WEI-CHOU, THE WATER CLOCK

The water clock drips the minutes away
drop by heavy drop.
The lamp goes out. There is no more oil.
The shadows seem to fly between the walls
of the garden,
crossing and recrossing in the moonlight.
A night bird cries.
I look from my casement into the brightness
of the moon.
The night will never end . . . will never end.
Oh, unbearable to be alone in life!
Desolation penetrates my very depths.

30. POEMS ARE WRITTEN IN VARIOUS SHAPES

Poems are written in various shapes,
Their messages clear,
But these are songs of love,
Diaphanous and free:
Remembering flowers when days darken,
Weaving moonlight into night's obscurities,
Knowing that drooping willows
Wake in the morning to dance.

During years, I have guarded these songs,
Precious, as white jade is precious,
Secretly cherished.
They are yours now . . .
They were always yours and mine . . .
But now I am fragile, I cannot protect them.
Keep them for your children.
They will learn from them
To what heights love ascends.

31. IRRESISTIBLE MAN

Irresistible man, most honored on the scroll of the East Hall,
At last we understand each other.
Today, face to face, each reads the other's heart.
See how the world makes itself new!
Every branch of the willow grove ends with a torch
In a blaze of sudden green.

32. IN THE SEASON OF FALLING PLUM PETALS

Unexpected as a blackbird with a spray of blossoms in his beak,
Your white flowers have come.
Although it is long since I have seen you,
In the season of falling plum petals
You think of our friendship.
A breath of air moves the flowers.
I lift them tenderly, remembering you.

33. TODAY, ALTHOUGH FAINT AND IN PAIN

Today, although faint and in pain, I greet the Duke.
A withering breath of wind strikes the resentful flower.
It is the autumn wind that blows before the winter.
While I thought that I was still in spring
The first snowflakes were whirling around my head!

34. THE LAST ROSE MALLOW

The last rose mallow has shed its petals.
Autumn withers the hills of Shu.
A messenger brings words of tenderness,
words of postponement.
He cannot come yet, but he will come . . .
Women know little of the inflexible rules of power.
Night after night one climbs the hill to wait.

Another spring has gone. The green of rushes
spreads along rivulets choked with petals.
Careless of brightness, forsaken in the moon
thousands of clansmen are grieving.
Raised sleeves hide desolate tears.
There is one who does not come through the Ch'in Pass.

35. THE EARLY SUN DISSOLVES THE MIST

The early sun dissolves the mist
that has covered the mountain.
All night I have listened to the wise,
yet failed to learn.
Dimly, darkly, the eternal pines
rise without effort from the vanishing fog.

36. THE SEEKING WIND

The seeking wind brings a breath
of distant bloom.
The jade chimes tinkle; then are still.
The wind moves beyond the casement
through tops of trees along the road.
All night it comes and goes
tossing the boughs, and crying rain

37. THE YEARS HAVE ERASED THE PATH

The years have erased the path up the mountain.
The gate to Kung Chih's compound is hidden by stout vines.
Little streams, swollen with rain,
escape their banks and swirl even into the doorway
of the great hall . . .
but on the mountaintop one steps into the sky!